Crystalline Crypt

Mary Coley

Mary Coley

This is a work of fiction. Names, characters, and incidents are products of the author's imagination or are used factiously and are not to be construed as real. Any resemblance to actual events, or persons, living or dead, is entirely coincidental

Crystalline Crypt

Copyright 2019 by Mary Coley. All rights reserved. No part of this book may be reproduced or retransmitted in any form or by any means without the written permission of the publisher.

Published by
P.O. Box 2517, Tulsa, OK 74101 USA
https://www.marycoley.com

ISBN: 978-1708958886

Other Books by Mary Coley:

The *Family Secret* Series (Mystery/Suspense):
Cobwebs (Book 1) Wheatmark, 2013.
Ant Dens (Book 2) Wheatmark, 2015.
Beehives (Book 3) Wheatmark, 2016.
Chrysalis (Book 4) Moonglow Books through KDP, 2018.

Mystery/Suspense

The Ravine. Wild Rose Press, 2016.
Blood on the Cimarron: No Motive for Murder. Moonglow Books through KDP, 2017.

Short Story Collections:

Beyond a Wild Sky. ML Coley. Create Space, 2013.
Secrets of the Heart. ML Coley. Create Space, 2013.

Non Fiction:

Environmentalism: How YOU Can Make a Difference. Published by Capstone, 2009

Mary Coley

Dedication:

I dedicate this book to my friend and critique partner, Mark Darrah, who pressed me to finish this book after a decade of starts and stops and delays, and to others who saw it in its early stages and insisted that I finish the story.

Writing a book is never easy. There are discouragements and roadblocks and distractions too numerous to name. I took this book to numerous workshops and critique groups as the plot was developing, working on it off and on because another idea for a book seemed more pressing. I'm happy to say it's finally finished.

Mary Coley

Acknowledgments

Once again, a big thanks to my husband, Daryl, and to my many supportive friends, both writers and non, who have encouraged me while writing this book.

I would be lost without my beta readers, who consider thoughtfully the plot and the characters even though the story is not yet fully formed or polished. They see through the chaff and help me home in on important questions, characterizations and story components. Thank you Sara Rupnik, Ann Fell, Jackie Darrah, Nancy Rosen and Nita Gould for your thoughts and comments.

I'd also like to thank the Oklahoma Tourism Department (one of my former employers) for promoting the beauty of my home state by providing a variety of information about the diversity found here. I could have selected so many places in Oklahoma as the setting for this story. I chose Tulsa for the beginning, and the area of the Wichita Mountains Wildlife Refuge and the community of Medicine Park for the last sections of the book. Urban and rural sections of the state both offer interesting history. From the Trail of Tears and the forced relocations of Native Americans in 'Indian Territory' to the Land Runs and settlement of 'Oklahoma territory,' the western frontier and its cattle drives, our history is laced with both intelligent and interesting individuals who made a difference in Oklahoma. Our culture includes European settlers who relocated here bringing their traditions, but 39 different Native American nations. These cultures have combined to provide a rich and colorful mosaic of life in a state which is blessed with four seasons and more diverse ecosystems than any other inland state.

Mary Coley

Cast of Characters

Jenna Wade – CFO at a Tulsa marketing firm, Empire Mktg

Sean Wade – Jenna's husband

Amanda (Mandy) Lyons – Jenna's best friend, account exec

Will – Mandy's boyfriend and Sean's best friend

Mike McNally – Mandy's friend, graphic designer

Mrs. Ida Childers – boarding house owner, Medicine Park

Nancy – waitress, Medicine Park

Dale and Max Hardesty – Jandafar B&B owners

Chad Hardesty – Max's brother

Lamar – cowboy at Jandafar B&B

Molly Bergen – missing

Sharon Bergen – missing

Crystalline Crypt

PART 1 - TUESDAY

~ Chapter 1 ~
Jenna

Jenna Wade didn't want to be followed. She slipped through the hidden rear exit from her sixth-floor office, took the elevator to the ground floor and left the building through the alley. Her pulse pounded as she pushed open her umbrella and plunged into the raging thunderstorm. The warm, wet air clung to her skin.

Her heart thumped too hard against her ribcage and her breath caught.

His note had come yesterday. She'd read it, then tucked it into a book on an overstuffed shelf in her home office.

The words burned a hole in her brain. She'd tossed, sleepless, all night.

Today her hands trembled. She couldn't focus on work. Did she really want to see him again?

What she wanted was for the endless nightmare to end.

She had to see him.

Fifteen minutes later, Jenna was peering at her destination when marble-sized hail dropped from the sky. As ice chunks slammed the sidewalk, she took shelter under the awning of the nearest shop. Jenna ducked her head and turned away from the storm. In front of her, narrow LED spotlights illuminated individual paintings in an art gallery window.

Jenna's heart stuttered. The awning over the storefront window next door snapped in the wind.

The dark painting pinpointed by one of the spotlights depicted a woman in a white dress trapped inside a glass crypt. Fear crazed her wide turquoise eyes and the white tips of her contorted fingers clawed at her unyielding prison. Her uplifted face, framed by white-gold hair, caught light beaming in from a single window, high in a wall.

The blond woman's face—*her* face.

Jenna's memories yanked her back two decades in time.

She smelled pine-scented air, dirt on her clothes and smoke from the burning cabin. She tasted his saliva on her lips.

Her stomach roiled and bile rose in her throat.

An hour later, Jenna paced her office, shaking. The painting had diverted her from her original mission in the arts district near downtown Tulsa. She didn't believe it was a coincidence that the meeting place and the gallery were on the same street. She had to talk this through. She couldn't keep the horrific painting to herself.

Jenna called her friend Mandy from her cell. "I need you, Mandy. Come now."

"It was me," she blurted after grabbing Mandy's arm and pulling her inside her office. She described the painting, adding, "They were my eyes, in my face."

Amanda Lyons shrugged. "Some artist has a hidden obsession with you." Amanda's shoulder-length auburn hair swung forward as she leaned against Jenna's desk.

Jenna wrapped her arms around herself and straightened. She'd said too much. She shouldn't tell Mandy she knew the artist.

He wouldn't have brought the painting to Tulsa unless he knew I was here.

Mandy frowned and pushed her hair behind her ears. "What are you not telling me?"

Jenna bolted across the room to the built-in bookcase lining one short wall. Among the many books filling the shelves—mostly annual reports and reference volumes—sat framed photographs of her husband and vacation souvenirs. She hesitated every few feet as she stepped from one end of the shelf to the other, letting her shaking finger trail the edge. She sucked in deep breaths. Her head filled with the faint odors of carpet shampoo and stacks of printed reports.

It was happening. She'd thought enough time had passed. She'd thought she was safe.

Safety was an illusion. Her life was an illusion. She'd held so many things so tight inside her for so long. She couldn't reveal any of them, even to Mandy, her best and only friend. She fingered a brightly painted carving of an armadillo from the Yucatan, purchased last year on a trip to Cozumel with her husband Sean, Mandy, and her boyfriend Will, Sean's best friend.

"Why didn't you call Sean after you saw this painting? Why didn't you go to his office?" Irritation was building in her friend's husky voice.

"I don't want Sean to know about the painting." Jenna set the armadillo back on the shelf and focused on a picture of the four of them at the edge of the ocean, lying in the frothy fingers of the sea.

And I didn't want him to know I'd been on my way to meet an old boyfriend.

"Someone uses you as the subject of a creepy painting and you won't tell Sean? You never keep anything from Sean. Call him. Now."

Jenna steeled herself to remain silent. There were many things she'd kept from Sean and Mandy.

The painting of the glass crypt is not just a painting. It's a promise.

"We should go back," Mandy said. "Find out the artist's name. I bet they innocently reproduced you from their memory. You probably met at some random event."

There's nothing innocent about that painting.

If someone from her past found her, she'd have to run again. From Sean, from Mandy, from her job. From everything. Like before. She couldn't risk what might happen.

She couldn't risk jail time.

"Forget it. I overreacted." Jenna hurried over to her desk and jiggled the computer mouse as she dropped into her chair. Her computer screen lit up. Her brain roared. *Why did I tell Mandy?* She had caved in a moment of panic—a moment of needing to tell someone about that horrible painting. She was so tired of keeping everything inside.

Why hadn't she learned over the past twenty years to keep her trap shut? It would never end. Not until she was dead.

There was no statute of limitations on murder.

~ Chapter 2 ~
Mandy

Mandy stewed over what Jenna had told her. Without details of what was depicted in the painting, Mandy's imagination soared. She pictured Jenna in scenarios from erotic fantasy trysts to lesbian love to historical remakes. She imagined her wearing an Elizabethan costume, as Queen Elizabeth I or Marie Antoinette, maybe Cleopatra.

Why had this painting upset Jenna so much?

Maybe the woman only resembled Jenna, looked enough like her to make Jenna *think* the painting was of her.

She doubted a vague resemblance would send Jenna into such a spiral. At her office cubicle, Mandy pulled a rain slicker from her narrow closet and grabbed her umbrella.

She rushed past Billie, the office assistant for her section. "Got to go out for foam core," she called. "In this weather, who knows how long it will take."

Mandy punched the elevator button. Jenna hadn't said where the gallery was, and Mandy hadn't asked why her friend was wandering around in the August thunderstorm. She hadn't been a good investigator; she'd left too many questions unasked. Her curiosity had been curbed by the stress evident on Jenna's face. She'd been concerned for her.

The Arts District, on the northside of downtown Tulsa, had expanded into former industrial buildings. How many galleries were there now? This could take hours.

On the sidewalk, rain splashed into puddles. She raised her umbrella, watched the car headlights reflect off the wet cement, looked down the sidewalk one direction and then the other. The weather was miserable. She wasn't sure she was up for this search.

Mandy stepped back into the building. Hubble, the security guard, stood behind his desk, grimacing as he stretched. He glanced at her, touched his cap, and looked below the desktop where every five seconds a bank of monitors switched from views of the elevator lobbies on the eight floors above to shots of the long hallways.

She should have googled Tulsa art galleries and made a list before she left her cubicle. Her thoughts raced. She'd have to do it the old way. "Do you have a phone book? Or the yellow pages?" She crossed the lobby to the desk.

"Sure thing. Not much of a phone book anymore. Businesses only. Have to use the Internet for anything else." Shaking his head, Hubble reached into a drawer and set a phone book on the counter. "Have a look." He grabbed a notepad and a pencil and laid them next to the phone book.

Mandy flipped through the yellow pages at the back of the volume. Under the "art gallery" heading, fifteen listings were potentially within walking distance, according to street names. It would take several hours to visit each of them if she did this alone.

The desk phone rang. While Hubble talked, she jotted down addresses. She waved at the guard, tore the page off the notepad, and left the building again. Standing under the building's portico in the rain-scented air, she called Mike McNally's office line.

"What are you doing?" she asked.

"Wrapping up the day." McNally spoke in a crisp, precise voice. "Ready to walk out of here. What about you?"

"I need help. There's something going on with Jenna." Her conscience twinged. Should she talk to Mike about this? Jenna didn't even know him.

"What did her Royal Highness do now?" His tone hardened, and Mandy pictured him taking off his glasses and leaning back in his chair to prop his feet up on the desk.

"She didn't do anything, but I need to check on something. You got a minute?"

"You got the money, honey, I got the time."

His suddenly energetic voice set off alarm bells in her head. He was tall, athletic and handsome, not to mention smart and eligible, but she didn't want to encourage him. "Mike…"

"Oh, right. Sorry. You and Will." He sighed. "Why doesn't Boyfriend Will help you out with this if you guys are so tight?"

"He's out of town. I need to move on this now, and I can't do it alone."

"Sounds intriguing. Give me more."

"If you have time—an hour, tops—we can do this and then I'll buy you a pizza. Deal?" She didn't like negotiating with Mike. Will wouldn't like it at all.

"Pizza and a beer," Mike countered.

"But just one beer. And we're done by eight, okay?" She didn't mean it as a question. Her voice was firm.

"Who are you, Cinderella?" he quipped.

"Mike!" Her voice sounded sharper than she'd intended.

"Meet you out front in ten."

She turned off her phone and immediately regretted calling Mike. She'd have to tell him what had happened, not to mention she was searching for the painting despite Jenna's command to forget it. She should give Jenna another chance to explain before she searched on her own.

Mandy called Jenna's office as she stared at the rainy street scene. Headlights glowed on the pavement and umbrellas bobbed on the sidewalks.

Jenna's voicemail picked up. "You have reached the office of Jenna Wade. I'm unable to take your call. Leave a message and I'll call you back before 6 p.m."

The phone beeped. Mandy glanced at her watch. 4:30. Had Jenna already left for the day?

"Jenna, it's Mandy," she said, keeping her voice low and even. "I'm still thinking about that painting. You sure you don't want me to go back to the gallery with you? Call me on my cell. Will's in Toronto for the week, so I'm going to pick up carryout and binge watch movies all evening. Call me back, okay?"

It wasn't a complete lie; Will was gone, and she probably would binge on chick flicks all evening—after she and Mike had found the gallery. Should she feel guilty for stretching the truth or omitting facts?

She wanted to help Jenna. She owed her. Jenna had always been there for her. Now she could finally repay her, even though Jenna hadn't asked for help.

Mandy grouped the galleries into two lists by address as she waited for Mike under the front portico. She also watched for Jenna. If her friend tried to return to the gallery alone, Mandy intended to go with her.

She considered what Will would say about her search. "If there is the smallest detail someone can't explain, you imagine an earth-shattering secret."

She did love mysteries. And Jenna's past was a big one.

Mike pushed through the revolving door and stood at attention in front of her. "Private McNally at your service. Awaiting the details of the mission." He gave a mock salute and ran his fingers through his black hair. "What's up?"

Mandy rolled her eyes but held her negative comment. She needed his energy for the search. "Jenna was caught in the hailstorm earlier today. She took shelter under an awning in front of a shop. The shop turned out to be an art gallery. And the picture in the front window was of a woman who looked like her. She came back dripping wet and freaked out. Called me to her office."

"She should have gone inside, asked who the artist was, gotten his number, and called him. Why didn't she?" Mike flipped up the collar of his black raincoat and opened his umbrella.

"I wish I knew. After she told me about it, she told me to forget it."

"Like that's going to happen. Your mind is a vault. And I mean that in a good way." He tossed her a charming grin, showing white teeth.

Mandy ignored him. His way of widening his eyes and leaning close made her uncomfortable. And it wasn't only because she was dating Will. "I've made a list of the art galleries within walking distance of this building. I've grouped them by street and divided the list in half. You head off that way and I'll start this direction. We're looking for a painting in the gallery's front window. The woman in it looks like Jenna."

"Right." Mike glanced at his list. "You have your cell?"

She nodded. "Call if you find it. And I'll meet you at Arnie's in an hour unless one of us finds it. Six o'clock, for pizza and *one* beer."

"Right, Pizza and *one* beer. You're such a downer, Mandy. What does a guy have to look forward to, anyway?"

Mandy opened Will's green golf umbrella and stepped out from under the portico. Her shoes made sucking sounds on the pavement as she trudged away from Mike and toward the first gallery on her list. A car roared past and threw a wave of water from the rushing stream beside the curb.

She was crazy for getting out in this unseasonably chill wind and relentless rain, all for the sake of a painting Jenna had asked her to forget. Didn't the calendar say it was August?

Someone had painted Jenna. Seeing the painting had broken down her friend's usually calm composure and air of reserve. Mandy had to see it.

She was curious about more than the painting. It could be a clue to the past her friend guarded so closely. Mandy knew a little about Jenna's college experiences, her fast romance with Sean, her struggles with an eating disorder, and her constant need to exercise. But she didn't know anything about how Jenna's parents had died or her life before that tragic event. Jenna had never even hinted at what had happened or how she had managed to continue life alone afterwards.

Thirty minutes later and several blocks away, Mandy was halfway through her gallery list when Mike called. She'd crossed a street with a half-dozen other umbrella-holding pedestrians when her phone played the OU Fight Song. She answered as the fourth "Boomer Sooner" blared.

"Find it?" she asked.

"No. And I guess you haven't either. It's wet out here. I think this warrants more than a pizza and *one* beer, Mandy."

"Find the painting, okay?" She stepped closer to the building to get out of the pounding rain. "How many more galleries on your list?"

"Two, and I'm getting closer to Arnie's. How 'bout you?"

"I'm coming up on my next to last one. There's no reason Jenna would be walking down this street unless she was on her way to that old building. What is that, anyway?" Mandy had noticed the three-story gray brick building as soon as she turned the corner. The shrubs in front were dead, and sick-looking vines clung to the façade.

"Old building? You mean the funeral parlor? There's an art gallery by Paducka's?"

"Hold on. Funeral parlor, a.k.a. embalming service? Creepy. Yes, there's a gallery on this street. Yolanda's Art."

Mandy peered at the storefronts as she walked past. "Cool buildings, but on the rundown side. Is this a historic district?"

"Probably too many buildings have been demolished for the area to qualify in its entirety. But who knows? I'm not a history buff. Bring on NASCAR if you want to entertain me, babe."

"So that's why women flock to spend their weekends with you, kneeling at your feet," she quipped, irritated.

"Hey, I'm keeping that spot open for you, love."

Mandy huffed. She'd fallen into his trap again, encouraged him to flirt with her. He needed to stop before Will got wind of it.

She studied the old funeral parlor at the end of the street, its limestone walls glistened in the rain. Tall windows stared like the vacant eyes of a giant spider, the glass panes reflecting racing gray clouds. Shivering, she turned to the front display window of the next gallery on her list. "Mike. Oh, wow." Chills raced down her back, and her hands and face felt icy despite the warm, humid air. Suddenly she understood Jenna's emotional response to the painting

"What?"

"You have to see this." She gave him the address.

The gallery door opened.

"Help you with something?"

The woman in the doorway had the reddest hair Mandy had ever seen. Lucille-Ball-red, clown-nose-red, not-natural-red. A quarter inch-wide black line extended across her eyelids near her stubby upper and lower lashes.

"Um. Just looking." Mandy returned her focus to the painting. Gooseflesh rose on her arms.

"You like that one?"

"The...lady in the glass...crypt?"

"Yeah, that one." Red chomped her gum. "Sweet, huh?"

"If you're a sadist." Mandy peered down the sidewalk and spotted Mike crossing the street at the corner.

"I got an interested party, ya know." Red put one hand on her hip and squeezed the other one into the pocket of her faded skin-tight jeans.

Mike jogged up, breathing hard. "Whew. Okay, let's see this painting of Jenna."

Mandy glanced at the woman in the doorway. Red's eyes were black holes. She stepped backwards into the shadows of the shop's interior.

Beside her, Mike choked. "Whoa. It *is* Jenna."

~ Chapter 3 ~
Mike

"Man, she's in a freakin' box. Suffocating." He couldn't take his eyes off the woman in the painting. Jenna was beautiful, but this artist had painted her like an imprisoned goddess. Silvery hair, flawless face, and an ooh-la-la body in a barely-there dress.

He sensed the woman lingering in the doorway and looked at her. "You work here?" She was older than she looked. Hair dyed; makeup too thick.

"Yeah." Her gum popped as she chomped.

An acidic taste filled his mouth. She was the opposite of the amazing Jenna. He could tolerate talking to the ugly woman if he didn't have to look at her. He pulled his phone from his pocket. "Who painted this?" Mike sought the artist's signature on the dark canvas as he turned on the phone's camera.

"No photos. Gallery policy. You're breaking the law. I'll call the cops." She stepped back into the dim interior of the gallery.

He tucked his phone back into his jacket pocket. "But it's for sale? How much?" Everything has a price, and this painting was worth buying. Then, he could look at Jenna's beautiful face every day. He wasn't the only man who wanted such an opportunity, apparently. "Hey, I have questions."

The doorway was empty. As he started toward it, the woman reappeared on the threshold. "The painting's been sold," she announced. The front door swung shut.

Mike leaped for the door, shoved it open and barreled inside. "Tell me who painted it. And who bought it."

The woman scurried to the front window, shoved aside the drapes and grabbed the painting off its easel.

He stepped further into the room, choking at a putrid smell which permeated the gallery.

"Who's the artist?" Mike squinted in the dim interior as he maneuvered around display tables of small paintings and jewelry to get to the window. With one hand, he squeezed his nostrils closed, but the odor was inescapable.

The woman clasped the painting against her chest as he neared the front window. Mike grabbed the picture frame. She pulled it away, but he snatched it again and wrenched it from her before darting across the room to a lamp.

Mike held the painting under the light, scanning for the painter's signature. A sloppily written name was barely legible in the purple-black background of the top left corner. He squinted. "Does that say Cha Har?" He shifted the painting closer to the lamp's bulb.

The red-haired woman glared. "Give me that, or I'll call the police." She seized the picture and hurried toward the rear of the gallery.

"I need the artist's information. I want him to paint another picture of someone in a glass box. Like Mandy here." Mike's footsteps thundered on the wood floor as he followed the red-haired woman.

"Shhh." Mandy shushed him from the front of the gallery.

He was breaking a cardinal rule of investigation: giving out too much information. Now the woman knew *Mandy's* first name, and she knew that both knew Jenna, the woman the artist had painted. He didn't care. He wanted the painting.

"I'd like to contact Cha Har, the artist. I need an address, phone number, or maybe a website?" No artist would place something in a gallery, probably on consignment, and not leave contact information.

The woman's lip curled. "The shop is closed. Leave." She snatched a worn umbrella from a stand full of them and jabbed the tip at him. "Now."

Mike lifted his hands. "Okay. You don't need to poke me. You're driving away a potential customer. And you're unlikely to have many more until you get rid of that horrible smell."

The woman shrugged. "The dog got sprayed by a skunk. Then he got wet in the rain. You need to go."

Behind the desk, something thumped the floor. Mike peered around the furniture. A large curly-haired dog lay with its head on its paws.

"Come on." Mandy grabbed his jacket and urged him toward the door. He avoided paintings on tables and others stacked against the walls as she hustled him across the gallery.

"I'm coming." As he moved, he watched the woman behind them and the umbrella spike she brandished. He stumbled over the doorsill.

The red-haired woman slammed the door. Latches clicked into place.

Mike glanced at the gallery window. The spotlights went dark.

The falling rain had lightened into a mist, but gray clouds still rolled across the sky.

"What do you think about that painting?" Mandy walked away from the gallery.

Two long steps and he'd caught up with her. "Can't say I blame Jenna for freaking out about that bizarre painting." His heartbeat quickened as he remembered the terrified look on the woman's face—Jenna—imprisoned in the glass crypt. *Nice.*

Mandy pushed the *walk* signal button at the corner streetlight.

"We're headed to Arnie's, right? A pizza and a beer. *One* beer." Mike shook the rain drops off his umbrella and twisted it closed. He wanted more than one beer. He wanted a pitcher. And he wanted that painting. If he couldn't have it right now, he'd have to settle for spending an hour with Mandy.

Could be good.

Sun rays streamed beneath the clouds, turning the glistening world golden. Steam rose from the sidewalk.

Mike slipped off his raincoat and folded it over his arm. August in Oklahoma. The last place on earth he'd be now, if the choice had been his to make.

"Weird painting," he muttered out loud to Mandy. "No doubt that was Jenna in that crypt, screaming. She makes a beautiful blonde. Must have iced her blood." He glanced at Mandy. "You know Jenna pretty well, don't you? You guys do lunch, have weekend spa dates? What else did she say about that painting?"

"She wouldn't talk about it. Wouldn't even tell me what was happening in the picture. Only that it was her."

They stepped through the doorway of the tiny establishment into Arnie's air conditioning. The smells of garlic bread and bubbling tomato sauce floated on the air. Mike's mouth watered. He'd skipped lunch and kept working to maintain his dedicated employee persona. Six months with the firm. What an assignment. What a charade.

Not much longer.

He waited with Mandy in the entry as his eyes adjusted to the dimness. and then moved to an empty booth by the front window.

Mike slid in and grabbed the beer menu. "Call Jenna and tell her you've seen the picture. Ask her the story behind it. Otherwise, she won't bring it up again."

"She'll be upset we searched for it. And especially upset that I told you." Mandy ran a finger over the smooth highly varnished tabletop.

"Don't tell her. She gets upset, it's your job that's lost. Keep my name out of this, okay?" Mike closed the menu and tucked it behind the salt and pepper. The next 24 hours were going to be interesting.

Mandy looked up. "She's not going to fire either of us over a painting. And besides, Allen Germaine's the boss. She's just the newly promoted CFO. Did you know she has a back exit to her office?"

"A back door." Mike stroked his chin. "So, when we think she's in there working away, she might not even be in the building. Wish I had a back door." He knew about the door. He'd even picked it open to get into her office—although he hadn't found what he was looking for.

A waitress walked up to their booth.

"Killian's," Mandy told her.

"Harp," Mike said. "No, make that a Snakebite. And the Special Pizza, hold the anchovies." The waitress hurried away, and he checked out her athletic legs and curvy bottom. *Might be worth pursuing another time.*

"I had no idea there was a back door until today." Mandy closed the menu. "Jenna admitted she left that way. The storm hit; she found the painting. Why was she on that street in the first place? Where was she going? The places I saw are not the kind of shops she frequents. That big mortuary down at the end...an old apartment building or hotel on the other side of the street..."

Mike took a long draw from the beer the waitress deposited in front of him. "Probably half-rented and the other rooms reserved for day use. So where was she going on her errand?"

He already knew. And he'd known what gallery the painting had been in as soon as she'd told him about Paducka's Funeral Parlor. He had a good idea what was going on in both buildings. He'd played along, trying to make the most of a stormy stroll through the Arts District.

Mandy shrugged. "Why was she there? It's not her kind of neighborhood."

"So, was she there to visit the hotel, or the mortuary? What do you think?" He was interested in Mandy's thoughts, although they were irrelevant to the situation. He wanted to engage her, make her feel comfortable, maybe even make her fall for him. That wouldn't be so bad.

Mandy shrugged. "Neither. I don't know. And it bothers me that suddenly the picture was sold, and the shop closed. Do you think another buyer was inside, waiting for us to leave?" Mandy sipped her beer. "Did you notice how many paintings were in that place? They were stacked everywhere. I wish we'd had time to find more paintings by the same artist."

Mike leaned back in the booth. Mandy was rambling. He needed to get her back on track. "Hey. You and Jenna are buds. Give her a call and ask questions. Do it." He suspected Jenna wouldn't answer her phone this time. And he suspected Jenna would claim not to know the artist.

"Okay, okay." She dug in her purse for her cell phone, pushed it on and glanced around the room as she held the phone to her ear. "No answer. And her voice mail message didn't play."

"Okay. Call again, later. Want to play a game of pool while the pizza cooks? Table's open."

They scooted out of the booth.

Without warning, something slammed into the front window, breaking it and sending shards of glass inward. The blast knocked them to the floor.

~ Chapter 4 ~
Mandy

Mandy covered her head as window glass shards pelted down. The waitress dropped a tray of beer-filled glasses. Liquid splashed Mandy's pants and shoes.

Mike groaned.

She glanced at him on the floor next to her. Blood dripped down his left cheek from a cut under his eye. "You're hurt. We need to get out of here." Mandy reached for her raincoat in the booth and grabbed Mike's arm before rushing for the front door with a dozen other patrons.

Outside, turmoil erupted. People scattered. Sirens wailed in the distance. Seconds later, a fire truck rumbled past and turned left a block away. A crowd was gathering at the corner.

Mike grabbed her hand and jogged that direction. Behind them, someone screamed.

A second boom shook the plate glass windows in the storefronts. They covered their heads as shattered glass pelted the sidewalk. A second fire truck rounded the corner, horn blaring. Smoke drifted past.

At the corner, police were stringing a line from a stoplight pole to the door of a corner shop, limiting access to the growing crowd. Down the block, flames licked at the front of a building, and shot from broken windows. Firemen dragged hoses from the fire trucks, hooked them to hydrants and pulled the flattened hoses across the street to aim at the blaze. The hoses filled and water gushed toward the building.

The art gallery was on fire.

Boom! Shock waves slammed into them. Mike grabbed Mandy's arm and pulled her close.

A second explosion rent the air.

Mandy turned. A man vaulted through Arnie's doorway, jacket ablaze. He dove to the sidewalk and rolled. Smoke billowed from the windows.

Sirens blasted. A police car screeched up to the curb.

Mike pulled her across the street and into an alley a half-block away. She pried his fingers off her arm and rubbed at the soon-to-be bruises.

He grabbed her shoulders. "Someone blew up the art gallery. We were there. Someone blew up Arnie's. We were just there. What are you not telling me about this painting of Jenna?" Blood dribbled down his cheek.

"It was a painting—you saw it." Another police car roared past them, siren screaming. "This has nothing to do with the painting or us. This is crazy."

Mike loosened his grip on her shoulders. "Convince me of that, would you?"

Something whimpered in the alley behind them. Mandy scanned the shadows where a shape huddled near a trash dumpster. She darted toward it as a car with a noisy motor inched past the alleyway.

"It's that dog from the gallery." Mandy knelt beside the animal as the car drew even again with the alley entrance.

Something whizzed through the air between her and Mike.

Mandy curled into a tight fetal position beside the dog. As a child, she'd gone target shooting with her dad. She knew what a gunshot sounded like.

Motor idling, the car waited at the end of the alley.

Head low, she clamped her hands against the back of her skull. She squeezed her eyes closed. She wished she'd had a chance to tell Will she loved him.

Minutes passed. Mandy's mind raced, she remembered good times with Will, and with Jenna. Would her life end here?

The engine chugged away from the alley entrance. She lifted her head. Mike lay curled a few yards away.

Mandy crawled toward him. "Mike! Get up. We've got to get out of here!"

He didn't move. Blood trailed down his face and onto the sidewalk.

"Mike!" Mandy leaned over and felt his breath on her cheek. When she laid her head on his chest, his heart thumped.

A flesh wound oozed blood above his left ear. Mike groaned and opened his eyes. He blinked and rolled onto his back.

Something cold touched Mandy's neck. The dog. The animal whined and scooted close, panting and shivering. The dog was as scared as she was.

The stench of skunk was overpowering but she pulled the hairy animal to her anyway. "It's going to be okay." She wished she believed that. Mandy stroked the animal and watched Mike rouse himself.

"Her cell phone goes right to message." Mandy laid her phone on the coffee table and looked at Mike, stretched out on the sofa in her living room.

He stared at the large dog lying on the floor wrapped in towels. "I could be dead." His hand dropped from the white bandage she had placed over his head wound after a thorough disinfecting. "And you were more concerned about rescuing this mutt."

"You've said that fifty times now. We could both be dead." She collapsed into an overstuffed chair and lifted her legs to the ottoman. "And as far as the dog goes, we couldn't leave him there. The gallery is gone, and that woman is either dead or in the hospital. You should have let me call the police."

"What, and tell them the fire and the explosions were because of us? That's paranoid." Mike shifted his legs and groaned. He squeezed his eyes shut. "Besides, I had that run-in with cops back in college—no need to dredge it up again. And there are all those unpaid parking tickets…"

Mandy swiped her forehead, pushed her fingers into her scalp, and rubbed in a circle. A headache pounded behind her eyes. "We should have gone to the hospital."

"They'd report it to the police. It was a random drive-by shooting. How many of those do we get a week around here? Ten or more? We were in the wrong place, wrong part of town. We don't know why the art gallery exploded or exactly what happened at Arnie's."

The dog whimpered.

"It's all right, fella. Once you dry out from your bath, you'll feel better." Mandy sniffed her hands. A faint skunk aroma remained despite the peach-scented shampoo she'd used during the dog's second bath, after his tomato juice rinse.

Mandy moved away from the dog and picked up her cell phone. "Turn on the news and see what they're saying while I try Jenna again."

Mike grabbed the television remote from the end table.

Jenna's phone rang and rang. No answer. No message.

"Why is she not answering her phone?" Mike bellowed as he punched buttons on the remote control.

"I don't know." Mandy had never known Jenna not to take her calls. And why was her voicemail not picking up?

Mike lay back against the sofa pillow and closed his eyes. "This isn't good."

Mandy glanced at the clock. In a few more minutes, the ten o'clock news would come on.

"...an inferno has now engulfed half a city block in downtown Tulsa. More details in a few moments, at the top of the hour," the newscaster said as the TV came on. The credits for the previous program rolled up the screen.

"An inferno," Mike repeated. "Lord Almighty."

Mandy's cell phone rang.

"Mandy, is Jenna with you?" Jenna's husband's voice sounded thin and strained.

"No. What's wrong?"

"She didn't come home from work today and she didn't call. She's not answering her cell. And voicemail is off. Is she working late? Have I forgotten she had a late meeting or something?"

Mandy paced across the room. "She was at work. I talked to her mid-afternoon, three or so."

"And was everything okay? Did she mention plans for after work?"

Mandy's thoughts tumbled. Jenna hadn't wanted Sean to know anything about the painting. Now Jenna was missing. She closed her eyes. The headache pounded.

"Mandy, did something happen today?"

She pictured Sean in his living room, perched on the edge of the sofa cushions, a worried expression on his face.

She glanced at Mike. His eyes were closed. "Sean, maybe you should come over. Mike McNally's here and we need to talk to you."

"Who's Mike McNally? Where's Will?"

"Will's in Toronto." She paused. "Have you had the news on?"

"No. Is there something about Jenna?"

"Not exactly, but turn it on, would you? Channel 6." The station was showing footage of the downtown gallery fire, with police and firemen at the scene. "Are you on Channel 6? You see the fire they're showing?"

"Yes. What does this have to do with Jenna?"

"Listen for a minute, okay? Stay on the phone with me but listen to the newscaster."

The broadcaster told how an incendiary device had leveled an art gallery and the loft apartment above it while also causing minor smoke damage to adjacent buildings and the businesses they contained. At this time, there were no injuries reported.

"What does this have to do with Jenna?" Sean demanded again.

"Listen, please."

"In a possibly related development, a similar explosion and fire occurred seconds later and three blocks away at Arnie's Pizza. About 6 p.m., eyewitnesses report someone threw an object through the window before the explosion. Several patrons were transported by ambulance to St. John's hospital, where they are undergoing treatment for first- and second-degree burns.

"Arnie's owner told Channel 6 that the building where Arnie's is located was insured. Inspectors have not yet assigned a value to the cost of this fire."

"Was Jenna there, was she hurt?" Sean blurted.

"I'll tell you all I can." Mandy explained about Jenna and the painting, as well as the experience she and Mike had at the gallery. As she spoke, the dog got up, shook, and plodded over to her. He let out a big sigh and lay down at her feet.

"I don't see what these fires have to do with Jenna," Sean said. "It could have been coincidence. You were in the wrong place at the wrong time."

She cleared her throat. She wanted to believe that. A coldness spread through her. "When Mike and I were leaving the area after Arnie's exploded, someone shot at us." Mandy reached down and petted the dog's head. His curly hair was still damp. The faint scent of peaches floated up to her.

"Random drive-by? This is crazy, Mandy. Have you talked to Will?"

"Not yet. There are too many coincidences. It couldn't have been an accident, and if you look at Mike's scalp, where a bullet grazed his head, you wouldn't think it was an accident either."

"What are you saying?"

"I'm telling you what happened. And I've been trying to call Jenna, too. There's no answer."

"This is crazy. I'm going to her office. I'll call you later."

~ Chapter 5 ~
Sean

Sean Wade knocked on the wide glass door of the office building. Inside the lobby, the night watchman sat at the front desk. The watchman looked up.

"Help you?" The man's voice came through the intercom on a panel next to the door.

Sean held up his driver's license. "I'm Jenna Wade's husband. Has Jenna been in this evening, since the building closed?"

The night watchman hurried to the door. He unlocked the locks at the bottom and top of the door and held it open for Sean.

"She hasn't come in. But I didn't see her leave, either. She may still be up there. Somebody did come in as I locked up. Don't recollect I've seen him leave, either. Haven't made my second rounds yet, but it's time."

"Could I walk upstairs with you? Jenna's not answering her phone and I'm worried."

The man relocked the bottom of the door. "Not against any rule I know of. I'd be glad for the company. Empty buildings are a bit creepy at night."

"Jenna's probably fallen asleep in her office." Sean hoped that was all this was.

"Let me lock the top of this door again. Wouldn't want anybody slipping in while I'm away from the desk." The middle-aged man grunted as he stretched to engage the upper lock.

After the door was secure, Sean followed the man across the wide lobby. His stomach clenched. He didn't like what Mandy had told him, and he didn't like the fire footage they'd shown on the nightly news. Mandy's suspicions could be paranoia, but Mandy wasn't prone to that. He didn't know about Mike; he'd never met the man. The worst thing was that he didn't understand why Jenna wouldn't want him to know about the painting.

"Are there fire exits on every floor?" Sean asked as they passed the stairwell.

"Oh, sure, gotta be, fire code and all." The watchman led him toward the elevator. "Four stairwells, four doors at the bottom of the stairwells, two open to the lobby, two outside in the alley. But you can't come in from the alley, least not unless someone was holding the door open. No doorknobs on the outside. We have cameras on those doors, and we make a videotape. They check it every morning, file it for six months, erase it, and use it again." He pushed the elevator button.

"So, we could check to see if she left that way?"

"Could. But not 'til Monday morning, when Ed Hubble comes in. He's in charge of building security and he works weekdays. I'm the evening staffer, Monday through Friday, 6 p.m. to 2 a.m."

The elevator doors opened, and the two men stepped in.

"What floor? I usually start at the top and work my way down, but you may not want to do the others with me."

"Thank you. My wife's office is 616, in the center on the east side of the building."

The man punched the button for six and detached a huge ring of keys from his belt. "Keys are color-coded with these plastic rings. If I can remember the right color for the floor, I'm in good shape."

Sean faked a smile. He didn't like this. There was a back exit. Why would Jenna need to sneak out? And why had she been in that rundown neighborhood on a stormy day? It had been hailing, for God's sake.

The elevator doors opened on the sixth floor to the noise of a vacuum cleaner. The janitor nodded at them and continued down the hallway. "Okay, you said east side." He stepped off the elevator to the left, Sean followed a few steps behind. They plodded down the gray carpeted hallway beneath silver LED light fixtures.

Framed employee pictures hung along the hall interspersed with photos of award-winning art used in advertising campaigns. Jenna's picture wasn't included in the display. She had a phobia about portrait photographs. Never wanted a solo picture taken, and only with a group if it wasn't to be posted on social media.

She had to know she was beautiful and that he was proud of her. What was the harm in showing a photo? Was it superstition? She'd never said.

"Here we are." The watchman selected a key and unlocked the office. The door swung open and the overhead light switched on automatically.

Sean blinked. He stepped in. The bookshelves were bare, and so was the top surface of the desk. All personal items—pictures and mementos—were gone. The office appeared unoccupied.

"Where's the back door?" Sean crossed the room and ran his fingers along the back edges of the wooden bookshelves.

"Behind this panel." The night watchman joined Sean on the back wall and touched the adjacent bookcase. One wall panel slid open. "Here."

They stepped out of the empty office and into an uncarpeted hallway.

"Whose offices access this hall?" Sean demanded.

"Your wife's and those two on the other side of the hall. The CEO and the COO." He pointed to the doors on the opposite side. Sean dashed to first one and then the other, turning the handles, pushing and pulling on the doors. Neither budged.

His head pounded. Why was her office empty? Where was his wife?

"Where does this go?" Sean indicated another door with a jerk of his head. "We've been married ten years," he said to himself. "Where is she?"

"This door goes to a small elevator and the stairway access." The watchman cleared his throat. "And ten years is a while. I imagine you're surprised."

Twenty minutes later Sean Wade parked at the curb in front of his house. He turned off the engine. The house was dark.

He grabbed his cell phone and touched Mandy's autodial.

"The office was empty. Nothing there," Sean blurted when Mandy answered. The car and the world beyond its windows made a slow whirl.

"I was there at 3 o'clock this afternoon. No way she could have cleaned out her office so quickly," Mandy insisted. "The bookshelves were jammed with books. Her desk was a mess. There were stacks of files on the floor. You were in the wrong office."

"The night watchman let me in. Her office was empty." To Sean, it sounded as if his voice was coming from somewhere other than his own body.

"I don't know what to say."

"Tell me more about this painting."

Mandy took a deep breath before she spoke. "The woman looked like Jenna. She was screaming, trying to claw her way out of a glass crypt. The rest of the painting was distorted, with lots of black and blue and gray smears, maybe dark furniture. Some light beamed in from a high window. Rays were falling on her face."

Sean shut his eyes, fully visualizing the painting Mandy described. He'd seen it himself over a week ago in that gallery.

"Did she ever mention someone painting a picture of her?" Mandy asked. "Or that she knew an artist?"

"No." Sean's voice dropped. His wife kept things from him. He knew that. Sean rubbed his forehead. He didn't like thinking she'd left him, but the police would focus on that possibility. And there was a 24-hour rule, wasn't there? She was an adult, perfectly free to disappear for that long before foul play was suspected.

"God, Mandy! Where is she? The police will say she cleaned out her office and left. They'll investigate our bank accounts and the company funds. They'll think she was embezzling, and I was involved, too." He groaned. "This is bound to effect my job."

"What if she didn't go willingly? What if someone kidnapped her?"

"Why would someone do that?" His voice was high and loud. Kidnap her? They didn't have much money—and she had no family. Still, his body chilled.

"You'd be more likely to know that than me." Mandy's voice was quiet and low.

Thing was, he didn't. *Damn it!* "But she talks to you about everything."

"I know a few things about college, things that happened before your marriage. But when I suggested that maybe someone from high school who remembered her had done the painting, her face turned white."

"Then you know we met after college," Sean said. "We were both on our own, and the past didn't matter. Her folks are dead. No siblings. She described her life as mundane, nondescript, of no interest. She was alone in the world. I became her family. But now I find out she was keeping something pretty big from me." He rubbed at the back of his neck. Why had the painting spooked her so much?

"Did she seem upset about anything lately?" Mandy asked.

Sean scooted out of the car. "No. I'm racking my brain trying to figure this out. Do you remember if there were other people in this painting?" He stared up at his house. From what he remembered, only Jenna was in the painting.

"I'm not sure. The painting was such a shock, and then the gallery employee grabbed it and Mike snatched it back to search for the name of the artist."

"I'm at the house now, Mandy. I'm going to check inside." He scanned the first-floor windows, then the second floor. "I'll call back."

A small light flickered in the upstairs bathroom window.

The streetlight cast shadows beneath the tall pin oak trees in the front yard. Sean jogged across them toward the house. That light in the window could have been a reflection from across the street, or from a car turning into a driveway the next street over.

The light glimmered again, this time through a different window. Someone was moving from room to room on the second floor of the house. Jenna? A burglar?

Sean reached the front door, unlocked it, and stepped inside. He darted to the alarm box to punch in the code. When he flipped open the box, the blinking light that signaled the alarm was operational was unlit. The alarm was off.

"Jenna?" He called her name. She had to be here. "Jenna, where are you?"

No one responded in the silent, dark house.

If Jenna was here, she would answer him. She would call out, turn on a light, or hurry to him. That is, she would have done one of those things if everything was all right.

Whoever was here, it either wasn't Jenna or she wasn't alone.

The revolver he practiced with on the gun range was in a box in the utility room. His other gun was in his briefcase, in his car.

Sean slipped through the dark house, his hands gliding along the walls, guiding him through the familiar floor plan. He crossed the open doorway to the kitchen and made a quick right into the laundry room. He closed the door, flipped on the light, opened the storage cabinet, and stretched to reach the top shelf.

He couldn't feel the gun box, but it could have been pushed to the back of the shelf.

Jenna kept a stepstool in here, collapsed and tucked between the dryer and the wall. She was forever running to get it to reach a tall shelf or the back of a cabinet.

Sean unfolded it and climbed the two steps to peer into the deep shelf. He pushed aside a pile of rags and a couple of empty cell phone boxes. No gun box. No gun.

Something scuffed the floor out in the hallway. Sean backed down the stool and crouched.

The door opened. A gun blasted.

~ Chapter 6 ~
Mandy

"He's not picking up." Mandy paced the living room, keeping the phone to her ear. Eventually, she disconnected and dropped it onto the ottoman. "We should drive over there, Mike."

"Did he ask us to drive over there?"

"No, but he's not answering. Something's wrong."

"Maybe Jenna came in and they're talking. Maybe they're arguing. Maybe they've gone to bed. It isn't any of our business."

Mandy wanted to agree with him, but an alarm rang inside her head. "It doesn't feel right. Don't you think he would have called me if he'd found her, if everything was all right?"

At her feet, the dog whined.

"Well, let's see. Would he expect you to drop everything in your life because of this weirdness with Jenna? You have, haven't you?"

"She's my best friend, Mike."

"Your best friend, but she's got a secret big enough to make her run for it. Like she's in the Witness Protection Program or something. Didn't you tell me she didn't have any relatives? No one from her family came to her wedding when she and Sean got married? Now that's shady, if you ask me."

"It's sad. Can you imagine not having any family?" Mandy would be in the same position if not for her aunt. She looked down at the dog. He responded with a tail wag and a sigh.

"Can you imagine leaving your job, your husband, and your best friend without saying a word? Apparently, she's pretty good at not only imagining, but doing," Mike quipped.

Mandy grabbed a sofa pillow and heaved it across the room at him. "Damn you. You have no idea how upsetting this is. Go away. You're not helping."

He caught the pillow, tucked it behind his head, adjusted his body, and extended his legs. "I'm helping by keeping you from going off the deep end. Since Will's not here, somebody has to keep you sane."

"I am sane."

"I'm not sure anymore. Not to mention you brought that stinky dog home and gave it a bath."

"I'll call animal control tomorrow. Someone will report him missing. I think he's a goldendoodle, and they're expensive."

"Expensive? Smelly, if you ask me. Not a dog lover."

"Well, I am. You need to go. I'm not kidding."

He stood. "Okay. But first, promise me—and Will, since I'm speaking for him in his absence—you won't go over to Jenna and Sean's house. Not unless one of them calls and invites you. Okay?"

Mandy clutched the bed pillow to her chest and rocked back and forth. Her boyfriend Will's voice, even over the telephone, comforted her and calmed her down. "Will, it's all so crazy. I have to do something."

"Nothing you can do. And you weren't invited. Besides, it's late. Wait until morning. Then, drive by. You may hear from one of them in the morning."

Will was calm, but his voice sounded odd. Was he disturbed about Jenna, too?

"You know, that empty office..." he began. "Do you suppose the guard opened the wrong room? Maybe Sean gave him the wrong office number? Chances are this is a series of coincidences."

"You can't tell me that painting was a coincidence. It was weird."

"I'm not saying it wasn't. You said it depicted a woman inside a glass crypt. Features distorted. It could have been anybody. Too bad the gallery's gone. I would like to see that painting."

"Believe me, it wasn't pleasant. Dark colors except for the light from above. Old-fashioned. Almost Baroque. Not your style of painting. Certainly not a Van Gogh or a Cezanne."

"I appreciate other artistic styles besides the Post-Impressionists."

"I didn't know you cared much about art, Will."

"There's a lot you don't know about me, honey. Maybe we should start taking care of that when I get back next week. We haven't spent as much time together lately as I'd like. We ought to think about moving in together."

"What?" The fluttering in her chest was not a new sensation. Had she heard him correctly? Did he really want to take the next step? Did she?

The dog jumped up on the bed and laid his big head in her lap.

Mary Coley

PART 2 - WEDNESDAY

~ Chapter 7 ~
Mandy

Mandy woke to her alarm and rain lashing the window. Another unusually wet August day. Four more days until Will came home. He'd kept her up late on the phone, talking about sharing an apartment or house. It had wiped Jenna and her disappearance temporarily out of her mind. But in the daylight, with the prospect of going into work and finding out whether Jenna really was gone, the feelings of anxiety and fear rushed back.

The dog shifted against her and thumped his tail. Mandy had to find out who he belonged to. She ran her fingers through the curly blond hair on his head and scratched his long ears. He grunted and looked through shaggy bangs at her, his tongue lolling from his mouth. She pulled him close and examined him for an owner's tattoo. It was possible he had a microchip.

An hour later, Mandy walked down the long empty hall in Empire Marketing. Where was everybody? Had she forgotten it was a holiday? She remembered—there was a sales conference downtown, most of the salespeople were attending. Marketing staff wasn't included.

She glanced into one empty office after another. Few

employees were at work, but the office doors were open. Company policy: office doors to be left open, inviting fellow workers to stop in unless you were in conference.

Jenna didn't have an open-door policy. As one of the fiscal managers, she had the right to privacy. Her phone calls and her work in general were done behind closed doors. Primarily, Mandy thought, to prevent the spread of rumors of financial problems.

She took the elevator up to the sixth floor and strolled toward the gatekeeper stationed outside the executive offices. The assistant, Mark Barnes, was one of several accountants who tracked client account expenses and payments. He worked primarily for Jenna.

Barnes glanced up from his computer as Mandy approached, his face blank. Usually unfriendly, he'd joined the marketing firm a year ago. Mandy agreed with Jenna's assessment: he had his sights set on inhabiting one of the offices for which he served as gatekeeper.

"Jenna in?" Mandy stopped in front of his desk.

"Who?" He blinked.

The guy needed to clean out his hairy ears. "Jenna. Mrs. Wade, CFO. Office 616."

He looked at her blankly. "Mrs. Wade no longer works here." His gray eyes were cold behind the lenses of black glasses. The corners of his mouth turned down.

Jenna no longer works here? A dozen questions popped into her head. "Wh— What do you mean?" She stammered. Her heart stopped beating.

"I'm not at liberty to say." Barnes grinned, baring his large white teeth.

He was feeding off her surprise like a vulture. She wouldn't give him the satisfaction of asking any other questions or displaying any emotion.

Mandy did her best to saunter nonchalantly down the corridor, away from the gatekeeper. She plucked her cell phone out of her jacket pocket and called Mike's number.

"Mike McNally. How can I help you?"

"Mike, Barnes just told me Jenna no longer works here."

"Seriously?"

"I'm calling her house." Mandy hit Jenna's home phone number on her speed dial.

On the other end, the phone rang and rang again. No one picked up.

She tried Jenna's cell. A recorded voice announced, "This number is no longer in service. If you dialed this number in error, please hang up and try again."

Mandy plunged down the stairs to her floor and jogged the empty hallway to her cubicle. The message light flashed on her desk phone.

As she reached for the phone, someone pounded on the cubicle panels.

Mike stepped in. "Anything?"

"Jenna's cell phone has been disconnected. And no one answers at their house." Mandy slumped into the padded desk chair.

Mike leaned against her modular desk. His forehead furrowed. He touched the bandage taped across his left temple. "What do you think is going on?"

Mandy frowned. "Something's terribly wrong."

"No kidding."

"You agree? You no longer think this is all coincidence?"

"Do you have Sean's cell number?"

Mandy grabbed her phone, pushed Sean's autodial, and listened to the recorded message before leaving her own. "Sean, it's Mandy. Call me, please." She disconnected. "Let's go over there."

Mary Coley

~ Chapter 8 ~
Sean

Someone must have hit him over the head with a hammer. That was the only explanation for why his head felt as it did. But it didn't jive with his memories, and it didn't jive with where he found himself.

The room was unfamiliar, with hotel furnishings. White sheets and a duvet cover tri-folded at the end of the bed. Curtains with a gray geometric design covered one entire wall, but most likely, the window was much smaller, centered in the wall behind only the central portion of the drapes.

He tried to drill through the pain in his head to remember why he was here. Slowly, his mental fog thinned. He'd been at the house, looking for Jenna. Someone was upstairs. He was on the step stool in the utility room, looking for his missing gun when the door opened.

Sean checked one arm and the other, threw off the sheets and checked his legs and torso. Most likely the large bandage on his left thigh covered an injury. He remembered a gun blast, didn't he?

And he remembered Jenna, there, in the house.

The fog thickened again. He'd taken something. And now he couldn't remember.

"Damn it!"

He needed to remember. He rubbed his temples, squeezed his eyelids together.

Jenna had been there. She had cried when she realized she'd shot him. She'd helped him to the bathroom, where they'd cleaned the wound.

But she hadn't come to this hotel room. He'd come alone, then taken a tablet to ease the pain and help him sleep. He looked around the room for a sign someone else had been here. Nothing. He lowered his head to the pillow and sniffed. No scent of Jenna's shampoo. No scent of her at all.

Wisps of the memory fog began to dissipate.

Last night, before the pain pill had kicked in, he'd thought long and hard about her empty office. Two years ago, they'd created a contingency plan. It was always possible that he—and therefore they—would have to be on the move quickly. She'd allowed him to keep a few secrets. She'd requested it; said she didn't want to know everything. In exchange, he had to stop asking for details about her past.

Jokingly, he'd said, "Are you wanted?"

And jokingly, she'd said, "I hope so. You want me, don't you?"

Ten minutes later, they'd continued the conversation. "I would like to know if you were involved in criminal activity."

Her eyes had clouded over. She'd never gotten around to answering the question, even though he'd clarified that his own activities were not criminal. In fact, they were the opposite. He was undercover, an insurance fraud investigator.

His wife was intelligent and capable. He wished he also knew whether she was in danger. With all his connections, it should be easy to find Jenna, but he sensed there was a time frame, something she had to accomplish in a short few days. And she didn't want his help.

Sean eased out of bed and limped to the bathroom shower.

The explosion at the art gallery, followed by the explosion at Arnie's and the drive-by shooting all shouted illegal activity. Most likely at the gallery. It was a cover for something, probably art fraud. Copies, replicas, maybe pastiches or even false documents of provenance.

The Tulsa Arts District was up and coming, and that little gallery was no doubt on someone's list to buy and renovate. The district was featuring small museums, including collections from Tulsa musicians. Galleries showcasing local artists as well as southwestern and Native American art were located on every street.

He'd been at Yolanda's before, looking for fakes after his company had been alerted that someone here in Tulsa was dealing in fraudulent art.

Sean had a few calls to make before trying to learn more about the gallery destroyed in last night's fire.

He should have bought the painting the first time he'd seen it, weeks ago, when this investigation began. Even if he hadn't bought it, he should have asked about the artist. But he hadn't. He didn't want to call attention to himself, making it possible he would be recognized during future visits. He couldn't create any possible tipoffs.

The woman painted clawing the sides of the crystalline crypt *had* looked like Jenna. Except for the platinum blond hair.

~ Chapter 9 ~
Mike

Mike parked his truck near the curb across the street from the Wades' two-story craftsman-style house. Although the rain had stopped, the street was slick. A rivulet ran beside the curb.

When Mandy started to get out, Mike put his hand on her arm. "Wait. Let's check it out first," he suggested. "Looks deserted." There was no need to barge in. Who knew what was happening inside? Sean Wade was no idiot.

They waited. A dark-haired woman pushed a stroller down the sidewalk. Not bad looking. She'd lost her pregnancy weight. She leaned over and spoke to the baby.

A small boy on a bicycle with training wheels wobbled down the sidewalk. The kid's safety helmet looked too big. Mike had never worn a helmet, and *he'd* never scrambled his brains by falling off his bike as a kid.

Behind the boy, an elderly man wearing a rain jacket hurried to keep up. His shirt protruded in the front with his beer belly. Mike would never allow himself to develop a pot like that.

A florist's delivery truck passed, and a plumbing service van. *Ah, the joys of home ownership.*

"I'm going to ring the bell. See if Sean's there." Mandy announced as she slipped out of the truck. "You coming?" She walked in front of Mike's truck and started to cross the street.

Tires squealed as a white SUV accelerated down the street. Mandy leaped for Jenna's front yard seconds before the vehicle zoomed past without slowing. A few houses down, the SUV made a U-turn.

Mike hopped out of the car and dashed to Mandy. He huddled over her as the roaring motor neared again. "Crap!" Mike protected his head with his arms.

The vehicle, a GMC Yukon Denali with a chrome cattle guard attached to the front bumper, zoomed past.

Nothing happened.

Mike released the breath he'd been holding. "You okay? Too close for comfort." He checked the street. No Denali. He reached for her hand. "Let's go," Mike urged as he helped Mandy stand.

"You go back to your place. This is my deal. Jenna was my friend. I won't let her down." Mandy crossed the lawn toward the porch and the wide oak front door.

Mike didn't want to go inside. But how would it look if he let her go alone?

She pushed the doorbell. A few seconds later, she pushed it again. "There's no one here," she announced as she dug in her purse. "But I have a key, and I know the security code."

Mike glanced over his shoulder at the street. "Then why are we waiting around out here? That crazy driver might come back."

Mandy inserted the key and pushed the door open. She darted across the wood floor to the keypad. The alarm blinked silently. She punched in the code. "Sean? Jenna?" she called. "Anyone here?" Her voice echoed through the still house.

Mike closed the front door after glancing at the street again. "Now what?"

"We look around. Upstairs. Let's check their bedroom."

Mike trailed behind her as she raced up the stairs to the second-floor landing and into the first open doorway. Mandy didn't need to know he'd been here before. But not in the daytime. No one had been home then, either.

"In here." She led him into the master bathroom and the adjoining closet. Racks of clothes hung in the closet, and every inch of space on the shoe shelf was full. Suitcases were stacked on the upper shelves. "She didn't leave here on her own, or she would have taken a suitcase."

Mike considered the king-sized four-poster bed. "Bed probably wasn't slept in. If Sean was here, he didn't stay. The comforter isn't even wrinkled."

"Or else they made the bed this morning," Mandy said.

They stepped out into the hallway and checked the other bedrooms and adjoining bath. Back downstairs, Mike followed Mandy through the living room, dining room, and the office.

Mail had been piled in the center of Jenna's desk, and her closed laptop had been pushed to one side. Mandy thumbed through the stack of mail. "The usual bills."

They walked to the kitchen. Mike glanced at the notes and photographs stuck by magnets to the refrigerator door before pulling the cabinet doors open one after another.

Mike remembered the layout of the house. Laundry room down the hall, and the garage. He headed that direction, pausing to open doors to closets and to the half-bath. He opened the door to the laundry room and looked inside. "Mandy?"

When she appeared in the doorway, he pointed to a spatter of dark red that clung to the painted wall. "What's this? And this?" Mike motioned to the tile floor.

Dark red spots trailed into the hallway and toward the small half-bath. They stepped carefully around them. The bathroom was spotless, the blood trail ended. When Mike opened the door to the garage, Sean's black BMW was parked on the left side of the large space.

Out on the wet street, tires squealed.

Mike jabbed the garage door opener panel beside the back door. He dashed to the front of the garage and ducked beneath the rising door.

"What the hell—" Mike yelled. "Stop!"

The white Denali slammed into the back of Mike's little truck.

"Hey!" He shouted.

The Denali changed gears, backed up, and slammed into the side of the truck.

Mike charged into the street. The vehicle's engine roared. He glowered as it sped away.

The Denali had crumpled the driver's side door, flattened and mangled the front left tire. The bed of the truck tilted.

Mike fisted his hands. *What the —?*

~ Chapter 10 ~
Mandy

Two hours later, the same policeman who had responded to her 911 call at the Wades' house dropped Mandy off at her office.

Poor Mike. She had dragged him into this fiasco, and he was paying the price. First his head, then his truck. The Denali had been a battering ram. It had left the scene, while Mike's truck had been towed off so an insurance adjustor could determine if it was totaled.

When Mike was finished at the police station, she'd pick him up and take him to his apartment.

Hopefully Mike would tell them everything, including about last night's drive-by and his head wound. The police might consider last night's event random, but they'd file a report, creating a record of the incident. Mike would get a lecture for not going to the hospital for treatment and for not reporting the shooting immediately.

Mandy passed her assistant Billie without a glance. She wasn't in the mood for meaningless greetings.

Billie cleared her throat. "Mr. Germaine is looking for you, Mandy. Better go by his office. ASAP. He isn't happy."

"Good," Mandy said. Germaine might have questions for her, but she had questions for him, too.

On the sixth floor, a new employee sat at the desk Barnes had occupied earlier. After the assistant announced her on the office intercom, Mandy pushed through the glass double doors and into the huge white-walled office. Germaine, the CEO of the company, Phil Macon, the COO, George Young, Director of Marketing, and Barnes were seated at a table in front of the bank of windows on the far wall. Their looks followed her as she crossed the room.

"Ms. Lyons," Mr. Young said. "This morning, top representatives of the Straightaway firm came to meet with you. You were not here to update them on their marketing campaign. They received no analytics. Therefore, they have declined to exercise their option to renew their marketing contract. Where were you?"

Mandy sucked in a quick breath. She'd completely forgotten the meeting. Earlier in the week, she'd worked on the Straightaway analytics and prepared their report. It was in a folder on her desk, easy enough for Billie to have found and provided to the client. She probably hadn't been asked.

She stared pointedly at Barnes, and said, "The report was on my desk. Billie could have retrieved it." She swallowed. "I apologize for not being here. My best friend, Jenna Wade, is missing. According to Mr. Barnes, she no longer works here. Her cell phone has been disconnected, and I can't reach either Jenna or her husband. I'm concerned. I want to know what happened to Mrs. Wade."

"Mrs. Wade resigned late yesterday. Her departure had to be handled immediately for security reasons," Mr. Germaine said. "Mr. Barnes, who is highly qualified, will step into her position."

All four men turned stone faces toward her. The scent of cigar smoke wafted past as the air conditioner kicked on.

"But—"

"You were absent this morning without authorization," Mr. Young lectured. "And you jeopardized an important client relationship. If you don't get this account back for us today, we'll have to let you go. Is that clear?"

Cold spread through her body. "Absolutely." Mandy left the room, chewing her lip.

Straightaway was one of her borderline accounts. The owners were condescending and arrogant, but they'd been pleased with both the marketing plan she had developed and the initial ad slogan. If they were shopping around and had found someone else they wanted to work with, there wasn't much she could do. The marketing/advertising business was cutthroat. Clients came and went every day of the week. How could they hold her completely responsible for this client's decision to move on? Mr. Young knew she'd been working on that analytics report. He could have asked Billie to find it. He could have handled the meeting.

She stomped to her cubicle. If she'd had an office door, she would have slammed it. The message light blinked "2" on her desk phone.

She retrieved the messages by speaker phone.

"Mandy?" a voice whispered. "I need your help. Please. Go to Jandafar. Find Lamar. By Saturday—" Jenna's voice cut off.

Jandafar? Lamar? She had no idea what—or who—Jenna was referring to. Saturday was three days away.

Message two played. Silence, and then a click as the caller disconnected.

Jandafar. Was that a place? And who, or what, was Lamar?

She grabbed her large carryall, stuffed it with the personal items from her top desk drawer, and marched out of her cubicle.

In the hallway, she stopped. She returned to her desk and flicked on her computer.

Mandy clicked onto the internet and typed "Jandafar." The screen filled with possible search results, including several foreign sites. She scrolled down through the list but found none that indicated any such place in the United States.

Maybe the name wasn't a city. It could be the name of a school, or a hotel, or even a development. How was she going to find it?

Jenna's office was empty. Her belongings could be anywhere. But Jenna's personal items would still be in her home; there could be something about Jandafar there. Did Sean know about Jandafar, or had she also hidden this from him?

Mandy made a snap decision, and it seemed right. She didn't like this work atmosphere. She had savings, enough to hold her for a few months. Right now, she couldn't see past what was happening with Jenna. Her friend was the closest thing to a sister she'd ever had. She couldn't lose her.

Her cell phone rang and the caller ID flashed *Animal Control Tulsa*.

"That large shaggy dog you called about earlier today? Still no lost dog reported. I'll keep your info for three days in case we get a call. If you want to bring him in, that's what we're here for. Otherwise, if you like the dog, I'd keep him."

She hung up. What would she do with a dog? It had been years since she'd had a pet. What would Will think? She tucked the picture of her and Will into her bag, as well as a few books and a glass apple paperweight.

Jandafar. The name tickled her brain. She'd heard it before. Where? Mandy rubbed her temples.

Jenna Wade was the first person she'd met when she'd started work at Empire Marketing Strategies. The two of them had literally bumped into each other when she'd come for orientation and had ended up having lunch together. During that conversation, something had passed between them, a spark of like minds and possible friendship. They seemed to have enough in common, emotionally or intellectually, to be friends.

Jenna Wade lived in the present. That first day, she'd made it clear: except for the immediate past, the past didn't matter. She and her husband Sean had been married ten years after dating a short time. Love at first sight. She'd shared that her parents were both deceased and that Sean was her only family. Mandy had wondered what had happened, but she didn't ask.

Now, Mandy reflected that in the years she'd known her, Jenna had never so much as mentioned her parents in passing. She'd called her life "boring" and insisted that nothing important had ever happened.

But somewhere, at some time, Jenna had mentioned Jandafar. When?

~ Chapter 11 ~
Jenna

Dark clouds still loomed above the rolling prairie landscape outside the car, leaving the grasslands in shadow. An occasional mercury vapor light on a thick pole shone in the false twilight. Animals grazed in verdant pastures. Farm trucks and SUVs drove the road with her. Jenna constantly checked the rearview mirror for headlights, potentially someone following.

She considered what could lie ahead of her and shuddered. She might not survive this confrontation. But she wouldn't live as she had been. For twenty years, she'd been looking over her shoulder. For the first ten, she'd remained aloof from the world. Then, she'd found Sean. She didn't want to lose him or the life they'd built. She had to confront the past. And then she had to tell Sean.

Unable to go forward to the unknown, her mind scurried back over the past thirty-six hours.

The note arrived with a small bouquet of daisies from a local florist. Jenna looked up the sender's address in the reverse directory. Paducka's Funeral Parlor? What was *he* doing there? For that matter, what was *he* doing in Tulsa?

As the enormity of it hit her, her hands shook. He shouldn't be here. He shouldn't have contacted her. After twenty years, she'd never expected to see him again.

She carried the flowers into the ladies' room down the hall and stuffed them into the trash bin. She couldn't look at them, and she couldn't risk that anyone else would see them and ask about the sender. Mandy especially.

Jenna closed her eyes. Her heart hurt. Pain pulsed up to her head. She didn't want her friendship with Mandy to end. She didn't want her marriage to Sean to be over. She didn't want this phase of her life to end. She'd made a big mistake coming back to Oklahoma. The past had caught up with her.

Immediately after she received the note, she knew what she had to do. There was no way to save what she had built. Once the truth was exposed, she couldn't risk being anywhere her face might be recognized and then tied to the crime she had supposedly committed.

Twenty years ago, Idaho had seemed far enough and secluded enough. Survivalists lived there. Everyone respected each other's privacy. They wouldn't care what she had done, or what someone said she'd done. She could make a life.

Waitressing wasn't easy. Guys hit on her all the time, but one sweet woman took her under her wing, invited her for dinner, and told her all about the online courses she was taking to better herself.

Jenna signed up for college courses the next day. She excelled at math; that was a logical choice. She couldn't be the veterinarian she'd wanted to be; that was a clue they could use to find her. She'd been the one who rescued abandoned animals, who nursed injured birds and rabbits.

But she made a mistake in Idaho. She missed friendly people and allowed herself to be drawn in. Apart from her sweet woman friend, people protected themselves from others, didn't reach out, maintained a barrier. She thought she wanted the same thing, but she discovered secluded people might have warped ideas. Without the balance of alternative thoughts, people became shuttered in their thinking. Polygamy was illegal in the law books.

But her sweet friend's husband based his life on early Mormon theology, and it turned out her friend was okay with a sister wife.

The move to Kansas had to happen to finish her degree. A resident summer semester at the university was required. The transition to KU had been easy at first. She liked being around younger people again. She was aloof to men but had girlfriends. The night before graduation, one of them had shyly come on to her during a party and asked if she was a lesbian, too.

Jenna clammed up and left the party. A lesbian. That was what they all thought? She'd successfully camouflaged what she was. She accepted her diploma and moved to Arkansas the next day.

Jenna came back to the present. She'd been on her way to Paducka's to meet him after all these years. She knew it was the wrong thing to do. If he'd found her, the others might find her, too. She shouldn't go there, shouldn't let him see her.

If nothing else had warned her, if her internal warning bells had not pealed loud enough, the crazy weather should have kept her from going. But it hadn't.

Hail slamming into her had caused her to seek shelter under that awning. She had no idea the building was an art gallery.

The painting had scared her so much she hadn't gone on to meet him at the old funeral parlor, even though it was close by. The paranoia that still lived in a cavity of her brain wondered: had he hoped she would see it when she came to see him? Was there a message in the painting?

If she hadn't seen the picture first and had gone on to meet him, what would have happened?

She couldn't think about any of those things. She should never have come to Oklahoma with Sean. Dear Sean. What would she do without him?

She'd fallen for him, and he for her. They'd married. During their years in Little Rock, her silence about the past had begun to eat at her relationship with Sean. She loved him. He'd thought Tulsa might be a better home. She'd never even suggested that it wasn't. Had she not known deep inside that it would dissolve the fragile life she'd created?

Once in Tulsa, she'd hungered for friendship like she'd hungered for a lover. Sean had satisfied both needs for years. But finding Mandy, trusting Mandy so completely, had been her saving grace when she'd been getting close to the edge. She truly was her best friend, much more of a friend than Jenna's sister had been growing up.

She shouldn't have told Mandy about the painting. But finding it and knowing the message the artist might be sending her, was too much. At least she'd stopped herself from blurting out everything. Maybe it had been because of fear Mandy would judge her if she knew what had happened, fear that Mandy wouldn't believe in her innocence. Mandy might abandon their friendship if she knew what Jenna had done.

Jenna rubbed her forehead. The car whizzed past another light pole.

A sob caught in her throat. She hadn't meant for the gun to go off, but her hand had been shaking. Hopefully, she'd cleaned Sean's wound completely and there'd be no infection or permanent damage.

Her destination had to be near, and there'd surely be a mom-and-pop roadside motel with a vacancy. From what she'd read, most of those places were inhabited by sex perverts, people who couldn't reside anywhere near a school or a playground or a place where kids lived. Sleeping in a room for the night with a pervert next door could be tolerated. What choice did she have?

~ Chapter 12 ~
Mandy

Mandy zipped her carryall closed. Will wasn't going to like what she was doing. But she couldn't see any other course of action. Surely when they talked it through, he would understand and support her decision.

With her carryall on one shoulder, she left the office. She wouldn't be back. Billie wasn't at her desk. For a minute, she regretted leaving without even telling her administrative assistant goodbye, but there wasn't time to find her, and she didn't want to run into Germaine again.

She rode the elevator down to the parking garage and rushed to her car, where she stowed the carryall in the backseat.

Mandy sat behind the steering wheel for a few minutes, uncertain of her next step. She wanted to return to the Wades' house to search, but the memory of what had happened to Mike's truck was fresh. And she needed to go back to her place to let the dog out. She'd left him in the kitchen with a water bowl and several old towels for a bed.

She called Mike's number on her cell phone. When his message clicked on, she waited for the beep. "Mike, it's me. I had the privilege of being called in front of Germaine this morning, right after I came in. I'm officially on notice. Apparently Straightaway is defecting. But I also had a phone message from Jenna and a hang up. Call me."

Mandy started the car and zoomed out of the parking garage. Her stomach twisted with sudden anxiety. She checked her rearview mirror, then the side mirrors. There didn't seem to be anyone following her.

She drove the few miles across town and turned down the Wades' street. Ahead, a moving van sat angled into a driveway, partially blocking the street. The Wades' driveway.

Mandy drove closer to the house and parked. Workmen were carrying out the living room sofa, and another hoisted Sean's favorite chair into the van. Yet another man balanced the coffee table on his broad shoulders. She bolted out of the car and onto the driveway.

"Who's in charge here?" Mandy demanded.

One of the workmen glanced at her as he carried a large box toward the van. "Inside, lady." He motioned toward the open front door.

Mandy stepped inside. The living room was already bare of furniture. She crossed the room to the kitchen and found two men wrapping dishes and tucking them into boxes on the counter. Another man ripped tape from a roll to seal the box.

"Who's in charge?" she asked again.

The overweight man with bloodshot eyes looked up from the box as he sealed it with tape. Sweat rolled down his face and neck. "That would be me."

"Who hired you to move this stuff?"

He studied her. "And you are?"

"I know the Wades, and as of yesterday, they weren't moving. I think you are trespassing, and I'm going to call the police." She took out her cell phone.

"I have the papers right here. No need to call the cops." He pulled a thick square of paper from his shirt pocket and unfolded it. "Sean Wade. You see?" He turned the paper towards her.

Sean's signature looked official, but she couldn't be sure the signature was really his. "Where are you taking their stuff?"

"Storage. The Wades are moving out of the state. We're supposed to pack it all and get it to the storage unit today. A rush job. No time to talk." He grabbed another piece of packing paper and rolled a glass in it.

Two men sauntered into the kitchen, picked up the round kitchen table, and carried it out of the room.

Mandy hurried into the utility room. The wall and floor, where the blood stains had been yesterday, were clean. She leaned against the washing machine. She had no idea where to look for information about Jandafar.

Down the hallway, the bustle of packing and moving continued.

Moving out of the state? She didn't believe it.

Had Sean found Jenna?

It was unlikely she'd find what she needed in the laundry room, but it was worth checking. Since the room doubled as a safe room, Jenna might have stored important things here. Mandy opened the cabinet and peered in, then scooted the step ladder over and climbed it to check the upper shelves. Spray cans and chemicals.

"Hey. Who are you? What are you doing here?" The man who claimed to be in charge eyed her. Mandy stepped off the step stool.

"I'm Mrs. Wade's best friend. She borrowed some things and I'm getting them back before you pack them up."

"They're in the laundry cabinet? You should go." The man jerked a cell phone off his belt and jabbed in a number.

"I'll grab the blouses she borrowed and be on my way." Mandy lunged from the room, avoiding the man's attempt to grab her arm. She took the front stairs two at a time and rushed down the hall. The linen closet door stood open; the shelves empty. A few steps further, the storage closet doors were also open and the shelves empty, wiped clean. She ran to the master bedroom and into the master closet. Clothes still hung on the racks, but the shelves above, where Jenna had stored out-of-season clothes and shoeboxes, had been cleaned out.

A burly moving man followed her into the closet. "Boss says to get you out of here. He's called the police."

Mandy plucked a few items from the clothes rack. "These blouses are mine." She pushed past him and raced from the bedroom.

She clattered down the stairs, the man only a few steps behind her. She dashed into the room Jenna and Sean had used as an office. A young man with long hair was packing books away, clearing the shelves of photographs and knickknacks.

Quickly, she scanned the titles of the remaining books. *Natural History of Oklahoma*? As far as she knew, Jenna wasn't into natural history. Mandy removed the book from the shelf and clutched it to her chest with the clothing she had grabbed from upstairs.

"What are you doing?" the worker asked.

"Just leaving." Mandy rushed down the hallway and out the front door. Two men were loading the washing machine into the moving van.

Mandy pitched the clothing into the back of her car and threw the book onto the passenger seat. She floored the accelerator and zoomed out of the neighborhood.

Her cell phone rang.

"Where are you? What are you doing?" Mike's voice was tense.

"I've been to the Wades' house. A moving crew is packing everything up, taking it to storage. And the blood stains are gone."

Mike's voice quieted. "Where are you now?"

"Driving. Just left. They called the police. The man in charge had a contract, signed by Sean. I'm not positive it was his signature, though. Where are you?"

"Finished at the police station. Can you pick me up? Since

my truck's a crumpled heap in the police impound, it's difficult for me to meet you anywhere."

"Okay. Be there in about ten." Another call was beeping in on her phone. Will's name flashed on the digital screen. "Gotta go."

She clicked over to the new call as she pulled to the curb and parked. "Hi!"

~ Chapter 13 ~
Will

He heard her voice and the pain in his gut eased a bit. She was safe. She hadn't done anything irreparable yet.

"Hi yourself. What's going on? Tried your office line. Billie said you were AWOL and Germaine's not happy." He didn't know Allen Germaine personally, but Mandy had told him plenty of stories about him.

"Germaine and I have parted ways. I walked out." She chuckled.

"You've quit? Mandy?" Will's voice rose. Maybe she *had* done something irreparable. Quitting wasn't something she'd normally consider without pondering for a long time, making a pros-and-cons list, and consulting her horoscope. But the past 24 hours were unusual. Starting with that damn painting and going straight to explosions and drive-by shootings.

"Doesn't sound like me, does it?"

At least she agreed with him on that. "No."

"Things are not good here, Will. Jenna's disappeared and so has Sean. Her office is empty. Her cell phone has been disconnected. Sean doesn't answer his phone, and now moving men are packing up their things. And somebody totaled Mike's car early this morning while we were at the Wades' house trying to find Sean."

Will processed this information. Jenna had disappeared.

Sean had disappeared. It had been 24 hours since he'd talked to his buddy. Sean's daily call was behind schedule, but not enough to be concerned. However, the moving van was a problem. For Sean to pull the plug meant something truly big had happened. Was it the painting or something else?

"Mike again, huh?" He knew she would believe he was jealous, that she would believe the worst of him, even without cause.

"Aren't you worried about Sean and Jenna? Will, they've vanished." Mandy's voice had a quiver to it.

"They'll turn up somewhere, eventually. I've known Sean for a long time. He'll get in touch."

"If you've known him for a long time, tell me where he is. And tell me why he didn't seem to know anything about where Jenna might have gone. He was worried last night."

"There's a lot he doesn't know about Jenna. She's a big mystery to him. That's part of what makes her so intriguing. But it's getting old." He was exaggerating, but all was not roses in paradise for the Wades.

"They were having marital problems? She didn't say anything to me."

"And she wouldn't. She didn't talk much about the first twenty or so years of her life. What did she do? Where did she live? Who were her friends? How can you trust somebody like that, Mandy?" He'd never trusted Jenna, but she was married to his best friend. He tolerated her, and he often reminded Sean that he'd married a wild card.

What had happened during all those years Jenna wouldn't talk about? Did Mandy know something he didn't? "Did you and Jenna ever talk about keeping secrets from a spouse or significant other?"

"We talked about whether or not your spouse should know everything about you. I told her, only the important things."

"What's important? Previous relationships, lies you've told, drug use, crimes you committed?" Will drummed his fingers on the table where he sat. He wasn't sure he wanted to have this conversation right now, when he couldn't see her face.

"Jenna told me she believed it wasn't necessary to tell everything if it didn't have anything to do with you now and what you want out of life and who you love."

"Was Sean demanding she tell him about her past?" Will knew Jenna's secrets were an issue, but he couldn't imagine his friend insisting his wife spill her guts if she didn't want to. He loved and respected her.

"Jenna told me nothing earth-shattering had happened, she just didn't like remembering those years. The past didn't make any difference to her and Sean as a couple."

"Anything else?" Will's fingers drummed faster. He had to get to a meeting, but he wanted to hear Mandy's response. He had his own concerns about the secrets he was keeping from Mandy.

"The big question is, can a marriage, or any relationship, survive if there are big secrets between the couple? I personally don't think so." Mandy's statement hung in the air. "My heart aches for Jenna. Her secrets don't matter to me."

He felt as if he'd been speared. The two of them had talked only a little about high school and college experiences. It sounded like Mandy was wondering if he was keeping secrets from her. "We need to talk more about this, honey. But I'm wondering, did she ever say anything concrete about her past?"

Mandy clicked her fingers. "That's it. She told me once she never wanted to hear the name Jandafar again. But she said it on her message today. She told me to go there."

Jandafar. Will's mind whirred. Pieces of separate puzzles were coming together. He'd heard that name before, too. Will's concern grew.

"Mandy, listen carefully to me."

"I'm listening, Will. I'm also thinking. This is confusing."

"Could be you've got to let her go." His fist clenched; his knuckles were white.

"Let her go? You mean, accept she's disappeared and something has happened to her? How can you ask me to do that? She's my best friend!"

"Did it ever occur to you this might be dangerous? Your buddy Mike's car was totaled. And he was shot. The two of you could have been killed in the explosions. Is this worth losing your life?"

She didn't respond.

"Do you not realize what the thought does to me?" The words poured out of him. "And I can't be there with you! Damn, Mandy. I love you—and you're driving me crazy. If I could catch the first plane back to you I would, but then both of us would be unemployed. Think about what you're doing."

~ Chapter 14 ~
Mandy

Mandy closed her eyes. This was all too much. Jenna had confided in her, when she so rarely shared anything with anybody. And she had called this morning with a desperate plea. *Jandafar. Lamar.* What did those names mean?

And what about the book? She grabbed it from the passenger seat and flipped the book open. The name "Molly Bergen" was scrawled across the inside front cover. Who was Molly Bergen? A friend? A relative?

"Are you there?" Will asked.

"Will, I'm sorry. I'm upset. I wish you were here. Mike's not much help."

"Who is this Mike person, anyway? You've never talked about him. Did I meet him at an office party?" Will's voice had an irritated edge to it.

"He's someone I get thrown into projects with. He's a creative—a graphic artist. Not my type."

"Oh, so I have nothing to worry about except that the two of you are getting blown up together and shot at."

"I think Jenna's in trouble."

"I'll come home. You may be in danger and I'm too far away to help. If you won't stop looking into this, I'm on the next plane. I'm serious."

If Will left this conference, he'd lose his job. And he was right: both unemployed would be bad news. Even if she gave up her apartment and lived with him, it would be hard to pay the bills.

"Please don't leave the conference," she begged. "I don't want you to risk your job for this. My job wasn't all that great. But you love your job. Don't sacrifice it because of me." She swallowed hard. "I'll tone it down. I won't do anything dangerous, just research, okay? I'm going to try to find out about Jenna's past. Get a handle on what that painting might have meant to her. Okay?" She was promising him something she probably couldn't do.

"Tone it down, baby, please? I'll be there Sunday."

Through the phone, Mandy heard a door close, and voices.

Will's voice quieted. "Maybe I'll hear from Sean. Maybe we'll both find out what happened. You know, he can run his insurance fraud investigation business from anywhere. Something scared her, for God knows what reason, and he's pulling things up and moving to a different locale. Simple explanation, Mandy."

"You make it sound simple. But it doesn't explain everything." Mandy started her car again. "I'll check in with you tonight. What time is your dinner?"

"I should be back in my room by ten o'clock. That's Eastern, an hour ahead of you, remember?"

"Sure. I love you, Will."

"Me too, Mandy. Be careful."

Mandy clicked off the phone. She signaled and pulled into traffic. What if Will was right and Sean and Jenna had decided to move because Jenna felt threatened? It was a logical explanation, and a lot less scary than thinking either one or both had been kidnapped or fallen victim to a dangerous plot.

She checked her watch. Mike would be hanging out in front of the police station, waiting.

~ Chapter 15 ~
Mike

Mike got up from the bench in front of the police station and sauntered to Mandy's car. "'Bout time. Get delayed on the highway?"

"Will called. He wants me to drop this whole thing. Says it's too dangerous."

"Well, frankly, even though I haven't met your boyfriend, I think he's right. I wish he'd talked you into dropping it before my truck was totaled, and before my head injury." He latched his seat belt and checked his head in the vanity mirror. "The cop had lots of questions. He didn't like the idea that the drive-by happened near the two explosions and we didn't report it."

Didn't like it was putting it mildly. His questioning had been relentless. But Mike had stuck to his story.

"You told them everything?"

"I would have been crazy not to. Most likely, I'd be sitting in a cell somewhere singing for an attorney." The lies rolled easily off his tongue. Tell them everything? They didn't know the half of it. And neither did Mandy.

"Did they believe you?"

"Let's say they didn't have anything on me, no reason to associate me with either explosion. I was clear enough about the fact that I'd been in the neighborhood. An innocent bystander. So, is Will coming back to sit on you?" The boyfriend could be a problem. Mandy as an information source would probably dry up.

"I promised I'd lighten up. Stick to research. So, research it'll be. I didn't have much luck finding anything at the house. The moving process was too far along. But I grabbed this book. Struck me as odd Jenna would have it on her bookshelf."

Mike took the book and quickly flipped through the pages. "*The Natural History of Oklahoma*? Yeah, I'd say that's strange. She's not even interested in animals and plants and stuff, is she?"

"That's why it seemed odd. And look at the name on the inside cover. Molly Bergen. Ever heard of her?" Mandy asked.

"Can't say that I have. Weird. Maybe it's Sean's book." He set it down on the console. Molly Bergen. Would Mandy find the connection between that name, Jenna and Jandafar? He hoped not.

"Don't think so. He's not a nature guy either. But there's a reason it was there. Maybe there's a connection with Jenna's message, the names Jandafar and Lamar."

His throat clenched. With the internet, it was too easy to find anything. People included. Like himself. "Is there a library in our future?" He hated libraries. Too quiet, and too many stale old books and dried-up librarians.

"Maybe. Aren't you going back to work?" Mandy flipped on her blinker and took the ramp onto the inner dispersal loop that circled downtown Tulsa.

"Hey, that's an idea. I've taken a sick day. Head injury, remember? What's your excuse?" He had called the office from the police station to check in and give his reason for not returning to work. The last thing he needed was his so-called boss on his back.

"I think I've been fired, or maybe I quit before they actually fired me. Anyway, with Jenna gone, there's no one to convince me to stay."

"You probably won't miss much except your gym membership. It's a cool gym."

"You would bring that up. And you're right. I should go

clean out my locker before they decide not to let me into the building."

"Drop me off at my place, would you? I called the office and told them I'm too dizzy to even ride up an elevator." He needed to make some calls to clear up a few things, like why the idiot had totaled his truck.

His compensation for this so-called "little" job had gone up about twelve grand.

~ Chapter 16 ~
Mandy

Mandy's footsteps echoed in the empty women's locker room of the employee gym. It was too early for mid-afternoon Pilates classes. Chlorine and sweat permeated the air.

The locker she shared with Jenna was on the far end of the first row. She worked the combination lock and opened the gray metal locker.

The top part was hers; the bottom, Jenna's. Her workout clothes and gym shoes were stacked neatly on the floor of the locker. Mandy grabbed the gym bag hanging from the back-panel hook and stuffed everything into the bag.

Jenna had tucked two pairs of socks and a blue sports bra into a net bag on a side hook. As Mandy removed the bag, an envelope fluttered to the floor.

Mandy opened the envelope flap and removed a picture. Two blond-haired girls of about the same size stood with their arms locked together in front of a man and woman. Behind them, wooden steps led to the porch of a house.

Did Jenna have a sister?

Mandy tucked the photograph back into the envelope and stuffed it into the gym bag. Behind her, voices sounded in the hallway. She removed the lock from the handle and stepped into one of the dressing rooms.

Two women came into the area. Door locks clicked on two bathroom stalls. The women's lighthearted conversation continued.

Quietly, she slipped out of the locker room. As she passed the windows onto the swimming pool, she glanced in. Daylight from the skylights reflected on the smooth water of the empty pool. She would miss her swims and her workouts. But there'd be another gym, someplace else, just like there'd be another job.

But she didn't expect to ever have another friend who cared about her like Jenna.

Mandy pitched the gym bag onto the passenger seat, started her car, and drove out of the parking lot to the street. The clouds had thinned, but puddles still lingered near the curbs. Behind her, tires squealed. A white Denali loomed in the rearview mirror.

Mandy changed lanes twice and turned a corner before the SUV had time to shift to her lane and follow. She drove into a convenience store parking lot and parked between two panel vans, then ducked low in the seat.

Two minutes later, her cell phone rang.

"So, what are you doing now?" Mike asked.

"I'm avoiding that white Denali. They tried to follow me. And who knows what they might have had in mind—a little road rage? I'm sitting it out in a QuikTrip parking lot." She dug into the gym bag and removed the envelope and the picture. "I found something interesting in our locker at the gym."

"What?"

"A picture. I think it might be Jenna with her family, the mom and dad, and maybe a sister. Do you know if she had a sister?"

"You're asking me? Don't think I ever actually talked to her..."

"Right. So why *are* you risking your life and your property to help me with this?" After she had talked with Will this morning, she had begun to wonder why Mike cared about what had happened to Jenna. Was it only because Mandy had brought him into it?

Mike cleared his throat. "Didn't you ever hear of someone doing something helpful for the sake of being helpful? Give me a break." Mandy snickered, and he chuckled. "Seriously, though. You've been my buddy at work, unlike a lot of people. I'm glad to help. Even though your man Will might knock my lights out when he gets back from wherever he's gone. That is, if we're still alive."

"Still alive?" Surely it wouldn't come to that.

"We haven't backed down. That's why they're tailing you. You want to swing by and pick me up?"

"I've one other stop to make. Give me an hour."

Mandy turned on her air conditioner as she drove to the Barnes and Noble. The temperature was climbing, and the humidity was high. She pushed her hair off her forehead as she climbed out of her car in the parking lot. She took off the jacket she'd worn to work and pitched it into the backseat. Today was the last day she'd wear that for a while.

Inside the bookstore, the scent of books filled the air, along with the bold aroma of coffee from the small café in the front corner. Half the couches and tables in the cafe were full.

Mandy hurried to the travel section. She pulled several books from the shelves and checked their indexes. She didn't find any entries about Jandafar.

A man got up from one of the overstuffed armchairs at the end of the bookshelf. She grabbed another book off the shelf, *Bed and Breakfasts of the Western U.S.*, and sat in the chair. As she flipped through the thick book, her mind worked.

Jenna was in trouble. She'd seen the painting and the photograph. And she had the book, *Natural History of Oklahoma*. Then there was the message from Jenna on her phone at work. Were these things connected?

Mandy checked her cell for voicemails. No messages. She repeated the procedure with her office phone. One message.

"Where are you, Amanda? This is the last straw." Allen Germaine's clipped voice dripped disgust. "Unless you are sucking up to the Straightaway owners, this absence is inexcusable. Call me immediately."

She turned off the phone. *Inexcusable.* A lot of things were inexcusable. Over the past hour or so, Mandy had gotten used to the idea of not working for Germaine. She would feel like a traitor to herself if she subjected herself to his abuse again.

She turned to the directory's table of contents. As she scanned the listing of inns in the Oklahoma section, one name jumped off the page at her.

Jandafar Hills.

Mandy turned to the page the index indicated. A locator map and travel directions told her how to get to Jandafar, in the Wichita Mountains, southwest corner of Oklahoma. So would the Maps app on her phone. Not that long of a drive—she could be there in 3 or 4 hours.

She thought of Mike, waiting for her at his apartment. Mike's truck was totaled. He had a head wound and a headache because she had dragged him into this. Mandy appreciated the help he'd given, but she needed to move on. Alone.

"Oh, you love to stay at B&Bs, too," the clerk observed as Mandy paid for the book at the front counter.

Mandy grinned. "I've found an interesting one to try that's only a few hours away."

~ Chapter 17 ~
Sean

The massive headache had begun to ease. Sean leaned back in the desk chair of the hotel's business office, where he'd been making phone calls for the past several hours. There wasn't any time to waste. He had to get a line on Jenna's whereabouts quickly. He might have to pull in favors and disrupt typical workdays, but it had to be done.

His first call had been short.

"Has a claim been filed for the fire at Yolanda's Art gallery?"

Tony, the supervising adjustor at the insurance firm who had initially hired him to check out the gallery, knew next to nothing. "We received notification, but no one has been sent to document what was destroyed. You remember the extensive list of inventory? Two experts verified almost everything, but there were items locked in the storeroom they were going to examine today."

"Any idea what those items were?"

"Documents. Sketches purported to be Renaissance. A Baroque they wanted to auction, Lorrain, I believe. And sketches from the Realism period, unverified artist."

"Next steps?"

"A site visit and an interview with the fire marshal."

"Keep me informed."

He scribbled several pages of handwritten notes, then made

a series of internet searches before ordering lunch. After eating, Sean placed another call.

A gruff voice answered. "Yeah?"

"Sean Wade. Have you finished loading the truck?"

"'Bout done."

"Any issues?"

"Some broad showed up. Your wife's friend. She grabbed a few blouses from her closet. Ran out after that."

Mandy. Her boldness surprised him, but his tension eased. She was looking for his wife, too. He needed all the help he could get.

"Thanks for getting this done so quickly."

"No problem, Mr. Wade. We're here to do what needs to be done when it needs to be done. That's my job."

He referred to his notes and made several other internet searches. After each, he wrote another line or two of notes.

His next call forwarded to voicemail. He waited until after the beep and left his message. "Will, I hope you've talked to Mandy. I had to pull the plug. If I remember right, you get back Sunday? I'll check in with you. Meanwhile, keep tabs on her. She could be stumbling into a dangerous situation."

His mother answered the fourth call, breathless. "Hi honey. I'm in the middle of my stretch class. This one's a killer. Can I call you back?"

"Call my cell, Mom. We're not at the house. Whenever you have time."

The last call, made precisely at 3 p.m., was redirected three times before a voice finally answered.

"Yes, Sean."

"I may need a few days. My wife is in trouble. I have to find her."

"Not a relationship issue, I hope?"

"Something from her past. I'll have a handle on it soon."

"Your presence at the raid is not necessary, if it comes to that. Good luck. You're covered, if need be."

He disconnected, pushed away from the desk, took his assigned gun from his briefcase and slipped it into his shoulder holster.

~ Chapter 18 ~
Mandy

At her apartment, after taking the dog out, Mandy changed her clothes, slipping on capris and a short-sleeved T-shirt. She curled up on the sofa, opened her laptop, and googled "Jandafar Hills Bed and Breakfast."

The inn's website was first on the list of Google's suggestions. She clicked the link.

"This historic Inn, formerly the ranch house and cabins of a guest ranch, features a scenic view of a valley in the ancient Wichita Mountains of southwestern Oklahoma. Travelers will find their visit an introduction to the spectacular granite mountains and unexpected vistas of this wild corner of the state. Should you want to spend a night or two in the Charon's Gardens wilderness area nearby, make your reservation at least six months in advance."

She scanned the rest of the article. "After being purchased by Dale and Max Hardesty in 2009, the Inn reopened to the public and has won accolades as one of the best Oklahoma Inns in the area."

The website pictured rustic cabins tucked on a forested hillside, as well as a large lodge. Other photos of the stables and riding trails offered evidence that horses were still a large part of the operation, even though Jandafar had ceased operation as a dude ranch years ago.

Mandy took out the photo and stared at the much younger Jenna. Had it been taken at Jandafar Hills? Had Jenna's parents died there? She needed to find old newspaper or periodical files from the late 1990s.

The dog bounded up to the sofa and laid his head on the seat cushion. Absentmindedly, she scratched his head. What was she going to do with him? Taking him to the dog pound was an option, but the idea made her heart hurt. He was growing on her. She liked having him for company.

She refilled the water bowl and left the dog in the kitchen.

It had been months since Mandy had gone to the nearest branch library. When she drove up, only a few cars were parked in the lot, even though it was the middle of a hot August afternoon.

Inside, the musty smell of old paper and old ink blended with lemony wood polish. Beautiful wooden library tables had been replaced by folding tables covered with rows of computers. Six of the stations were filled with library patrons either looking for a job or surfing the web. Here and there, reading chairs and small tables were still available for those who wanted to investigate a shelved book and take notes. Mandy slid into an empty chair at a computer and opened the library catalog database.

She searched for Jandafar in the periodical section of the catalog and had a hit.

Jandafar was the name of a guest ranch in southwestern Oklahoma that had been open from 1976 to 1992 and was operated by the Farmer family. One article featured a picture of the ranch house, with a family identified as the Farmers on the front porch. Once again, Mandy studied the photo from her purse. She couldn't be sure that the buildings in the two photos were the same, but the construction was similar.

Mandy conducted a few more word searches, still looking for references to the Farmer family and their ranch but came up empty.

She turned the computer off. A man slipped into the chair next to hers, bringing with him the smell of cigarettes. She glanced at him. Beard stubble, at least a four-day growth, dotted his jawbone. Bushy eyebrows hung over blue eyes. He looked at the photograph on the library table beside the computer, and then at her.

"You must not think bullets and wrecked cars and missing people are scary enough," he whispered as he reached across to her mouse; the cursor darted across the screen to the exit button and the screen blackened.

Stunned, Mandy grabbed the photo and tucked it back into her purse. Her breath caught in her throat.

His left hand slammed down on hers. "This is the last warning. Whatever you think you know about your friend, you're wrong. Forget her."

Abruptly, the man crossed the room and exited through the front door.

Mandy sat frozen at the computer. When her heart had stopped racing, she glanced around the room. No one was paying any attention to her, and the man was either gone or waiting outside. She called Mike. His recorded greeting played. She disconnected without leaving a message. Less than two hours had passed since she'd talked to him. He had no car, and he was supposed to be waiting for her. Why wasn't he answering the phone?

Outside the library, she scanned the parking lot. There was no sign of the Denali, and she didn't see anyone sitting in a car, watching. She dashed to her car, slid in, and started the engine.

As she turned onto the street, a black pickup truck drove up behind her. Blocks later, the truck continued to hug her rear bumper.

At Mike's apartment complex, she slowed and turned in. The truck followed. She stopped at the building's entrance. The pickup pulled right behind her and honked. The driver's door opened and the man from the library got out. Mandy pressed the accelerator. Her tires squealed as she exited the parking lot and turned onto the street. She shot across traffic in front of a solid line of cars.

She sped down the street, glancing often at her rearview mirror. By the time she turned a corner to circle the block, the vehicle had not yet merged into the line of traffic. She worked her way back around to a major thoroughfare and accelerated away from Mike's apartment.

Had something happened to Mike? He was a grown man; he made his own decisions. But the fact was, if he'd been hurt again, she was to blame.

She debated placing a 911 call to report a disturbance at Mike's apartment. Mike had talked with Detective Larson earlier, and the detective's reaction was disbelief. What were the chances that he would take her seriously if Mike was in danger again?

Mandy stopped at a traffic light. She checked the mirrors for a white SUV or the black truck that had been tailing her and saw neither.

She turned the corner and took surface streets to downtown Tulsa.

The neighborhood where the art gallery had been located looked better in daylight than it had the stormy evening before. She drove slowly past the remains of Arnie's Pizza and turned down the street where the gallery had been. In front of the blackened remains of the building, yellow police tape stretched across the sidewalk. Not much was left except burnt bricks and fallen timbers.

Did the fire have anything to do with the visit Mike and I made to this place? Someone had displayed a painting in the gallery, and the person in the painting looked like Jenna. Why blow up the gallery? Why not buy the picture and leave? No one would have been any wiser. The painting would vanish.

She steered into a metered space by the curb a block past the gallery. On the same side of the street, a series of shops—shoe repair, alterations, a Chinese takeout place, a CD exchange—were scattered between various unidentified storefronts. Farther down the street sat Paducka's Funeral Parlor.

From the safety of her car, she studied the oldest structure on the street. Even if she hadn't known it was a mortuary, she'd have thought the place was creepy. Curtains were cinched tight behind grimy second story windows. Leaves littered the wide steps leading up to the double front door. Even from here, she could see a crack spider-webbed across the narrow glass window at the top of the door.

Mandy thought of yesterday afternoon's storm. What was so important that Jenna had left work during a storm to come here? Jenna's destination could have been one of the other businesses.

A bell rang as Mandy opened the door to the shoe repair shop, and an elderly man pushed through the curtain separating the reception area from the working section of the shop. "Help you?" He glanced at her empty hands and scratched the thinning hair on top of his head. "Picking up?"

"I'm wondering if you have a client that—um—" This was stupid. She had no picture of Jenna, no idea why Jenna might have come here. Certainly, if Jenna had ventured out in a storm it wasn't because of a pair of shoes. "Oh, never mind. You know the gallery a few doors down? Do you know if the woman who worked there was injured in the fire?"

"Don't know. Didn't hear about any injuries."

"Did she have a dog? A goldendoodle, maybe?"

"Never saw her with a dog. Our paths didn't cross. I stay busy."

"I'm sure you do. Thanks for your time." Mandy left the business.

Next door, a neon sign flashed "Alterations." Bright orange drapes hung in the front windows, serving as a backdrop for torso mannequins wearing articles of clothing. Little signs pointed to hems and sleeves and side seams, listing the price for each type of alteration.

A buzzer sounded as the door opened. A young woman with thick glasses, her hair in a long brown braid, looked up before turning her wheelchair around to face the front of the shop. "Hello." A brown, black, and white Australian shepherd trotted around the counter and stood next to her chair. The woman stroked the dog's head, then wheeled toward her.

"I'm wondering about a friend of mine," Mandy said. "She might have been here yesterday, late afternoon. About my height, dark hair, beautiful blue-green eyes, thin. She's missing. Do you remember seeing anyone like that?"

The woman patted the dog's head and wheeled closer to Mandy. "I don't recall anyone. Did something happen to her?"

"I'm trying to find out if she was in this neighborhood yesterday."

The woman shook her head. "Sorry, can't help you."

"Thanks anyway. Say, I saw a stray goldendoodle on the street yesterday. Do you know who it might belong to?" The woman was obviously a dog lover. She would know if other workers on the street had dogs.

"No idea. We get strays. Never understood how anybody could dump a dog. But it happens."

Mandy left the shop. She paused before the next doorway. The sleazy hotel looked like a bad movie set with grimy windows and a small handwritten sign that said, "Rooms by the Night or by the Hour."

Mandy thrust her hands in her pockets. She didn't want to know if Jenna had been there. She liked Sean, and Jenna and Sean made a great couple. There was no reason for Jenna to have gone into the fleabag hotel.

"Need something?" A man pushed past her, opened the door, and paused in the doorway. "Come on in. You alone? I can fix that for ya, if ya want." He grinned, showing empty spaces between several of his teeth.

Mandy rushed down the street.

The sign in the window of the Chinese takeout place said, "Closed," and the door didn't budge. Briefly, she stepped into the CD exchange, a used bookstore, and a thrift shop. None of them seemed likely places Jenna would have visited.

That left the mortuary. She crossed the intersection and stopped in front of the steps.

A metal sign hung over the door. *Paducka's Funeral Parlor. Serving the Community Since 1922.*

A hundred years in the funeral business. What could be more depressing? Why would Jenna come here? Once again, she wondered what she could ask to find out if Jenna had been here. As Jenna's friend, she should already know the answers to questions such as: Was my friend planning a funeral? Who died?

The reality of her friendship with Jenna hit her with full force. She knew very little about her secretive friend. How could that be when they'd been friends for all these years?

Paducka's front door yawned open, and a handsome young man—a blonde Greek god—stepped outside. "Something I could help you with?"

Mandy stared. If ever there was a reason for Jenna to come here, he might be it.

"I, ah... I'm admiring this old building. 1922, huh? Your family owns this?"

He grinned, revealing beautiful, perfectly straight front teeth that glistened. "Only for a few years. But the business was operated by the same family for over eighty. We're renovating."

This funeral director was handsome enough for women to consider dying to get in, she thought. But was he handsome enough to have tempted Jenna away from Sean?

"Come in. I'll give you a quick tour. We're not actually open for services yet. Modernizing." He motioned her up the steps.

What harm would there be? It was a creepy old building, but she wanted to see what it looked like inside. Now was her chance.

Her cell phone rang. Mike's number flashed in the display panel. "Excuse me a minute," she said. "Hello."

"I thought you were picking me up." Mike sounded irritated.

"Hold on a second." Mandy turned back to the blond man at the top of the steps. "Maybe I'll take the tour another time, thank you," she called up to him. "I'll come back. Really."

She crossed the intersection and walked toward her car. "Mike, are you okay?"

~ Chapter 19 ~
Mike

"Why wouldn't I be? I'm sitting here waiting for you. What's happening?" Mike's irritation level was peaking. What did she think he was, a dog that would patiently wait for her to pay attention to him?

"To start with, a goon at the library threatened me. Then, this truck followed me to your apartment. Did you see anyone? I debated calling the police."

He glanced at the street from his seat on a bench in front of the apartment complex. "If anyone came looking for me, I missed them. I walked to the corner deli for a sandwich. You said you'd be here in one hour, not two."

"I'm sorry. I drove downtown. Thought I'd visit a few shops near the gallery, try to figure out who Jenna intended to visit before she saw the painting. That funeral parlor was interesting. A handsome funeral director could be a possibility. I don't have anything concrete."

Sheesh. She'd gone investigating without him. Why? Was she suspicious of him? "Are you coming to get me or not?"

Mandy hesitated.

He could imagine what she was thinking. He was a stranger; he shouldn't be involved in something so personal.

"Mandy, I thought we were working on this Jenna thing together." He scratched his forehead, where the bandage irritated his skin.

"The man at the library scared me. I'm afraid you're going to be hurt even worse if you keep trying to help me. I should go on alone."

"You're not serious." He stood and paced in front of the apartment building. "That could be dangerous. You're safer if I'm with you."

"I can't risk you getting hurt again. You've already helped too much."

"You want to help Jenna. I want to help you help her." He softened the angry edge he felt. He couldn't believe she would go on without him.

"Jenna is my best friend. I owe this to her."

"Tell me something I don't already know. I'm your friend, aren't I?" He didn't like to beg, but he didn't see much choice at this point.

"You have become a friend, yes, but we're tied together by our work situation—or we were until I quit. We've never seen each other outside of work events."

Mike had nothing to say to that. It was true, even though he wished it wasn't.

"I don't mean to hurt your feelings, Mike."

"I can handle it, Mandy," he blurted. He had to try a different tactic, get her to listen to him again. "Be honest with me, and with yourself. Why are you willing to risk yourself for Jenna?"

That was a legitimate question, and one he'd like her to answer.

"She was the first person I met at work. She was friendly. I needed that. I needed to feel I fit in."

"There's more to it. She isn't that nice to anybody." He had let resentment creep into his voice. He hoped Mandy didn't hear it. Jenna had never even said hello to him.

"My aunt raised me, and she told me how important it is to stick by your friends. She said you should never let a gully open up between you and someone you cared for. I don't want a gully between me and Jenna."

"Sounds like your aunt was a sentimental cowgirl," he scoffed. "Gully?"

"Don't make fun of me. My aunt had lived through it. She and my mother fought and fell out of touch. My mom and dad died, and she never had a chance to set things straight. She still regrets it. I don't want to experience that with Jenna."

"I think I hear violins," he teased. Surely this sentimental crap wasn't the only reason she'd become friends with Jenna.

"You're rude."

Her voice had changed. He was losing her. "No, really, Mandy. Sisters having a falling out is a lot different than two people who have been friends for a few years breaking off a friendship because one of them goes racing away for who knows why."

An engine turned over in the background. Mandy's car. She was on the move again, and she wasn't going to take him with her.

He had to find out if she had located Jandafar. "What about Jandafar? Are you going to try to find it?"

~ Chapter 20 ~
Mandy

"Probably." Mandy reached over and opened *Natural History of Oklahoma*, which still lay on her passenger seat. She thumbed through the pages. A large section of pages divided itself from the rest, and the book fell open. Something was stuck tightly down into the binding. She opened the folded piece of card stock.

With a purple pen, someone had written, "Come to me! It's been so long. 2 p.m. tomorrow." The writer had noted an address.

"Are you still there?" Mike asked.

"Uh, Mike, sorry. I'll have to call you back." Mandy disconnected.

She reread the note, turned the car off, and retraced her steps down the street.

In front of the old square building, a block past the blackened ruins of Yolanda's Art gallery, she stopped. The address on the card was the location of Paducka's Funeral Parlor.

The Greek god funeral director answered the antique button doorbell seconds after she pushed it. "You've come back. I knew you would. Come in, please. I'm Adam Hughes." He extended his hand as she stepped through the doorway.

"Pleased to meet you. I'm Mandy Lyons."

"I think you're sight-seeing, more than needing my services. Unless I'm reading you wrong," he said, grinning.

...ke to know more about your business." She took in ...d stairs and thick drapes over each door opening. A wooden floor stretched past the stairs into a dim hallway. ... music played through an intercom system, and vases of flowe... graced tabletops on both sides of the hall, scenting the air. The place had the look of a mansion rather than what it was. "This is a magnificent building. Must take a lot of people to keep your business going."

His teeth caught the light from the crystal chandelier above them when he smiled. "My brother and I own this building. He and I will be the primaries once we get the business going again. My great uncle purchased it late in life but neglected to develop the business when his health declined."

Mandy listened with one ear, focused on the mortician's face. Had this man or his brother written to Jenna? "Are there women on staff? Potential clients—my aunt, for example—might prefer to deal with a woman at such an emotional time."

Hughes smiled again. "Are you asking about your aunt, or are you wondering about employment?"

She forced a laugh. She'd play along with this angle. "I am between jobs right now, but I do think older ladies like my aunt would want a woman's support during the funeral planning process."

"Good enough. I have employment applications in the office. Follow me." Hughes pushed aside one of the thick burgundy drapes to reveal a door. He opened it and motioned her through.

They strolled down the long hall past several closed doors before he opened one and stepped inside. Gas logs blazed in the fireplace despite the August heat outside. The classical music she'd heard in the foyer was also wired into this room. Unpacked boxes sat on the floor in front of bookcases already full of bound volumes. From the age and condition of the hard covers, many of them would be welcome in an antique bookstore.

Several paintings had been stacked against one wall. The front painting looked like a Thomas Moran landscape, like the beautiful works she'd seen at Tulsa's Gilcrease Museum. They couldn't really be Moran's, not here in this rundown funeral parlor.

"Ah, you notice art. Shades of the Romantic art movement, mid- to late-19th Century. Moran possibly? Sorry to say, it's a copy." Adam Hughes moved a stack of magazines from the seat of a leather wingback chair and motioned for her to sit. "Where did I stash those employment forms?" He opened the middle drawer of a wooden file cabinet behind the desk.

As he searched for the paperwork, he held himself straight, artificially so, as if he were on display.

She shifted on the leather seat and her stomach clenched with the realization that no one knew she was here, all alone with this stranger. Maybe Jenna had been on her way here yesterday afternoon. Hours later, she had disappeared. Mandy stood.

Adam Hughes turned back to her and held out a paper. "Here it is."

Mandy folded the form and tucked it into her purse. "Thanks. I'll fill it out and return it soon."

"Do you have time for a tour? It's a great old building. The apartments on the third floor haven't been occupied for a long time, except for the one my great uncle lived in. They'll become state-of-the-art lofts. Want to see them?" He smiled his dazzling smile again. He was George Clooney handsome.

"Another time. I have an appointment."

Hughes followed Mandy out of the room and down the hallway.

She glanced inside the only room with an open door. The glass crypt on the display table in the center of the room was illuminated by a crystal chandelier. Goosebumps broke out on her arms.

She jumped when a hand touched her shoulder.

"We plan to carry unique caskets. That's a crypt from our crystal line. They're used mostly in family mausoleums. Ever seen one before?"

"No." Mandy's heart thumped. Had Jenna been here? Had she seen this after, or before, the painting? Her breath caught in her throat.

"Let me show you the unique features." He stepped past her and into the room. Lamps blazed and the chandelier brightened.

"I'll pass." She hurried away from him to the hall door and shoved aside the drape.

"I'll see you out," Adam Hughes called from behind her.

"I can find my way." Mandy crossed the foyer to the front door. She couldn't get outside fast enough.

"Hope to see you again. I think my brother will agree the business needs a woman's touch, an emotional élan. Thanks for coming by." He called to her from the entry.

Mandy didn't look back. She stopped herself from taking the steps two at a time and charging across the street before looking both ways for traffic. She raced to her car, slid in and locked the doors. Her hands trembled.

The room at Paducka's Funeral Parlor could have been the setting for the painting of Jenna screaming, trapped in the glass crypt.

~ Chapter 21 ~
Mandy

Mandy thumbed through the bills in the cash pocket of her wallet. She had $33 in bills, about two dollars in change, her ATM card, and her MasterCard. And she was on her way to southwestern Oklahoma, 200 miles away.

No one on the planet had any idea where she was going, except maybe Mike. Will would have no idea where to look for her. Should she call him? He had already threatened to return early, told her what an idiot she was for pursuing this. He was going to be mad when she returned, even if she made it back before he did.

She pushed his name on the dashboard Bluetooth phone display. His voice message played after three rings, and the beep sounded.

"I'm sure you're in a meeting, honey. Things have gotten weird here. I can't get hold of Sean. Their house was emptied by movers this morning. Some goon threatened me in the library. I think I've figured out where and what Jandafar is. It's a B&B in southwestern Oklahoma, used to be a guest ranch. I think maybe Jenna vacationed there as a teenager with her parents. Something happened, and I'm going to go find out what. I'll call you later this evening from Medicine Park. It'll be late."

She chose her next words carefully. "I know you're disappointed in me. But I think Jenna's in serious trouble. I've got to help if I can. Hopefully, it'll all be over by the time you get back on Sunday. Love you. Talk to you soon."

She disconnected. Her phone battery indicator hovered in the red zone. She didn't want to be without that lifeline, and she plugged her phone into the car charger.

Mandy knew she was doing the right thing, but Will might not see it that way. He was protective of her. Their relationship had become serious, even though neither of them had wanted anything serious at the beginning. Did he love her enough to get over his disappointment that she had gone against his wishes?

Mandy stopped at her apartment to get the dog, clothes, and a few necessities from the bathroom, then at a nearby QuikTrip to grab a small bag of dog food. She merged onto I-44, the Turner Turnpike, and headed southwest toward Oklahoma City and eventually Lawton and the Wichita Mountains. She hadn't been to that part of the state in years, but the first 90 miles of the journey through forested eastern Oklahoma was rote.

The interstate passed over hills and into valleys, all of them lush with green pastures or covered with forest trees of oak and ash. Cattle and horses grazed in the pastoral setting. The dog remained curled in the passenger seat, his head on the center console, his eyes watchful.

An hour and a half later, she drove through Oklahoma City, navigating crisscrossing highways to get on another turnpike that would take her to the southwestern corner of the state. At a gas station, she studied the map she kept in the glovebox. She could have used the Map feature on her phone, but she liked seeing the names of all the small towns just off the highway, towns like the ones where her parents had grown up. Back on the road, the turnpike stretched to the straight blue horizon. The temperature had risen into the nineties, much more typical for late August weather than the previous gloomy days.

An hour later, the dropping sun hung low enough that she flipped down the sun visor. Her stomach rumbled, and the gas gauge showed only a quarter of a tank. When she reached Lawton, she stopped at a truck stop with a Subway deli located inside. A sandwich and potato chips were as much as she could afford until she could find an ATM.

Mandy walked the dog in a grassy area to do his business, gave him water, and slid back into the car. Her cell phone rang.

"Where are you?" Will demanded.

"Lawton," she said. She didn't give him time to respond. "I think Jandafar may be somewhere northwest of here, near the Wichita Mountains Wildlife Refuge. I know it's crazy, Will. But I'm worried about Jenna."

Will was silent on the other end of the line. She waited.

"I can't believe you're going ahead with this," he finally said. "You may be putting yourself in danger, and yet you don't know for certain anything has happened to Jenna."

"It seems that way. But I have this feeling she's in trouble, and the only one to help is me."

"I don't want you to go on alone, Mandy. I'm coming home."

"But I don't want you to miss your meeting. It's too important." He had told her his future with the company hinged on this meeting. A lot of the upper execs were there, and his presentation could earn him a promotion.

"It is. But so are you. Don't you understand what you're putting me through right now? If I must pick between you and my job, I pick you."

She sucked in a quick breath. She'd been waiting to hear those words. Why did he have to say them now? She bit her lip. "I'm doing this on my own, Will. You don't have to be here. I can find Jandafar. I can get the local police involved. I won't do it alone, I promise. I'll probably be in Tulsa by the time you are on Sunday."

"What if it's not that easy? What if you don't find Jenna, or any trace of her?"

Mandy didn't want to think about that. She had to find Jenna. Hadn't her message said, "by Saturday"? It was late Wednesday. She started the car. "I need to get back on the road again, honey. I'll call you when I get settled in a motel tonight."

Will didn't respond.

"Are you there? I said—"

"I heard what you said. Please don't do this."

"I love you, Will. Talk to you later." She disconnected.

In the sky, the wispy clouds had turned pink and deep rose. She drove toward Medicine Park. The sky glowed, bathing the road and the surrounding farmland in golden twilight. Her stomach felt hollow despite her recent dinner. Will was mad at her.

Headlights gleamed in her rear-view mirror. A big sedan had crept up behind and was now only a few feet from her rear bumper. Her heart skipped. A truck coming from the opposite way came too close to the center line, and she jerked the wheel to the right, afraid the driver was navigating into her lane. The shoulder of the highway buzzed under her right tires; she corrected, pulling back into her lane. The sedan behind her accelerated into the passing lane, honking. She took her foot off the accelerator. Thank God the guy was moving on. She didn't want him on her tail as she drove these last few snaky miles.

The car completed the pass and returned to her lane. Brake lights glowed red, and the vehicle's speed dropped below the posted speed limit.

Now the driver wanted her to pass. Another car was behind her, hugging her rear bumper. A line of traffic came towards her in the opposite lane of the two-lane road. The car honked. She raised a hand in exasperation. The sedan in front slowed even more. Her speedometer read 50 mph. She tapped the horn. Brake lights glowed.

There was an opening in the oncoming traffic. She put on the turn signal and started to pull out. A horn blared. The car behind was attempting to pass. She jerked the wheel and got behind the slow sedan again.

Another opportunity to pass the car opened. The next oncoming vehicle, a semi, topped a hill a mile away. She pressed the accelerator and started to pass. The sedan sped up. She accelerated, and the other car matched her speed.

When she looked over at the vehicle, the driver grinned.

Mandy pressed the brake pedal to drop back as the approaching semi neared. But the sedan slowed, too. She tapped her brakes. The big car matched her pace.

The approaching semi-tractor trailer driver laid on his horn. Mandy panicked. The sedan would not let her back over.

Mandy swerved to the left shoulder and off the pavement into the dirt. The semi blew past, horn blaring as she skidded to a stop.

Dust swirled around the vehicle. When it had settled, the big sedan that had forced her off the road was parked yards ahead on the opposite shoulder.

A car topped the distant hill. As it grew closer, the blinking lights on the top of the black and white car came on. It pulled in and parked at an angle beside her.

The sedan on the opposite shoulder eased back onto the road and drove on.

Mandy jumped from her car and hurried to the officer as he got out of his vehicle. One of his hands rested on the butt of his pistol.

"That guy tried to run me off the road," she shouted, pointing down the highway.

The patrolman glanced at the retreating vehicle and shrugged. "You're parked on the wrong side of the road, Miss. I'm going to have to cite you for that."

"The man in that car wouldn't let me pass. Then he wouldn't let me pull back into the lane. A truck was coming. I had no choice but to pull over to this shoulder. It was that or die in a head-on collision."

"Please return to your vehicle. I need to see your license, proof of insurance, and registration."

Exasperated, Mandy led the officer back to her car. She stretched across the passenger seat to the glove box for the requested documents. The dog watched with big eyes. "Seriously, sir, the man tried to make me have a wreck. He should be the one who receives a citation."

The policeman studied her, shone his flashlight at the dog, into the backseat, and around the car's interior. "Wait a moment, please."

He returned to his patrol car with her documents. Mandy waited. Her cell phone rang.

"That was lucky," a man's voice said.

"What?" Her blood froze.

"The cop. Lucky for you. It should have ended there, with you dead." With a click, the call disconnected.

She touched the call back button with trembling fingers. The message screen read *Number not available.*

"Did you get the license number?" The police officer leaned over to peer into the window. She jerked. "The tag number of the vehicle playing cat and mouse with you. Did you get it?"

"Of course not! I was too shook up. And he just called me on my cell phone." Her voice squeaked.

"Must be someone you know. Did you recognize his voice or get a look at him?"

"No."

The radio clipped to his shoulder crackled and he stepped away.

He tapped on the side of the car door. "I'm going to let you off the hook. Sounds like you have a problem. If I were you, I'd get off the highway for the night. You can follow me into Medicine Park. Flash your lights if you see the vehicle." He glanced at the dog and smiled. "My girlfriend has a goldendoodle. Smart. What's his name?"

Mandy glanced at the dog. Name? To name him would mean he was hers. If he wasn't hers, whose was he? She said the first thing that came to mind. He was big and white. "Moby."

"Like the whale. I like it."

Hands shaking, Mandy followed the policeman back onto the highway. She focused on the cruiser's taillights trying not to think about what could have happened out on the road with the truck if she had not pulled off. She glanced down every side road as they neared the small town. She shivered despite the hot air outside the car. She rolled down her windows.

In Medicine Park, the patrol car turned down a street and parked in front of the small police station.

As the policeman walked toward the station, she called to him. "Can you suggest a place to stay?"

"Straight on in town there's a small motel and cabins to rent. Not the big chain operations, but clean. And they won't care about Moby if you're only staying one night. You didn't see the car as we came into town?"

Mandy shook her head.

"Maybe the guy had enough cat and mouse." He walked over and handed her a business card. "Call if anything happens tonight, or if you spot his vehicle. Highway games are dangerous."

She read his card and shoved it into the unused ashtray on her console.

"Thanks, Officer Findley. I appreciate it." She drove away from the station, still glancing down alleys and side streets, looking for the dark sedan that had run her off the road. When she saw a sign advertising cobblestone cabins, she turned in.

At the office, she paid for one night's stay in a tiny cabin. The clerk, an older bald man wearing coveralls, smiled at Moby.

"Your dog well-behaved?" he asked as he handed her the key to her cabin.

"Never had any trouble with him chewing anything he shouldn't." The man had no way of knowing she'd known the dog less than 24 hours.

After parking in front of the tiny cabin, she snapped the leash onto Moby's collar and let him sniff around the landscaping while she noted the unusual red cobblestones that made up the cabin's exterior walls. The air was quiet and still, and at least 90 degrees. Hairs rose on the back of her neck. Was someone watching her?

She rushed back to her cabin. Moby trotted in behind her, jumped onto the bed, circled, and lay down. She pushed the deadbolt into place, latched the chain, and fell onto the queen-size bed beside the dog. Her hands trembled.

What had she gotten herself into? Someone had tried to kill her.

~ Chapter 22 ~
Will

Will closed the door to his hotel room and sat on the bed. He was still unsettled by his last conversation with Mandy. Despite what he wanted her to do—had insisted she do—she was going right ahead with her plan to find and rescue Jenna.

What was it with her? Was a friendship so dear to her she'd begin a dangerous rescue mission with no preparation?

Mandy had no idea what she might be getting herself into.

He and Sean had talked about what might happen if Jenna realized her cover was about to be blown.

Of course, she didn't know they both knew who she really was. That would have defeated the purpose of the charade all three of them were playing. But now Mandy had intruded, and the game was heading in a direction they had not foreseen.

He pushed a button on his cell phone. The screen read, "Calling Mandy."

"Hello?" she sighed.

"Where are you? What's happening? I thought you were going to call?" The words exploded from his throat, and he wished he could erase them from the airwaves, as if they'd been written on a dry erase board.

"Sorry, I just arrived. A jerk tried to run me off the road on my way here. I followed a policeman into town."

"This is insane. You're making me crazy." And she was. He was bonkers. He'd never expected to begin to care for her so much, to want to protect her, to love her. How had this happened?

To a certain extent, he was in control of his emotions, as he tried to stay in control of everything he did, and said, and even thought. But with Mandy, it wasn't easy. At first, he'd been just going along, wanting to provide part of a couple Sean and Jenna could interact with. But things had changed. It had become something more.

"Have you heard from Sean?" Mandy asked.

Initially, Will had insisted there was nothing to worry about with Sean. The short voice mail from Sean gave nothing he could share. "When I call his cell, I get his message. The house phone has been disconnected."

"You finally agree with me this is odd?"

"He's done this before. They've suddenly decided to move someplace else, and Jenna has gone along with it. He doesn't have to check in with me for approval. Tulsa is the only place we've lived in the same town since college."

Will scratched an imaginary itch on the back of his neck. He would feel better about all of this if he had talked to Sean. The message Sean had left him this morning had told him little.

"Okay. You've said that before." Her voice sounded lonely and sad. "Maybe I'm wrong to have come here. Maybe I should have flown to Toronto to be with you. Maybe I should be back in Tulsa looking for an apartment we could share."

Panic surged through Will's brain. This was not the way he wanted the conversation to go. He wanted Mandy to stay in Tulsa and mind her own business. It would be a disaster if she flew to Toronto. "Go home to Tulsa, Mandy. Wait for me there."

"Can you think of anything that might help me? Did Sean ever talk about Jenna's past or mention any secrets she was keeping?"

She was ignoring his advice. He heard the earnestness in her voice. It speared right through the walls he'd built. He took a deep swallow before he lied again. "He didn't know much about what happened with her parents or her sister other than that the parents died so she was an orphan."

"So, she did have a sister. What happened to her?"

"Sean told me Jenna hadn't seen or heard from her sister in twenty years." At least that wasn't a lie.

"Maybe the painting sent Jenna a message about her sister?"

That painting of the glass coffin was a problem. He couldn't figure out where the painting fit in, or why it had frightened Jenna so much. Maybe Sean knew, but since they hadn't talked... He had to continue to believe that within a few days, he'd hear from his friend. "You saw the picture. Did it send you a message?"

"Someone is in danger. Someone who looks a lot like Jenna. What if it wasn't Jenna, but her sister? What if it meant her sister was in trouble? Maybe she's running to help and not running away."

"She could have read something into the picture, whether that was its purpose or not. It could be a sicko's fantasy." He hoped what he was saying was true. He liked Jenna. She was the perfect balance to Sean. They both tolerated each other's secrets. Will still wasn't sure Mandy could handle *his* secrets. "I don't want you to stay down there alone. I'm worried about what you might find. Go back to Tulsa tomorrow."

He heard a whine in his voice, which he didn't like.

"If it's any comfort to you, Will, I'm worried, too, and I'm being careful. Jenna asked me to come, and I'm going to follow through even though I don't have much to go on."

"Mandy, is there anything I can say that will convince you to drive home tomorrow?" He anticipated her answer and wondered how he was going to cope with it.

"I don't think so. This B&B may be a dead end. I'll have no choice but to leave. At any rate, I'll see you Sunday."

That was it. What he'd said had made no difference. His heart was a lump in his chest. He took a deep breath and said, "Call me tomorrow, promise?"

Part 3 - THURSDAY

~ Chapter 23 ~
Mandy

Mandy looked out of her cabin window early Thursday morning, shortly after sunrise. Only a few cars shared the parking lot with hers, and none of them were white Denalis or sedans like the one that had run her off the road last night.

"Let's go find breakfast, Moby." The dog's tail wagged slowly. A drip of doggy spit rolled off the end of his tongue. She grabbed her purse and the directory listing Jandafar as a B&B and left the tiny cabin.

The August air was already warm. She rolled up her T-shirt sleeves.

Mandy strolled down the main street toward what might be a café. Patrons were sitting at outside tables. Hopefully, Moby could sit with her while she ate. She didn't want to leave him in the motel room. No telling what the dog might do when left alone.

Was it because both she and Jenna had lost their parents that the two of them had become such close friends? Mandy wished she knew the story behind Jenna's tragedy. Jenna had been old enough when her parents died that she'd lived on her own. What had happened to her sister? Mandy was grateful to have had her aunt in Austin and not to have been completely alone.

The last two years of high school when she'd lived with Aunt Grace, she'd been rebellious. Her aunt's constraints were suffocating. During college, she had pushed to have her own way on more and more decisions. But she'd stayed in Austin to be near where Grace lived and worked. Taking the job in Tulsa, a nine-hour drive from Austin, had been her breakaway move. Her aunt had finally stopped trying to direct her life. She sent cards on holidays and called weekly, but she left all decisions up to Mandy and rarely berated her.

How would Grace react if she knew Mandy had quit her job to search for Jenna? Most likely, there would be panic in Grace's voice as she asked questions. Then, silence. If Mandy didn't comment, Grace would realize her words had no effect. The topic of conversation would change to something safe, and within a minute the phone call would end.

Like Will, Grace would want her to return to Tulsa.

Two of the outside tables were unoccupied when Mandy reached the cafe. She stepped inside and waited until someone noticed her by the *Please Wait to be Seated* sign. Moby sat obediently behind her.

"Hey there." Middle-aged, dark hair streaked with a few gray strands, the waitress was still slim and healthy-looking. "I'm Nancy. Table outside is open, since you've got your dog with you."

"Thanks. I'll have coffee and a water with lemon. Two eggs over medium, bacon and biscuits, no gravy."

"I'll bring it out in a jiffy."

Mandy stepped back outside and settled into a chair at one of the sidewalk tables. Moby lay at her feet. She opened the Bed and Breakfast directory and read the directions to Jandafar Hills. It was several miles west and north, an easy drive from Medicine Park. She flipped through the directory and found other lodging facilities, cabins, and cottages, in the surrounding area.

Nancy, the waitress, placed a mug in front of her.

"You worked here long?" Mandy asked, closing the directory.

"A while." She filled Mandy's coffee mug. "My folks moved here when I was in high school. It's peaceful here, and this café stays busy. Tips are decent."

The waitress worked her way down the sidewalk, checking other outside customers, refilling coffee mugs. A few minutes later she came back to Mandy. "You visiting?"

"Thinking about looking for work around here," Mandy said. It was becoming easy to lie.

"What kind of work?"

"I've always thought a bed and breakfast would be a great place to work. Smaller than a motel, something along the lines of an inn, or maybe even a dude ranch. Any place like that around here you could recommend?"

Nancy quickly surveyed her tables. "There are small lodging operations here in town. Not sure anyone's hiring. But there's Jandafar Hills outside of town. Used to be a dude ranch. Turned B&B several years ago. Don't know if they need any help. Summer's winding down, but fall is still busy around here. You could try there."

"Good people to work for?"

"I've never heard anything one way or another. They seem to do well in the summer. Locals use their gazebo and dining hall for parties, reunions, weddings and things. Owners are Dale and Max Hardesty. They probably wouldn't mind if you drove out and asked about work. I might even have a flyer with their listing in the brochure rack. I'll check."

"Thanks." She liked the feel of the town. Peaceful and quiet.

Minutes later, Nancy slid a plate of food in front of Mandy. "Here you go." She handed her a double-fold flyer listing area bed and breakfast inns. "This has directions. It's a twenty-minute drive from here, twisty road, but beautiful vistas of the Wichitas."

"Any history about the place I ought to know? Ghosts or anything? I'm superstitious."

"Never heard anybody talk about ghosts. Seems like a woman died on a trail ride back when it was a dude ranch. And there was a fire out there once. I never paid much attention. Might ask the Hardestys." Nancy tore Mandy's bill off her order pad and handed it to her. "I'll be your cashier."

"Thanks." She thought about what Nancy had told her. A woman died, and there was a fire. Did Jenna have anything to do with either event?

Mandy glanced at the brochure as she ate. It listed area lodgings, including Jandafar Hills Bed and Breakfast Inn. If she was truly looking for a job, she'd check all those places.

A white Denali with tinted windows and a chrome cattle guard maneuvered into a parking space in front of the café.

Mandy's appetite disappeared. She nibbled a slice of bacon, her gaze on the Denali. No one got out of the vehicle. She studied the other customers. No one looked interested in the giant SUV.

Nancy came outside and refilled her coffee mug. Mandy poked at the plate of food, ate part of a biscuit and a forkful of egg. She sipped her coffee and waited.

What were the chances this vehicle was the same one which had rammed Mike's car in Tulsa? She didn't see any dents in the front fender, but the cattle guard was scratched.

It could be a coincidence. Even so, she dreaded the short walk back to the cottage to get her car even though it was broad daylight and the café was full of people. Vehicles were driving by in the street. It seemed unlikely she'd be attacked here, now.

She pulled out her wallet and laid down the right amount to cover her bill and a tip. Then, she untied Moby's leash from the table leg and set off at a fast walk down the sidewalk. Twice she turned and looked back. The Denali remained stationary.

At the little cabin, she retrieved her things and turned in her key. She checked the street for the Denali. All clear.

In her car, she reread the directions for Jandafar Hills, then started the engine.

"Off we go, dog. Here's hoping we find Jenna today."

She drove down the street, past the café and the white Denali, and turned west out of town. Mandy opened the sunroof and cracked the back two windows. The road wound around hills or climbed them before descending into valleys. S-curves meant slow speeds.

Would Dale and Max Hardesty be able to tell her the history of Jandafar Hills? What were the chances they might know the owner of the book, Molly Bergen, possibly a.k.a. Jenna Wade?

Mandy drove the speed limit, enjoying the late August morning air and the verdant countryside. She'd negotiated the final part of a switchback curve when headlights flashed behind her, glaring in her mirrors. It was the Denali.

Her heart began a hammering rhythm, a crazy beat that crawled from her chest up into her head. Where was the next pullout?

Bang! The huge white SUV rammed her rear bumper.

Mandy slammed her foot down on the accelerator and pulled ahead for an instant, but the white vehicle was soon on top of her again.

Another jarring bump jerked her entire body. Her car skidded sideways. She twisted the wheel, trying to stay on the road, but the big vehicle butted her again. Her car pitched onto the shoulder and the right front tire thudded into a hole.

It shuddered, then pitched and rolled down an embankment.

"You're okay, miss. We're going to get you out and to the hospital. Do you hurt anywhere?" The speaker's voice sounded far away. "Miss? Miss? Look at me."

She worked her eyelids open. Her head pounded, and pain shot through her arm and leg. The car lay on its side, and the air bag and her seat belt were holding her in an impossible vertical position. "My arm hurts."

"What about your legs? Can you wiggle your toes?"

She could, but her legs hung at a weird angle and her knees hurt. "Yes, both feet. But I can't pull them out. I'm trapped. Where's the dog?" She tried to look for Moby, but her neck was jammed by the tight seatbelt and the inflated air bag.

"Dog's okay. He's up on the road. And we'll get you out. The door is smashed. We'll get our equipment hooked on and get it open. You sit tight."

"Not going anywhere," Mandy muttered, more to herself than to the EMT.

With a screech, the door opened. Arms reached in and a disembodied hand used a blade to deflate the airbag and slice her seatbelt in two. Another set of arms eased her out of the car and onto a flat carrier. They strapped her onto the board and hoisted her up the hillside to a waiting ambulance.

"I don't think the hospital is necessary. I think I'm okay," she protested. She could see the hospital bills now, and as of yesterday, or whatever date they used as her severance date, she no longer had medical insurance.

"We'll let the professionals at the hospital in Lawton decide. That's where we're headed."

"My dog?"

"We have a pet kennel for vacationers. Not too full since season's nearly over. I'm sure they'll watch him for you."

A policeman walked over as they shoved the gurney into the ambulance. "I'll follow you to the hospital. We'll need to talk there."

Three hours later, Mandy left the emergency room, discharge papers in hand. The policeman had brought her bag and purse, interviewed her about the accident, and told her which garage had towed in her car.

"Where can I rent a car?" she asked the volunteer at the information desk.

"Champion's Car Rental. Local operation, no Avis or Enterprise," the old gentleman said. He looked over his bifocals at her. "Had an accident, did you? Doing okay?"

"Yes, I'm okay. Banged up and sore. Do you have a number, or could I use your desk phone to call them? Do they pick people up?"

"I reckon we could talk ol' Doug into coming out to pick you up, since he's only a half-mile down the road. Let me call him."

An hour later, Doug, a skinny white-haired talker who winked at her after every sentence he spoke, had picked her up, taken her back to his shop, and rented her a 2015 Trail Blazer. She used her credit card. He didn't ask for ID.

"Your car's at Sparks, yeah? They'll get it drivable, but it may not be pretty. You staying around here? Not driving out of state, are you, Missy?"

She knew Doug would spread the word about her as soon as she had driven away from his car lot. Gossip was the lifeblood of small towns, and people kept score on who had the freshest gossip. She thought it was even possible that Nancy, at the café in Medicine Park, might have already started a gossip thread about her, and that Doug wanted to tie onto it.

"Might be looking for work. Was on my way out to Jandafar Hills when someone ran me off the road."

"Ran you off the road? Get a look at the idjit?"

"Wish I had, but no. They came up on me too fast. I was busy trying to keep my car on the road, but that big white SUV rammed me until I skidded off."

Doug shook his head. "Dammit. People can be fools on these roads, in such a hurry! Well, you be careful. And not just because you're in my rental. Got a cousin works at that burger place up in Meers. Been there? Worth stoppin' in."

"If I have time, I will. I may be staying for a while if I find work."

The man peered at her. "We'd be pleased to have you move here, and Jandafar wouldn't be a bad place to work. Dale Hardesty's a sweet lady."

"What do you know about the place? Any interesting history?" Nancy had mentioned a fire. Jandafar could be where Jenna's parents had died.

Doug lowered his head and squinted at her. "You sure all you want is a job? You a reporter?"

"No. Just looking for a job."

Doug frowned at her. "That right?"

"I'm superstitious. Sometimes I ask for morbid details when I ought to let it go. I'm not sure about Jandafar as a place to work. If somebody died there…"

"It was a long time ago. Bad cabin fire. Married couple with teenagers. The kids up and disappeared, figured that whoever set the fire took off with them, else they were completely incinerated. Never found hide nor hair."

Gooseflesh rose on Mandy's neck. "When was this?"

"Been a while. Fifteen, twenty years or so." He scratched his forehead. "Hmmm. Hadn't thought about that business for a while. Had a crime writer come through here a couple years ago wanting to dig it all up again. Don't think he got far with his investigation. We keep our calamities close to our chests. Don't do no good to talk about it. Won't make it go away, and leaves a bad taste in your mouth, you know?"

Mandy signed the paperwork.

"Oh, don't you worry about that business. It was a long time ago. Where hasn't somebody died on this planet? Ghosts must be floating all around us. You get on out there and talk to the Hardestys."

Doug stood in the doorway of his office as she trudged out to the rental SUV and waved goodbye. She'd head for Jandafar again. But first, she had to swing by the police station, get directions to the kennel, and retrieve Moby.

At the police station, she looked for Officer Findley, but he was off duty. She was directed to the local animal shelter.

Moby greeted her with a bark and frantic full-body wags. She was glad for the dog's companionship. It would have been nice if Will was here, or even to have had Mike's company.

The advantage with the dog was that he never disagreed with her or told her what to do. She slipped gingerly back into the rented vehicle. Her muscles had stiffened and every joint screamed.

~ Chapter 24 ~
Jenna

Sweat glued her dark hair to her forehead. The panic receded, and her breath came evenly again.

She was all right.

She was still safe.

It had been a close call, hearing them nearby, looking for… her?

What if she'd done the wrong thing?

What if the painting meant nothing?

What if finding it in that gallery was only a coincidence and not a message?

Why had she told Mandy?

She pinched her eyelids shut, but tears flowed anyway.

Why had she mentioned Jandafar to Mandy?

What if they killed her? What if Mandy came and they killed them both?

She started to hyperventilate again.

Deep breath. Slow.

Breathe in. Slow.

Count to ten.

Let it out. Slow.

Deep breath. Slow.

She was all right.

If Mandy came, she would not be stupid. She would ask the right people the right questions. Eventually, she'd come here.

Mandy would find her.

Sean was so used to being her everything, best friend, lover, confidante. He'd not been sure of Mandy or their friendship. But she needed her. Sean kept things from her, and she kept things from him. They had learned the boundaries. Mandy had been a good friend.

But she'd been getting tired of keeping the secrets. She'd felt a void where her past should have been. Too many things she couldn't share.

It had been a relief to get the note, to have contact from someone from the past, someone who might fill in the memory blanks from that night.

She'd been grasping at straws.

And now she'd never know.

What if she'd seen him and not the painting?

She'd been at another fork in the road and hadn't realized.

The tenseness left her body. She shifted on the hard surface, moved her head so that the folded blanket provided a thicker pillow. She was hungry, but she could do without food. After it happened, when she was still a teenager, she'd done it all the time.

Jenna slept.

~ Chapter 25 ~
Mandy

Her sweaty hands were slick on the steering wheel of the rented SUV. She accelerated slowly through the turns and glanced frequently at the rearview mirror. The car traveling behind her stayed well back. After one particularly sharp hairpin curve, she saw the sign: *Jandafar Hills Bed and Breakfast. Where Western Hospitality and Luxury Meet Good Food!*

Mandy turned onto the road, and its all-weather surface crunched beneath the tires. When she rolled down her window, hot August air rushed inside. Insect sounds—grasshoppers and crickets—came in with the air. Mandy breathed deeply.

Native trees, oaks and elms, grew thick beside the road, groupings of smaller trees clustered between them. Sumac bushes had begun to change colors, adding red to the mostly green landscape. The open country, broken by green hills and granite outcroppings, evoked memories of vacationing with her aunt. Cicadas droned from the trees.

She and Aunt Grace had spent a full week at a cabin somewhere around here the summer she was 14. Grace had napped and read, leaving Mandy to wander the countryside and ride horses at the nearby stable. She remembered the pungent scent of horse sweat and the aching soreness of her inner thigh muscles after hours on a trail ride.

She hadn't ridden a horse since that summer, and she and her aunt had never had the time to take a vacation together again.

The road curved and the trees thinned. She drove over a cattle guard and passed into an open meadow. Paddocks and barns spread off to the right of the road, and a large ranch house with a wide veranda on three sides sat at the end of the drive on the left. Straight ahead, a row of cabins perched on the wooded hillside.

A black and white border collie raced toward her, barking. The animal stopped and waited until she drew even, then ran beside the SUV as she continued up the road to the house.

In the seat beside her, Moby sat up and pressed his pink-brown nose to the passenger window.

She parked by the white gate in front of the ranch house. A sign near the veranda read *Jandafar Hills. Welcome.* The dog trotted to the gate and sat, ears pricked, waiting.

Mandy contemplated stepping out of the SUV, wondering how the collie would react to the energetic goldendoodle beside her.

A black-haired woman appeared on the front porch and waved. "Hello," she called. "Come here, Doobie. Good boy." The dog wagged its tail and looked from the woman to Mandy and back again before he trotted to the porch.

"Hi. Are you Mrs. Hardesty?" Mandy called as she scooted out of the SUV. "Wait, Moby." The big dog's tongue lolled out of his mouth, but he sat obediently in the passenger seat. He looked from her to the other dog, his body quivering.

"Yes." The woman brushed a loose strand of hair off her face and came down the steps. The dog, Doobie, walked with her. "How can I help you?"

"My name is Mandy Lyons. Nancy in Medicine Park told me you might be hiring. I came out to see what Jandafar Hills was all about." Mandy felt a twinge of guilt because of her lies, but the words slid out anyway. This lying was getting too easy. Why couldn't she tell this woman why she was here? She doubted she had anything to fear from her.

Dale nodded. "Actually, I saw Nancy this morning, and she told me about you. I also heard you had an accident on the road. You doing all right?"

"I'm okay. My car wasn't so lucky. I'm in a rental." Mandy motioned at the Trail Blazer and rubbed her injured arm.

"I see Doug Champion set you up with his favorite. Not just anybody he'll rent that one to. You must've impressed him." Her blue eyes twinkled.

"It's a lot nicer than my car. I'll have to figure out how to pay the bill to get my car fixed."

"Well, folks around here can be real neighborly. Don't be afraid to ask for help, and chances are you'll find someone who's willing to offer it. My name is Dale, by the way. Why don't you come inside, Mandy? You a coffee drinker? I'll get you a cup and we'll talk, see if I have any work you might be interested in. Nancy was right, I could use help."

Mandy carefully followed her up the steps and into the house, limping. Dale Hardesty looked to be about forty, but she trudged along like a much older woman. Her skin was makeup-free, and her cheeks were dotted with freckles.

Doobie lay down by the door, his head on his paws.

Wide windows let air and light into the house. Potted plants positioned on tables and grouped on the floor near the windows gave the house the oxygen-rich scent of a greenhouse. Warm oak floors glistened, and the scattered area rugs looked like Navajo weaving, with bright colors and intricate patterns.

Dale plodded to the kitchen and motioned to the breakfast table by the bay window. The aroma of something cooking—beef stew? —hung in the air. Mandy slipped into a barrel-style chair and stared outside. Green hills stretched into the distance, broken by stands of trees, the ever-present granite boulders, and horses grazing. Lush green lawn hugged the house. Water tumbled in a nearby water feature, cascading over rocks into a pool. Leafy foliage and brightly colored flowers—impatiens, she thought—crowded the flower beds and gave the place a garden-like feel. Birds and butterflies flitted around the pool, and a rabbit hopped up to the water.

"I love this view," Dale said as she set a cup of coffee in front of Mandy and sat down across from her with her own mug.

"I can see why. I wouldn't ever get anything done if I had this view. It's beautiful."

"Yes, it is. We felt so lucky when we found this place. Did Nancy tell you it had been a dude ranch?"

"She did. Had the people who owned it closed the ranch, or was it still operating as a ranch when you bought it?" Mandy threw the question out nonchalantly. She didn't want Dale to suspect her questions had a purpose other than conversation.

"A family operated it as a dude ranch for many years, but the ranch had closed. Another couple turned it into a B&B, but they wanted to retire. We came along at the right time and made them an offer. Everybody was happy. We only have a few horses now, and occasionally one of the hands takes visitors on trail rides. We don't advertise that."

"Those cabins on the hillside. That's what you rent?"

"Yes. Three are big enough for families, will sleep up to eight. The other two sleep four. We also rent three bedrooms upstairs to couples. Each has an adjoining bath. There are more cabins, but we don't rent those unless we're hosting a retreat, or maybe a wedding."

Had the cabin where the people died in the fire been rebuilt? The only way to find out was to ask the question. "Nancy told me there was a fire in one of the cabins years ago."

Dale sipped her coffee and looked out the window. The rabbit hopped across the lawn, stopping to graze as it moved. "The dude ranch closed not long after that fire." Dale fingered her mug, tracing one finger around the rim. "Another accident occurred earlier that same day. A woman died on one of the trail rides. A tragedy. The owners had insurance, and there was a settlement even though they weren't at fault."

"The families of those who died sued the ranch?"

"The woman's family did. Unfortunately, the couple that died in the fire didn't have relatives. Their two daughters disappeared that same night." She took a long swallow of coffee and rubbed her forehead with one finger.

Once again, the gooseflesh rose on Mandy's neck. One of those girls had been Jenna, she was certain of it. "You wouldn't happen to remember the name of that family, would you?"

"Why in the world would you want to know that?" Dale stared.

"Morbid curiosity, I guess. I have this thing about tragedies. I'm superstitious. My own parents died when I was young, and my aunt raised me."

"I don't know the name of the family. But there is a library in Lawton. They probably have newspaper files if you really want to know."

Mandy pushed back in her chair. "I think what I want to know is what job you have open."

Dale smiled. "It's a combination job, a bit of secretary and a bit of maid. We're headed into the offseason once we hit September, and my summer help has already gone back to college. The job includes room and board, which makes up for the pay. I'm afraid it isn't much more than minimum wage. But you do have half of a duplex cabin for your own, across from the stables. The cowboys live in a nearby bunkhouse. Two of the men stay on year-round, and three cowboys are summer positions only." She stood. "I'll show you the living arrangements if you'd like. Then I need to make lunch."

Mandy drained the rest of the coffee from her cup before following Dale to the back door and onto a rear deck. As Dale shut the door behind them, Doobie ran out, tail wagging. "Okay, you come with us," Dale said to the dog.

In the car, Moby was hanging his head out of the half-open window, his tongue lolling.

"We have a tennis court and a pool," Dale said, motioning beyond the house. "A sand volleyball court, horseshoe pit, and a fire ring. Our employees are welcome to use any of those at any time they aren't working. There's a whirlpool by the pool, too."

"Sounds perfect." Mandy was impressed with the cleanliness of the complex. The flowerbeds were well maintained, and every wooden surface had a fresh coat of paint.

They rounded the house and ambled toward the barns and corrals. Mandy could easily pick out the small bunkhouses where the help stayed. Unlike the cabins on the forested mountainside, the staff housing was surrounded by mowed lawns and flowerbeds.

"Here we are." Dale took a key ring from her pocket and opened the door. "Our summer girls left Sunday. I've not yet cleaned. Of course, I'd take care of that before you move in if you decide you want the job."

Mandy strolled through the cabin, taking in the furnishings. The red plaid sofa in the living room looked well-used and featured plump pillows covered in a lodge-style fabric. A wood fireplace with a stone chimney filled most of one wall. The small wood table in the kitchen had four mismatched chairs around it.

Dale opened another door and pointed into a cheerful bedroom. "You could have this half of the duplex, although both sides are vacant right now. You wouldn't be sharing the house until Thanksgiving, when we'll take on extra help for the holiday weeks."

Had she been single—without Will—and ready for an adventure, she would have gladly taken this opportunity. It would be the experience of a lifetime, getting paid to live in a beautiful place.

She turned to Dale and found the woman staring at nothing, eyes vacant.

"What do you think?" Dale asked suddenly in a flat voice, disconnected from the moment.

Had Dale figured out she wasn't looking for a job, but for information? She'd gotten the history she'd come for, but Jenna wasn't here, and there seemed to be no indication she had been.

"I'll think about this. It's a change for me. Can I let you know tomorrow?"

"Sure." Dale pushed her fingers into her forehead again. "People aren't beating down my door to work out here. But I have an ad breaking in the newspapers on Sunday. If you decide before Friday noon, I can pull the ad."

"I'll let you know tomorrow morning." Mandy rubbed her arm, keenly aware that this arm injury might make it difficult to accept this job even temporarily. Changing sheets would be painful, not to mention scrubbing showers and sinks.

"Great. Now, I've got to get back in and make lunch for the boys. You're welcome to have a look around if you'd like. If you're still here at 12, stop by the house and join us for lunch. You're certainly welcome."

"Thanks, Dale. I will look around a bit. It's been a while since I've been this close to nature."

Dale locked the door behind them as they left the cabin. "Hope to see you in a bit." She sounded exhausted.

"You probably will."

As Dale trudged away, Doobie ran out of the forest and trotted beside her to the house.

Mandy studied the distant hills. A bird flew from a tree, and when she looked up, the gray and white mockingbird swooped down and landed on the cabin's porch railing. It tilted its head, flapped its wings, and began to sing.

"I bet you or one of your relatives saw the fire, and everything that happened afterward," Mandy said to the bird. "Was that Jenna's family? Was it Jenna and her sister who disappeared?"

The bird spread its wings and flew away.

Mandy climbed the hillside carefully, her bruised legs alerting her that the slight incline was straining injured muscles. The little porch of each cabin contained two bent willow rockers. Gingham curtains decorated the windows. Outside each cabin, a picnic table and a charcoal cooker stood ready to grill hamburgers or hot dogs.

She strolled around the first cabin. Through slits in the window curtains, she determined the cabin had two bedrooms, a living room, and a small kitchen/dining area. Evergreen bushes grew close to the porch on three sides of the house. Flowers in whiskey barrel halves decorated the spaces between the bushes. On the fourth wall there was a back door and a small stoop. An air conditioner unit was positioned beside the back step.

Mandy walked on to the next cabin, a replica of the first, and noticed a 2 had first been carved and painted onto the logs beside the front door frame. A few steps further down the road, Cabin 3 looked bigger, probably a three-bedroom, as did Cabin 4. A parking area had been created by removing a few oaks beside the cabin. On the other side of Cabin 4, another log cabin perched on the forested hill.

Each structure was built about fifty yards from the next, far enough apart to offer those who sat on the porch privacy, but not so far as to seem isolated.

A blue jay cawed at her from his perch in a nearby pine, and a breeze licked her cheek. Mandy couldn't imagine a deadly fire in this idyllic setting.

An asphalt road curved up the hill to two more cabins, but Mandy took a shortcut through the trees to reach them. Last year's leaves and acorns crunched beneath her feet.

These two cabins were larger, perhaps even four bedrooms, and each featured two large fireplaces. Another cabin, hidden by overgrown bushes, stood a short distance away. Tree debris littered these shingled roofs and dust layered the windows. Dead beetles and other insects covered the sills. No one had occupied these cabins in recent weeks.

Mandy limped around each cabin, testing her bruised leg muscles. With forest scent filling her head, she stopped to listen to the birds and feel the fresh, warm breeze. Neither the main house nor the bunkhouses were visible from here. Far to her left, the trees opened into a clearing. Mandy meandered that direction, listening and thinking.

If this was Jandafar and Jenna had disappeared from here after the fire that killed her parents, why had she never told anyone who she was? And what had happened to her sister? She had hidden this secret for a long time. Why had Jenna suddenly asked Mandy to come here by Saturday?

She was here, but where was Jenna? There was no sign anyone else was staying in the cabins other than the staff. Two old Ford trucks were parked near the bunkhouse, and there were a couple of SUVs behind the ranch house.

Was she at the wrong place? Maybe this wasn't the Jandafar Jenna had meant.

When she reached the clearing, vegetation hid charred timbers and bricks. Half a chimney stuck up between young trees and bushes. One outer wall was mostly intact, making it apparent where the structure had been. Leaves and tree litter covered the floor, as did detritus that had either blown in or been carried by animals.

Had Jenna's parents died in this cabin?

Something glittered in the mess at her feet. Mandy swept the leaves to one side and uncovered a gold hoop earring. Untarnished, it didn't look like it had been lying there for twenty years. It looked like one of the hoops Jenna loved to wear on the weekends, when she wasn't dressed for business.

She tucked the earring into the pocket of her jeans. If Jenna had come here, where had she gone? Had Dale seen her?

Melancholy settled over Mandy. If Jenna had come back here, she must be an emotional basket case. Mandy had been unable to even consider passing the location of her parents' car accident for years.

The bushes rustled. Mandy froze, every hair on her body sensing danger. A ground squirrel poked his head out from the bush and scampered across the remains of the porch and over the sole remaining concrete step.

Mandy hurriedly limped her way downhill toward the ranch house.

~ Chapter 26 ~
Mike

Traffic moved too slow. Mike tapped the steering wheel with his fingers and glared ahead.

This is all wrong. The whole thing has gone wrong.

He fingered the bandage on his forehead.

And they shot me! That wasn't supposed to happen. Just a little scare, or so he said.

I could have died.

Not to mention what they did to my truck.

Totally unnecessary.

"Collateral damage," he said.

He'll pay for all the collateral damage when this is over.

He caught sight of a turnpike mile marker and calculated how many more miles until he reached Lawton.

Mandy will be surprised to see me, but I'll see him first. He needs to get a few things straight. For one, no more of these "accidents" that end up backfiring on me. And second, my cut includes Mandy. He gets his girl, I get mine.

That's the deal.

I won't let him forget it.

~ Chapter 27 ~
Mandy

Mandy stopped at the Trail Blazer on her way back to the ranch house and let Moby out. The dog raced in a circle, sniffing at everything, before he found a spot and did his business. Mandy filled the plastic bowl she'd brought for Moby with water from a convenience store bottle. Once the dog had drunk his fill, she put Moby back in the SUV again. "Just for a little longer, boy. I promise."

She rapped at the front door of the main house. Breakfast at the café had been hours ago, and she was hungry. There was no reason she shouldn't join them for lunch if she was careful about what she said. It would give her a chance to talk to Dale about the history of the place. If the cowboys were around, she might find out if they remembered the fire, or the family.

Dale opened the door and motioned her in. "Hello, Mandy. I'm finishing things up. The men should be here shortly for lunch. You can pretty much set the clock by them."

Mandy followed her into the kitchen. "Anything I can help you with?" The aroma of stew bubbled up from the stove.

"No. Cutting the biscuits. Soon as they're done, it'll be time to eat." She smiled at Mandy. "Tell me more about yourself. Where have you worked before?"

Mandy stepped over to the window. She didn't want to keep lying to Dale. The woman seemed trustworthy, but Mandy didn't know anything about her. "Actually, I'm in marketing. Left a job in Tulsa to move out here. I guess you could say I'm fed up with the corporate world. I want to try something simpler. And I love this part of the state."

"You wouldn't believe how many times I hear the same thing from the people who stay here a night or two. But they never act on it. They complain about being fed up, and how they aren't enjoying their life, but they aren't willing to take the risk to change a damn thing." Dale slid the sheet of biscuits into the oven. "You think you're ready to take that risk?"

"I like what I see here. But I'd like to hang around a few days and learn more. Could I—"

The back door burst open and loud laughter filled the room. Two men wandered in, joking with each other. When they caught sight of Mandy and Dale, their conversation stopped mid-sentence.

"Oh, hi, honey. Didn't know we had company." The older of the two men, who had a full head of dark brown hair, graying at the temples, stepped over to Dale and planted a kiss on her cheek. He extended his hand toward Mandy and focused deep brown eyes on her face. Sun had tanned his skin and wrinkled his face. "Hello. I'm Max Hardesty. Glad to have you here at Jandafar. Will you be staying long?" He pumped her hand up and down.

"She's actually looking for work, Max. From Tulsa," Dale explained.

"Tulsa! Well, that's a coincidence. Lamar and I were just talking about Tulsa." He nodded at the other man. "This is Lamar, our all-around hand. I think they'd call him a foreman if we were a working ranch. He takes care of the place for us and looks after the horses."

"Mandy Lyons. Pleased to meet you both." Mandy felt an electric connection as she looked at the second man, Lamar. His tanned face was lined from years of outdoors work, but she noticed his thick sandy blond hair and green eyes. He squinted at her, curious, and smiled before extending his hand. The man had needed a haircut a week or two ago; his hair curled over the tops of his ears and down onto his neck.

"Nice to meet you," Lamar said.

"Everybody washed? Lunch is ready as soon as these biscuits are. Five minutes?" Dale checked the oven before grabbing a handful of flatware to set the table.

The two men tromped out of the room.

"Don't know where we'd be without Lamar." Dale positioned the flatware next to white dinner plates.

Jenna had said, "Find Lamar." Did he know Jenna? Had he seen her this week?

"He's from around here?" Mandy asked.

"He and Max both are. But Lamar's the one who knows how to keep up a place like this. He worked here when it was a dude ranch. You know, he might know something about that incident you mentioned earlier. You should ask him."

She had found Jandafar and she had found Lamar. Both before Saturday. Would Lamar know where Jenna was?

"So—Mandy, was it? You're looking for work? What brought you out here?" Max Hardesty asked as he scooted into a chair at the dining table and picked up his spoon to tackle his bowl of stew.

Once again, Mandy wondered if she should trust these people, tell them why she was here, or continue to play games. Her bruised arm ached. Hardly a minute passed that she didn't think about the big sedan that ran her off the road. She could have been seriously injured. Did one of them already know why she was here?

She glanced at each face as she answered. "I love the Wichita Mountains, and I have fond memories of a vacation in this area when I was a kid."

"Oh, you like to ride?" Max crammed a biscuit into his mouth.

"When I was growing up, my family vacations usually

included a trail ride. I was about six the first time I rode, and I'm pretty sure that was someplace down here. We also traveled a lot to New Mexico and Colorado."

"Guess Dale told you that this place used to be a dude ranch. Lamar worked there." Max swallowed a spoonful of stew and buttered another biscuit.

The lines around Lamar's mouth crinkled as he smiled. "Once a cowboy, always a cowboy. I never wanted to be anything else."

Dale jumped into the conversation. "Mandy asked earlier about that fire and the accident with the woman who died all those years ago. I couldn't tell her much, since I didn't live here. Anything you can add?"

"Like what?" Lamar's smile died.

The three of them looked at her.

"Um, like what happened, or who they were, or anything. I'm hesitant—*superstitious*—about working someplace where there have been tragedies." Her mind worked to create a reasonable backstory.

"You afraid of ghosts or something?" Max asked. He sopped up the remains of his stew with a bit of biscuit.

Mandy shrugged. "Ghosts, memories, whatever you want to call it. You ever notice anything like that here? Anything weird or supernatural?"

"The only thing weird that ever happens is the bloodsuckers that want to come out here and dredge it up again," Lamar said. "Don't know why people keep wanting to talk about it. I don't." He pushed his chair back from the table and carried his empty bowl to the sink. "Thanks for lunch, Dale. I'll see to the horses. Then I'll be in the east pasture, Max, fixing that fence." He stopped in the doorway and turned back. "Oh, glad to meet you, Mandy." His look didn't meet hers.

"Thanks. Me, too."

Dale pushed out of her chair, grabbed her dishes and Mandy's, and carried them to the sink.

"So, Mandy, what are your plans? Where are you staying?" Max shoved his plate to one side, folded his arms, and leaned forward on the table to peer at her.

"No plans. Dale has asked me if I'd help for the weekend and stay in the duplex. I'd like to check out Medicine Park, meet more people. I've never worked as a maid before. Could you recommend places to check for work next week if the job out here isn't what I want?"

"A couple of mom-and-pop places rent cabins, and there's one of those roadside motor courts. Been here since the fifties. They've upgraded, and George and Marla keep it clean and neat. Mrs. Childers has a rooming house, might be cheaper, but you know, you get what you pay for. There's several eating establishments, three or four little gift shops—one sells only T-shirts. There's a coffee shop/bookstore, post office, city hall. The fire and police departments. Office for the weekly newspaper/gossip sheet. That's all we got." Max leaned back, balancing on the two back legs of the chair.

"While you think it over, you're welcome to stay here," Dale repeated. "A couple of the cabins are booked for the weekend. You could work for room and board for the next few days. First of the week, you can inquire at the other places. Only downside to being way out here is that we have spotty internet and phone service."

Mandy wanted to nose around the former ranch and to talk to Lamar. It sounded as if she might have to wait to talk to him until he'd finished his workday. She needed to find a newspaper archive, to learn about the fire and the woman who had died, since an earlier Google search had popped up no results.

The downside was driving into town. She didn't want to give anyone the opportunity to run her off the road again. Mandy could use the house phone to call Sparks Garage about her car and delay a trip into town until tomorrow. But she had to find Jenna. Tomorrow was Friday. What would happen to Jenna if she hadn't found her by Saturday?

"Mandy? Is it that tough of a decision?" Max's voice was sharp.

"Sorry. This is a big decision for me. I'm stressed, wondering about my boyfriend and what he's going to think about this. I don't think I'll be happy in a long-distance relationship."

"If you're in a relationship and you're thinking about moving this far away from it, I'd say you're not committed. Seems like there was a spark between you and Lamar. He's a good-looking guy," Dale observed from the sink.

"He is. Why's he not married?"

"Oh, he was," Max said. "Wife left him, took their daughter, relocated to Denver. The girl comes to visit a lot, maybe even this weekend. He's been bitter about it. And there's not too much in the way of eligible young women around here. At least, not until you showed up." Max grinned at her.

Mandy's face warmed. "If it's okay with you, I'll stay here, at least tonight. Get a real feel for the place. And could be I'll stay over the weekend to help. But I expect to pay for my room. I don't know that I'll be that much help to you."

Dale shrugged. "Well, I'll give you tonight for half price, and we'll negotiate the rest as the weekend happens. Give me a couple of hours of your time tomorrow to freshen up the cabins, make up the beds, and clean the bathrooms. Okay?"

They shook on it.

"Now, I've got bookwork to do before I drive into town to get groceries." Dale cleared the rest of the dishes from the table and carried them over to the sink.

"Honey take it easy. You know your headaches get worse when you do too much. This young lady has offered to help. Let her." Max kissed his wife on the cheek and left the room.

"He's right. I accept your help. You're welcome to go into town with me if you'd like." Dale rinsed the plates.

"I would like to pick up a few things." But mainly, Mandy wanted to ask around about Jenna and the tragedies at the dude ranch. "My dog's in the car. If there's a place I could leave him here, I'll ride with you. Is that okay?"

"Sure. We can put him in the tack room at the stable for the afternoon. He'll be out of the way and will probably love the smell of the place." Dale's eyes closed briefly, and her brow creased. "There's a shop next to the grocery that carries basics. Nothing fancy, jeans and tops, T-shirts. Give me thirty minutes and I'll be ready to go. Here's the key to bunk 2, the one I showed you. You can move your vehicle, if you'd like. I'll meet you back up here."

Inside the little cabin, Moby wandered around, sniffing. Mandy hoped he was housetrained, but she was ready to shoo him outside if he raised his leg.

When it was apparent he wouldn't make a mess in the cabin, she got out her cell phone. No signal. If there were any towers within twenty miles, the granite hillsides blocked the signal. She'd call Will once they were in town. Otherwise, she'd have to ask Dale if she could pay to use their landline.

Layered with quilts and two fluffy pillows, the double bed was as comfortable as it looked. The sheets smelled fresh and clean and were smooth and soft to the touch. She could sleep here for a night and hopefully find time to talk to Lamar. If he was the Lamar Jenna had told her to find, he could help find Jenna. Otherwise, she'd be back to square one. But how likely was it that there was more than one person in this area named Lamar?

~ Chapter 28 ~
Sean

Sean Wade slumped over his tiny table in the Starbucks and stared out the window at the afternoon traffic on Peoria in Tulsa's popular Brookside district. Over an hour had passed since he'd ordered his coffee, and the half cup that remained was cold, the same temperature as the air in the place, somewhere around 72 degrees.

He had played this whole thing wrong. He should have talked to Jenna. He should have told her more. Maybe she would have trusted him with her past. Then, she would have known he could help her find a way out. She hadn't needed to run.

Sean could make it right, he was sure. He thought he knew where Jenna had gone. Mandy was probably on the right track, going to the Wichita Mountains, going to Jandafar. But Jenna could have run in the other direction, away from her past, away from him and everything they'd built together.

A work assignment in the world of art fraud had brought them to Tulsa, and she'd been willing to come, even though it brought her back to the state she'd run from so many years ago. He'd expected her to tell him the story of her past. He'd waited for her to tell him. But she hadn't. He'd been trained not to reveal his thoughts or emotions but pretending he didn't know the tragedy she'd suffered was the hardest thing he'd ever had to cover up.

Sean had seen the painting of the woman who looked like Jenna when it first arrived at Yolanda's Art. He'd noted the resemblance, but his mind was focused on other things. The artist, for one. The similarity in the dark style of that painting, compared with others in the gallery—paintings he'd been watching and studying since coming to Tulsa—had convinced him that the artist of Jenna's painting, Cha Har, was the forger he'd been tracking.

The brushstrokes, the use of color and light, the Baroque-like style, as well as the fine details the artist had added to the woman's face had cinched it. The commonalities were conclusive.

Jenna knew Cha Har. The artist was connected to her. But even after she'd shot him Tuesday night, she had not revealed anything about the painting or the artist and her connection to him.

The bullet had grazed his leg, but he dove toward the door and knocked the breath out of his assailant. When he'd flipped the light switch on, she'd looked up at him from the floor and burst into tears.

"Jenna! My God." Sean had leaned over his wife and lifted her to a sitting position, cradling her in his arms and swaying as if she was a baby.

"Oh," she'd whimpered. "I could have killed you."

"But you didn't. It's just a scratch. What's going on?"

She'd evaded the question, pulling him out of the laundry room to the bathroom, where she'd grabbed the first aid kit from the cabinet. He'd questioned her as she cleaned the wound in his leg, but she had refused to respond. Finally, after the bandage was secure and he was standing, embracing her, she spoke.

"I can't stay here, Sean. They've caught up with me."

"Who?"

She shook her head. "I can't talk about it. Let me go, Sean."

He sat back, opened his embracing arms.

"I mean, I'm leaving."

"Jenna?"

"I can't stay. A moving company took my office things to storage. I quit my job. And I'll send you divorce papers to sign once I've found someplace to live. Don't try to find me, Sean."

"Jenna!" He'd reached for her as she brushed past him. "Where are you—"

She ran from him. He started after her, wincing at the pain in his leg. By the time he got to the front door, she was nowhere to be seen.

He'd done the only thing he knew to do that would help her disappear. He'd contacted a moving company to store their things and a realtor to sell the house.

He had no home to return to tonight. Everything was in motion.

Sean chugged the remnants of lukewarm espresso in his mug.

He had to find his wife.

~ Chapter 29 ~
Mandy

"I'm ready. Hop in. I've got my grocery list." Dale waved a piece of paper in the air.

Mandy climbed into the passenger seat of the truck.

"Did you get your dog situated in the tack room?"

Mandy nodded. "He was intrigued by all the smells, like you thought. He'll be fine." She dreaded the ride into town and back. Dale was bound to want to make conversation, and Mandy was afraid she might get confused about what lies she'd told and say something contradictory. At least she didn't have to drive or worry about being run off the road or rammed into a ditch.

Dale turned the radio up as they turned onto the country road and rolled down her window. Apparently, she didn't want to talk either. Mandy studied the countryside and hummed along with the music. Dale's face was set in a frown as she focused on the road into town.

"Meet you back here in an hour? Dry Goods is over there," Dale said as she parked the truck in front of the grocery. "If you get delayed, don't worry, I'll go get a soda pop. If I'm not in the truck, that's where I'll be."

Mandy headed to the recommended store. There was precious little time to accomplish all she needed to do in only an hour.

The shop's worn wood floor needed to be stripped and polished before it would resemble the popular wood floors in

Tulsa's posh department stores. The wall displays made it evident where the men's, children's, shoes, and women's departments were without the use of signage. Hardware section, appliances, and electronics filled one end of the building. It was a mini-Walmart without the smiley-face pricing signs.

She darted through the store to the women's clothing section and flipped through the rack of shirts and tops. A few garments fit her style, and after finding her size, she took them to the counter. "I need a few other things. I'll be right back."

Mandy gathered items from the cosmetics department and found a large carryall in the small selection of luggage. She returned to the counter and lay down her credit card.

"That it for you?" the checkout girl asked. She chomped her bubble gum, blew a bubble, chewed it up, and popped it between her teeth. Her lipstick and fingernails were painted a deep shade of blood red, and her eye shadow matched. The fake diamond stud in her left nostril wiggled as she chewed.

"Think so. Hope you take plastic?"

"Sure do. You're that woman who ran off the road headed up to Jandafar, aren't you?" She blew and popped another bubble.

Mandy peered at the girl. "Good news travels fast."

The girl smiled. "Small-town grapevine. Bet I know more about you than you know yourself."

"Oh?"

"You're from Tulsa. Got your name right here on the credit card, and it's the same as the name I heard over at the café earlier. Supposedly you're looking for a job, wanting to move here, but you don't have much luggage. Kinda nosy, asks lots of questions, mostly about Jandafar and what happened up there not long after I was born. People suspect you're a newspaper reporter. Gonna write a true crime article or dig up dirt about ghosts. That about right?"

Mandy frowned. "No, that's not right. I'm not a reporter of any kind or a ghost hunter. I'm curious, that's all."

The girl finally smiled, revealing black braces. "Uh-huh. Just 'cause this is a small town don't mean we're stupid."

How many times had the girl heard that sentiment?

"I never said anything about anyone being stupid. And you know what? It doesn't matter what you think you know. You don't know squat."

Mandy signed the credit card slip. She slipped the shirts and the other items she had bought into the carryall, tore off its tag, and left the store.

How boring life must be for these people if all they had to do was run down to the café and gossip about her. She paused on the sidewalk and looked up and down the street. Her next stop—at the newspaper office—would raise the red flags even higher.

Jenna's life might be at stake, one part of her brain argued. *You back down now, stop digging, and you may never find her—alive.*

But I've already found Lamar and Jandafar, the other part of her brain argued back. *I'll talk to Lamar tonight. First-hand information will be better than a news article anyway.*

She wanted to kick herself for not being more discreet. She'd asked the wrong person something and now the whole town was suspicious of her.

The cafe was across the street.

Mandy settled onto a stool in the middle section of the counter. About a half-dozen other people sat scattered around the eatery.

"Hey there, good to see you again. What can I get you?" It was Nancy, the waitress who'd been so friendly to her before, so friendly that the entire town knew who she was. But it could have been Doug at the car rental place, or someone at the hospital, or the guy who had pulled her out of the car, or... There was a long list of people she'd talked to. It might not be Nancy's fault at all.

"A Diet Coke. Thanks." Mandy avoided looking at the waitress. If she didn't know who she could trust, she wouldn't trust anyone.

"You okay? Heard about your accident. Sounds like you were lucky."

"It wasn't an accident. Someone ran me off the road. What I don't know is why. You knew I was going up there; you suggested it."

Nancy leaned over the counter. "You're thinking I told somebody, and they tried to run you off the road? Hm. Ever hear of paranoia?" Nancy marched over to the ice machine, filled a glass with ice, and shifted to the drink machine. She set the drink in front of Mandy and turned away without speaking.

Mandy sipped her cola. She hadn't handled that right, and she needed someone on her side. She suspected Nancy had told her all she knew about Jandafar in their first conversation. There was no need to try to dig up more info. What she did need was to convince people she wasn't a reporter. Maybe then someone would talk to her.

The next time Nancy passed she was carrying a big chocolate soda with whipped cream on top. Mandy spoke up. "Look, I'm sorry. I wasn't accusing you of anything. I'm scared and a little paranoid. I'd expect things like that to happen in big cities, but not in a small town. I came here to get away from crime and aggressive drivers. But I guess I didn't."

"Our normal way of driving is not to run people off the road. But there are idiots here, like everywhere. Usually they drive giant SUVs and trucks. Got something to prove, I guess." Nancy deposited the chocolate soda in front of a customer, removed used dishes farther down on the counter and rubbed the surface with her rag before she worked her way back to Mandy. "I'm sorry you were scared. And honest, I didn't say a word to anyone about you. But that doesn't mean someone didn't overhear our conversation."

On the ride back to Jandafar Hills, Mandy said nothing to Dale about what the shop girl had said or the words she'd had with Nancy. Dale probably had her own doubts about Mandy and her story, but Mandy planned to keep up her ruse, at least until she'd had a chance to talk to Lamar. Tomorrow, before she dug herself any deeper into this lie, and before Dale pulled her help wanted ad, she'd tell the Hardestys the truth.

That afternoon, as promised, she helped Dale clean the upstairs rooms which had been occupied the previous weekend. She dusted and vacuumed the rooms, cleaned the bathrooms and put fresh linens on the beds. It would have been easy, mindless work if her arm hadn't been so badly bruised. As it was, she gritted her teeth with each movement. The upside of it all was that the work gave her time to prepare to talk to Lamar.

He'd made it clear he didn't like people digging into either his business or the past. First, she had to get him to like her a little. She had to open up and talk about herself, had to reveal something personal. After dinner, she'd grab an opportunity to talk to Lamar alone. Then she'd throw out her ace and watch for his reaction.

Back at the ranch house, Mandy set the table and made a centerpiece from flowers Dale had collected. After mashing the potatoes, she kept an eye on the biscuits in the oven while Dale cooked chicken-fried steak.

Outside, Moby and Doobie raced around the yard. Initially, Mandy was concerned the dog might run away if he wasn't on a leash, but he stayed with Doobie, and Doobie was thoroughly attached to Jandafar.

Mandy felt guilty. Dale was trusting her, trying her out, seeing if they could work together. Their conversation was easy, and she liked the woman and felt concerned about her health. Dale looked exhausted and frequently seemed disoriented, probably from her headache medication. Mandy hoped Dale and Max wouldn't be mad when she told them the truth tomorrow.

"You know anyone else named Dale?" she'd asked as Mandy helped peel the potatoes. "I'm named after Dale Evans. She was married to Roy Rogers, but you're probably too young to remember them. Or even Trigger."

"I've heard of them, but you're right, I'm too young to have seen that television program. That was back in the '50s, wasn't it?"

"Late '50s, early '60s. The name Dale for a girl didn't catch on, though, not like other name crazes. When I met Max, he told me he loved that name. Kept saying I was his personal cowgirl and would never be anyone else's."

It seemed an odd thing for Dale to share, and if that's what Max had really said, a possible red flag indicating someone who was possessive and controlling. She avoided those attributes in men she agreed to date. Thank goodness Will wasn't like that—at least, he hadn't been until she started looking for Jenna.

"I love your place," Mandy said at dinner after they'd all filled their plates with a homestyle dinner of chicken-fried steak, green beans, mashed potatoes, and biscuits. "I can't imagine a more beautiful setting. The valleys and the old granite mountains. I can see why you love it and why you bought this place."

"We did fall in love with it," Dale said. "But Max was in love with it long before I was. He grew up in this area, so he knew it when it was a dude ranch even before Lamar worked here."

Another possible source of information. If she followed up on this information would it seem like she was snooping?

"I can't imagine growing up out here, in such a small town. Is it like they say, nothing to do as a teenager but drink and get into trouble?"

Max chuckled. "That's about right. This fella here and I both did our share of both, years apart. His uncle and I went to school together."

"Are most people ranchers?"

"Yup. That and business owners, catering to tourists," Max continued. "We've seen retirees moving in over the last ten, fifteen years. A few new houses going up. Construction business and land sales doing okay."

"We were lucky to get this place before the land grab was in full swing," Dale added. "And you wouldn't believe how often we have offers to buy it outright, sight unseen."

"I can see why you get the offers, and I can see why you don't want to sell. Like I said, I can't imagine a more perfect place to be." Mandy reached for the gravy and added a heaping ladle-full to her mashed potatoes.

"Where'd you grow up, Mandy?" Dale asked.

She was relieved for the opportunity to talk about herself. She hoped it would help Lamar lower his guard. Carefully, she chose facts to tell them, never revealing the real reason she'd come to Medicine Park.

"I've probably bored you silly," she said at the conclusion of her life's story. "But it's all brought me here. And I don't regret losing the job. I need time to figure out what I want out of life."

Lamar finished eating. He placed his silverware in the center of his place and perched awkwardly on the edge of the chair, ready to charge out of the room.

Would it be too obvious if she left right after him?

"No man in your life?" Max asked suddenly.

A smile spread across her face. "I have been seeing someone, but I'm not sure how he's going to take the sudden changes I'm contemplating. He's not too happy with me right now."

Dale patted her hand. "Well, if it's meant to be... You've heard it before. You do what you feel is best for you. If he's the right fellow, it'll work itself out."

Lamar stood and carried his plate to the sink. "Fine meal, Dale. Thanks. Think I'll go into town for a bit."

Mandy carried her plate to the sink too, reaching around Lamar to throw her paper napkin in the under-sink trash can. "I think I'll take a walk," she said. "Later, if I could, I'd like to make a few phone calls. My cell phone's not working out here."

"Absolutely. Come back in whenever you're ready. And don't worry about the charges. It's a business line, inexpensive." Dale nodded at the wall phone.

"Lamar?" Mandy left the house a few seconds after him, but the ranch hand was halfway to his cabin and the Chevy truck parked next to it.

"Yeah?" He stopped and faced her.

"If you have a minute, I'd like to talk to you." If Mandy failed to find out what she needed to know, she'd have to leave Jandafar. Lamar was her only lead.

"I got a minute. Shoot." He slipped his hands into the pockets of his jeans and stared down at her. The sun was dropping in the sky, and the early evening rays shimmered in his green eyes.

She swallowed. "Jenna told me to come here, and to find you."

His face didn't change. "Jenna?"

Mandy blinked. Of course, that wasn't the name he knew her by. "Maybe you knew her as Molly Bergen."

His eyes widened, and he pulled his hands out of his pockets. "Molly Bergen?"

"You remember her?"

"Molly Bergen," he repeated softly. "And how is it you know anything about Molly Bergen? She disappeared twenty years ago."

Mandy sucked in her breath. It was true. Jenna could be one of the girls who had gone missing after the fire.

"She told me to come here. Her name is Jenna Wade—that's the name she's using now. And I think she came here earlier this week. I think she's in danger."

"What magazine is it you work for again?" he sneered.

"No magazine. Honestly. I may not be here looking for a job, but everything else I've told you is true. I'm trying to find Jenna, or Molly, or whoever she is. If I don't, I'm afraid something bad will happen to her."

"Right. Well, you find another source for your little story. I've got better things to do."

"Lamar, wait. Please talk to me."

He whirled and stomped to his truck. Seconds later, the vehicle roared down the all-weather road.

Moby raced up to her, panting heavily; Doobie trailed behind. "Come on, boy. Time to put you up for the night." She rushed to her cabin, calling the dog to come with her. Once inside, she poured kibble into the dog bowl.

What now? Mandy hadn't expected Lamar's reaction. And she couldn't let it go.

"I'll be back in a while, Moby. Be good." Mandy hurried to her rented SUV, hopped in, and headed into town.

She had to catch up with Lamar.

~ Chapter 30 ~
Will

Will called Mandy's phone one more time, but there was no answer. She was either out of range or she wasn't taking his calls.

He paced the floor outside the conference room, holding his phone. Finally, he hit the autodial button for Sean.

"Hello, Will," Sean growled.

"Sean! My God, man. I've been trying to reach you. What's with the disappearing act? Mandy's gone AWOL looking for Jenna and I'm at my wit's end. I'm supposed to be in this seminar, but I can't keep my mind on strategies right now." Will ran his fingers through his hair and checked the hallway for anyone who might be listening in. "Where are you?"

"Still in Tulsa, but not for long."

"Where are you going?"

"Can't say. Not sure this line is secure. All I can say is that there are two hens on the same nest. Surprise, surprise. I'll have to get back to you after I've checked the henhouse to be sure all the chicks are accounted for."

The line clicked.

Will slid the phone into his coat pocket. Sean's cryptic message told him two things: Sean was headed to the Wichita Mountains where Mandy and Jenna were. And the case Sean had been working, concerning a forger replicating modern art pieces, was somehow tied in with Jenna's disappearance.

~ Chapter 31 ~
Mike

A horn blared.

Damn. Mike jerked the steering wheel to get the car back into his lane of the highway.

He'd fallen asleep again. His head hurt from the bullet wound, but he'd not given up or given in. He was going to see this through. They owed him money, and he'd be damned if he'd let them waltz off without paying.

He'd given them everything they'd asked for, all the info on Jenna he could uncover during the few months he'd been at Empire Marketing. He'd done surveillance outside—and inside—her house. He'd followed Jenna in her car, mapped her usual routes, noted her routines. And he'd called nightly to report his findings.

There was nothing more he could have done. The man was *not* going to stiff him.

He took a sip of coffee from the convenience store cup and cursed. Awful stuff. Cold.

It couldn't be much further. Dusk hovered over the countryside, casting everything in a golden light that this city boy was not used to seeing. "Country" was not natural as far as he was concerned. Give him pavement and high-rise office buildings any day. Creatures lurked out here on the open countryside.

No scaredy cat, am I? He slapped the dash and resettled in the driver's seat. This was easy-peasy. He'd be there soon, and tomorrow...

Mandy.

~ Chapter 32 ~
Mandy

Once she reached the outskirts of the tiny town, it wasn't hard to figure out where Lamar had gone. The sign flashed "The Corral" in red light bulb letters, and an assortment of neon beer signs glowed from the front windows of the old clapboard building. Lamar had parked at the end of the row of cars in front.

Mandy parked beside his truck and stayed in the Trail Blazer. It had been a long time since she'd entered a bar by herself. She didn't like the way people scoped out newcomers, judging, rating. She'd had the comfort of Will's presence for two years now, and it seemed odd to be entering a bar without him.

What was she going to do inside? March up to Lamar and demand he tell her about Molly? How likely was he to talk to her in front of his buddies if he wouldn't do it when the two of them were alone?

Another truck parked beside her. Two cowboys headed for the door. One of them glanced over his shoulder at her and smiled. Years ago, she might have been encouraged by that smile, but tonight, it made her feel sleazy and unfaithful.

She decided to stay put and wait for Lamar to come out. Hopefully he wouldn't stay until closing. She doubted she could keep her eyes open that long.

Mandy's cell phone had three bars worth of signal. She called Will.

"How are you, honey?" she asked when he answered. Her heart beat faster.

"I'm fine. How are you?" His voice sounded distant, as if he didn't recognize her voice.

"Are you busy?" In the background someone laughed, dishes and silverware clanked. Was he at the final banquet?

"Yeah." Now his voice was curt, and the pit of her stomach suddenly hurt.

"I drove into town, can't get a signal out at Jandafar Hills, so if you're busy, we'll have to wait to talk until tomorrow since I'm headed back there soon. Do you want to call me back?"

"Any news?"

"No, still trying to figure out what happened here. I think it involves Jenna's family, and that Jenna and her sister disappeared after a fire that killed her parents. No one wants to talk about it. They think I'm a crime reporter doing an exposé."

"Why don't you tell them the truth?"

She thought about telling him how she'd been run off the road, but that would mean another lecture, and Will would insist she drop this quest to find Jenna. She couldn't. It was only a matter of time until she figured it out. She would find Jenna.

"I will, tomorrow. Right now, I'm still digging at the truth."

"I've got to go."

"I'll call again when I know something. Planning to head back Sunday, if not before."

"Okay. Later."

The phone clicked in her ear.

Mandy slipped the phone into her purse. Her heart pounded, and her stomach churned. Will was mad at her.

A man sauntered past her vehicle toward the entrance to the bar. The way he walked, the way he swung his arms, and the way he carried his head reminded her of Mike, but Mike couldn't be here. He hadn't known where she was going. But he wasn't dumb. He could have made it here exactly the way she did. The information about Jandafar Hills was available to anyone who looked for it.

Had Mike come after her? She checked the missed messages list on her phone for a call from him. No messages since she'd left Tulsa yesterday. She had dropped off the face of the earth and no one gave a damn.

If Mike had decided to join her at Jandafar Hills, why hadn't he let her know he was coming? Wouldn't he want to meet up with her right away so they could search together? Maybe, she thought, unless he was still angry.

Or maybe the man only resembled Mike.

She slipped out of the SUV, locked the door, and walked to the entrance.

Inside, cigarette smoke hung in the air. A half-dozen men sat at the bar; a few single cowgirls flitted around the tables. In the pool room on the far wall, Lamar cued up the table and broke, scattering balls across the green felt surface.

Mandy scanned the room. Mike sat at a corner table, hands wrapped around a beer bottle.

She weaved between the tables to the man, pausing to study his face only a second before she dropped into the extra chair. "What are you doing here?"

He broke his stare to nod his head at an approaching waitress. "What'll you have, Mandy?"

"Nothing. Answer, please."

Mike flicked his hand and the waitress turned away. "I didn't like being dropped. This is as much my investigation as it is yours."

"What about your job?"

"What about it?"

"You quit?"

He smiled slyly. "I'm hurt, remember? Head injury. Can't work, doctor's orders. Doesn't mean I can't drive. Why did you come here without me?" His tone was hard.

"This thing with Jenna is my deal. She's my friend. You hardly know her. I don't understand why it meant so much to you to help me, especially after your truck was damaged and you were hurt. You should have been glad for me to continue the investigation alone."

"Do I have to spell it out for you? You're denser than I thought."

She stared at him, and he stared back. He reached across the table and brushed her arm with his fingertips. "I know you and Will are together. Doesn't matter to me. I'm willing to wait. It's time you knew how I felt."

She sat back in her chair. All these months, she'd thought he wasn't interested in her romantically. Yes, he'd flirted with her endlessly, but he'd never made a pass, never asked her out. Because of Will. He was waiting. Waiting. Wasn't that like stalking?

"I'm here to help you, Mandy. Will would be here if he loved you. He knows how important Jenna is to you."

Mandy's heart began to pound. "He wants to be here. But he has this meeting in Toronto. If he leaves, it may mean his job."

Mike played with his glass, sliding it around on the thick cardboard coaster. He took a drink and placed the glass back in the exact center of the coaster. "Toronto, huh. Are you sure?"

"Yes. I've called his cell phone and talked to him. He's in Toronto."

"Call his hotel." Mike's eyes narrowed.

"What are you suggesting?"

"I'm suggesting there are things you don't know about Will, like there are things you don't know about Jenna."

"And exactly how do *you* know?"

He tilted his head and smiled for the first time since she'd come into the bar. "Let's say that while I've been waiting, I've been investigating Will. I want the best for you, Mandy, and I'm not sure he's it."

"I don't believe you."

"So, you've gone from trusting me with important things, relying on me to help when Will won't, to suddenly not believing me? I'm telling the truth, Mandy. You have your phone with you?"

She lifted her phone.

Mike handed her a slip of paper. "He's supposed to be staying at the Rex, isn't he? Here's the number."

Mandy hesitated, then punched in the digits. When the operator answered with the hotel name, she asked to be connected to Will's room. He put her on hold and Mandy waited. When the operator returned to the line, he said, "There is no one by that name registered in the hotel. Could he be sharing a room?"

Stunned, Mandy disconnected. Her insides clenched. How could this be true? Only a few nights ago, Will had talked about moving in together, sharing every part of their lives.

"Are you okay?" Mike asked. He reached across the table for her hand.

Mandy shoved her chair back, bolted out of the bar, and raced to the rented SUV. Her hands quivered as she climbed in and grasped the steering wheel. Will had lied to her. Where was he? What was he doing?

Will had been talking all week about Jenna's secrets and how it had bothered Sean. But he was as guilty of keeping secrets as Jenna.

~ Chapter 33 ~
Dale

Dale Hardesty stared out the kitchen window at the expanse of grassland and rolling hills outside the ranch house. A golden light touched the earth as the sun sank farther behind the hills, but a headache pounded behind her eyes. The two analgesics she'd taken did not seem to be helping. The last few days, these headaches had become brutal. They'd been horrible today after the woman, Mandy, showed up at Jandafar.

She liked her, that wasn't the problem. But her suspicion that Mandy wasn't being entirely truthful about the reason she was here continued to grow stronger.

Max had been suspicious from the moment he met her, but that was not unusual. He didn't like strangers nosing around. He was overly possessive of her, always had been. He enjoyed their visitors to a point, if they didn't get too comfortable here, or too friendly.

Her husband knew she needed help for the coming weekend, but she suspected he would not want Mandy to stay on as an employee. She'd seen him look sideways at the woman, when he thought no one was looking. His jaw hardened, and that muscle in his cheek twitched.

His eyes had narrowed.

It was a look she didn't like to see. It made her afraid. She'd have nightmares tonight, no doubt, or crazy mixed-up dreams of meeting Max in Texas all those years ago, being swept off her feet and married within a month. They'd made a life there, until he decided to come back to Oklahoma. She agreed their home was beautiful. She agreed this was the perfect place to live.

They wanted children, but so far, pregnancy had eluded her. There was still plenty of time, the doctor in Lawton said. Plenty of time, even though something inside her seemed to be saying that time had run out. She was so tired all of the time, and she kept forgetting things.

She rubbed her head. The MRI last spring had not shown a brain tumor. But she was certain it was the only thing that could explain her partial amnesia, tiredness, and the headaches. She would try to find out later this year how much time she had. Knowing the truth would be a relief.

A gunshot boomed and she jumped, then relaxed her tightened shoulders. It was the television in the downstairs common room. When they had no guests, Max preferred that room's overstuffed leather chair and ottoman. He'd sit, legs up, smoking a damn cigar until she reminded him the place shouldn't smell like cigars when they had a no-smoking rule for guests.

Outside, a squirrel caught her attention as it raced across the phone line from the pole to the house. An owl swooped low to the ground. After a mouse, no doubt. Bats flapped around the mercury vapor light, catching mosquitoes and moths.

The screen door slammed. Dale listened. The TV was silent. Max had gone out.

Maybe when he returned, he'd be in a better mood.

~ Chapter 34 ~
Mandy

Someone tapped the passenger window as tears oozed over Mandy's lower eyelid and down her cheeks. She closed her eyes and shook her head, not willing to let Mike into the car. She didn't want to discuss this. She had to get her thoughts together. Her heart hurt, every bit as bad as in junior high when Casey Morton had broken up with her.

The tapping continued, more insistent, and when she finally opened her eyes, Lamar, not Mike, peered in at her.

"Open up," he mouthed.

When she unlocked the passenger door, he scooted in.

"You ran out," he said, frowning. "What's wrong? Who's that guy?"

"What do you care? I got the impression you didn't want to talk to me about anything." She glanced in the rear-view mirror at the black smear of mascara beneath her eyes and rubbed them with a tissue.

"Not exactly anything. Molly." He ran his hand through his hair, combing it off his forehead.

"Is that because you cared about her? My friend is missing. I need information."

"Word is that you've been asking about that fire and her family ever since you came into town."

"Nancy at the café told me about the fire. She also told me there might be a job at Jandafar."

"Nobody comes to this town out of the blue like you did. I'll answer your questions if you'll be honest with me."

"I need information about Molly." She wanted to trust him. But she'd trusted Will, and she'd trusted Mike, and neither one of them had been honest with her. She didn't want to play games anymore. She didn't like lying to people, trying to get them to tell her the truth when she wasn't willing to do the same. She wiped her eyes again. The scent of Lamar's woodsy, spicy aftershave filled the SUV.

Someone tapped on the driver's window.

Mike.

She rolled the window down a few inches. "I'm busy, Mike."

"Busy? You *are* a fast worker. I'm staying at Mrs. Childers' boarding house. When you decide you forgive me for cluing you in about Will, that's where I'll be. We've got work to do." Mike lumbered away.

Mandy rolled up the window.

She and Lamar sat in heavy silence.

"Who's Will?" Lamar asked a few minutes later. "And who was that?"

"You tell me about Molly, I'll tell you about Will. And about Mike."

Lamar stared grimly out the car window. "I've tried real hard not to talk about it for a long time." He peered into her face. "And I hope to God I'm not making a mistake by telling you. You're sure this isn't going to become a book or get on *60 Minutes* or something?"

"I'm absolutely sure."

He squinted. "I was working at the ranch that summer, right after high school graduation. The clientele was mostly families with little kids. Most families didn't stay more than a week. Sometimes a teenager showed up with their parents, usually bored stiff. It was hard to have a relationship but consorting with the guests wasn't recommended anyway." He cleared his throat. "Late that summer, the Bergens came. Their teenage daughters were knockouts. The other wranglers and me were typical guys. Whoever could score the fastest—it didn't matter which one of the girls." He shook his head and looked embarrassed.

"Which one were you after?"

"Molly and Sharon looked a lot alike, but Sharon was wilder than Molly. Molly liked to read, and she didn't go after us like Sharon did. Chad, the other wrangler, made out with Sharon the first night. I tried to hook up with Molly. She was friendly, but cautious. You could tell she wasn't out to score like her sister was, or like us guys were."

"You lost the bet."

"We all lost the bet. Middle of that week, Chad and I took a group on a trail ride. Fifteen riders, including Molly and Sharon. Two riders started to race. We weren't supposed to allow it. A woman fell from her horse and hit her head. She died on the scene."

"Nancy mentioned that to me. Dale Hardesty only knew the basics."

"Max moved to Texas that summer. He and Dale met in Texas. Actually, Chad is Max's youngest brother."

"Is Chad still around?"

"Lives about an hour up the valley. Don't see him much. He has a part-time job in town."

"So, tell me what happened with this race."

Lamar scratched his neck and cleared his throat. "That race was more like a catfight on horseback than a race. The husband egged it on. He'd been flirting with Sharon and his wife was jealous. After she fell off the horse, he threatened all of us, called his lawyer, filed a lawsuit that same day. That night, the Bergen's cabin caught fire. The parents burned to death and the girls disappeared. Vanished. We searched the area, and the search and rescue teams took it beyond the ranch's borders and into the Wildlife Refuge. They never found anything."

"That's horrible. How could they disappear without a trace?"

"The authorities ruled the fire an accident. Candle melted down and caught the tablecloth on fire, or so they said. But the biggest mystery was what happened to Molly and Sharon. Sharon was nearly 19, Molly a year or so younger. No one pushed the case with the local or state police. No one offered a reward. Once the locals dropped the search, no one cared."

"Why are you so hesitant to talk about Molly? It wasn't your fault."

"Chad and I were the last ones to see the girls alive. He and Sharon had been making out in our bunkhouse. I walked in on them. Later, I saw Molly with her parents at the dance. Didn't see either of them again." He peered at her. "What do you know about Molly Bergen? And who's Will? And who's that guy who upset you?"

Mandy had to tell him the truth, but not every detail.

"Will is my boyfriend. Mike just told me Will's been lying to me. He's not where he's supposed to be or doing what he's supposed to be doing this week."

"You two live together? Are you engaged?"

"We've talked about living together. That won't happen now unless he has a super explanation for lying to me."

"Does Will know why you're here?"

"Yes. He didn't like that I came alone."

Lamar's eyebrows lifted. "What about that other guy? Didn't you come with him?"

"I work with him. He…doesn't count. And I came here alone. I didn't ask Mike to follow me."

"But your man Will didn't rush out here to convince you to return to Tulsa when he found out you were here?"

She chose her words carefully. "He wanted me to stay in Tulsa. He didn't see any need for me to come here." Her heart pounded and her head hurt. Was this the end of her and Will? She had gone against his wishes, but he had lied to her. Could their relationship recover?

"It's your turn. Why are you looking for Molly Bergen?"

Mandy reached under the seat before she remembered that the book was in her wrecked car at the body shop. "I found this book. The *Natural History of Oklahoma*. The name written inside the front cover was Molly Bergen."

"But how did finding that book get you here?"

"I found the book in the home of my best friend after she disappeared. Not long after, I received a phone message from her that said, 'Go to Jandafar. Find Lamar.' I researched the name and found this place."

"Wait a minute. Your best friend had a book belonging to Molly Bergen?"

"Yes. But she doesn't use that name. She calls herself Jenna, and she's married to Sean Wade. And he's disappeared, too."

"You're telling me that Molly—Jenna—is still alive, but she's disappeared, and she told you to come here to find me?"

"Something is going to happen Saturday. That's why I left Tulsa so quickly."

"And why you didn't bring much with you."

She laughed. "That must be part of the story going around about me."

His eyes crinkled as he grinned. "Yeah. That and the part about you being paranoid and somebody running you off the road."

Her laughter died. "Somebody did run me off the road. They rammed the back of my car on an s-curve and I lost control. I rolled my car into a shallow ravine."

"Did you file a police report?"

"While I was in the hospital this morning. Haven't talked to them since, though. I left my cell number, but you know there's no signal up at Jandafar."

"Nope, nearest tower's down here, and the granite hills block most signals. There's talk about putting a tower farther out, but it hasn't happened yet. Until it does, we all have to use the landline at the ranch."

Two men left the bar and ambled past the SUV. They looked in through the windshield. "Woohoo, Lamar! Hook 'em horns!"

"Idiots," he groused under his breath. "What about this other guy, Mike, the one you were talking to earlier?"

"Mike's been helping me find Jenna."

"Because the boyfriend was out of town."

"It's not like that. We're friends. At least I thought so until tonight, when Mike told me Will's a lying jerk and he's been waiting for me to come around and date him."

Lamar nodded slowly. "Right. He clues you in and wonders why you're mad at him."

Mandy's throat closed and her eyes swam with tears.

"He thought he could show up here and win you over, help you find Jenna and cement a relationship."

"I guess so. Is that how men think?"

"Some men will do anything when they have their sights set on a woman."

Mandy had never imagined Mike had his sights set on her. They joked around a lot and he made innuendos, but she never took him seriously. "Did you have your sights set on Molly Bergen?"

He shrugged. "I was too young. But there was something about her. She seemed vulnerable, not like Sharon. Sharon was in a hurry to live."

"What about the husband of the woman who died? He sued the ranch and won, didn't he?"

"Unfortunately. He never forgave Sharon, blamed her openly until he left to bury his wife. The ranch owners settled out of court, but there was no way they could continue to operate the place. They had to take out second and third mortgages, and finally, they had to sell. The second owners made a go of it for a few years before they sold to the Hardestys."

"You mentioned other reporters. They were trying to find out what happened to Sharon and Molly?"

"Every few years, somebody digs it up again and they come, pretending to be tourists, snooping around the burned-out cabin, looking in the woods for skeletons uncovered by coyotes or a downpour. Some people believe the grieving husband set the fire, killed the parents and both girls, and buried them."

"Did the police look into that theory?"

"The husband was their primary suspect. But nothing ever panned out. They followed him around as long as they could stretch the department's budget, but the guy was from Abilene, Texas. Too many long-distance expenses."

"Jenna wanted me to find her by Saturday. Why that deadline?"

"It happened twenty years ago, right before Labor Day."

Mandy pulled in a deep breath. Her head spun with Lamar's revelations. How had Jenna been able to keep this horrific secret?

Her friend was Molly, she was sure of it.

But why had Jenna asked Mandy to come here? What was going to happen Saturday?

~ Chapter 35 ~
Jenna

Jenna huddled on the pile of blankets, sweat beading on her forehead.

Coming here had been a mistake. She hadn't accomplished anything, and she had destroyed her life in Tulsa.

It was all so messed up. The note, followed by the painting, had sent her into a spiral of despair. She'd been unable to ignore her past any longer. Her whole adult life she'd been running, pretending to be someone she wasn't, pretending that she hadn't done what she'd done.

None of the people who loved her and cared about her now—mainly Sean and Mandy, but probably Will also—would feel the same if they found out the truth.

She contemplated her next steps. She hadn't made a plan before coming here. Her only thought had been to get here and find her sister. She had to be here.

Her sister hadn't died in the fire. She was here, or somewhere near. Jenna had successfully run from the past, but she'd also eluded her sister, if her sister had been trying to find *her*.

Should she contact Lamar? Initially, she'd thought he might be the one who could help her the most. And she'd given his name to Mandy. But now she wasn't so sure. She'd suppressed her memories for so long, she was afraid they'd been altered, that what she remembered was either an exaggeration or an outright lie. Maybe what had happened was worse than what she had allowed herself to remember.

Knots tied up her stomach.

It was time to eat again, but there wasn't much food in the cabin. Condiments, mostly. Since last night, she'd had ketchup on crackers and the last third of a bag of popcorn someone had popped days—maybe weeks—ago and stuck on a cabinet shelf. She hadn't yet touched the small bottle of pickle relish in the refrigerator. She could try mustard and relish on crackers. It shouldn't taste that much different from a hot dog.

Her stomach rumbled. She clutched her abdomen. She had to eat, and she had to drink. She had to get out of the attic and do something.

~ Chapter 36 ~
Mandy

When Mandy's phone rang, she retrieved it from her purse. *Will.* She stared at his name on the display screen and let it ring again.

Lamar leaned over and looked at the screen. "So, you going to talk to the jerk? I'll excuse myself." He opened the door and got out.

She willed her voice to be strong. "Hello Will."

"Hello yourself. What's happening?" His voice was upbeat, unlike earlier when he seemed to have been bothered by her call.

"I'm in Medicine Park but still staying out at Jandafar Hills. I think this might be where she is, or will be, but I haven't found her."

"Are you leaving tomorrow?"

"Saturday's the day, Will. Some kind of deadline. I'll be home after that. What about you?"

"You already know that, babe. The meeting's over Saturday. I fly out from Toronto on Sunday."

"I thought you told me that you were staying at the Rex," she stated, her mouth dry. She dreaded confrontation, but she had to ask.

"Yes, that's where the conference is."

"But you're not staying there. I tried to call your room, and you're not registered."

"They put me up at the hotel down the street. They overbooked. It's a short walk. Not a problem."

Was it a lie? He didn't sound concerned. The explanation had come so easily. Had Mike upset her for no reason?

"Where are you really, Will?" Her voice didn't crack, thankfully.

"I'm in Toronto at the conference. What do you mean? What's up?" He was using his stubborn tone.

She knew him well enough to know he wasn't going to admit anything over the phone. It would turn into a shouting match, and neither one would win. There was no reasoning or explaining when he became like this. "Forget it. I was concerned when I couldn't reach your room. What's the name of your hotel, in case I can't get you on your cell?"

He hesitated a half-second too long. "You can reach me on my cell. Otherwise, it's the Beverly. But I may be able to move to the Rex, so don't freak out. Two more nights and I'll be back in Tulsa. Hopefully you will too. Tell me what you've found so far."

She told him quickly and cut the call short. "I need to go, Will. I need to get back up to the ranch, and I'll lose reception on the curves going through the hills. I'll call tomorrow."

"Okay. Tomorrow. Cell would be best. Love you."

"Me, too." She disconnected. The Beverly in Toronto. Relief moved through her. It was a reasonable explanation. She trusted him, but something felt different. He was no longer upset with her, no longer demanding that she go home or he would come after her. He was no longer talking about leaving the conference. His voice had sounded completely different. Something had changed.

She thought about going back inside the bar to find Lamar again, but his truck was no longer parked beside her. He'd left when she answered Will's call.

It was just as well. Her insides felt poured out, and she didn't want to talk. She started the SUV, intending to drive to Jandafar Hills.

Something jabbed her brain. Mike had come down here to help and to tell her about Will. Were his motives all good? Mike had played the white knight all week, helping her search for the painting, enduring the explosion fiasco and the search through the Wade's home the following morning. Now he had followed her to the Wichita Mountains.

She turned the SUV around. Mike was staying at Mrs. Childers'. Nancy, the waitress, had pointed down the street the opposite way from Jandafar when she had suggested the boarding house as a place Mandy might stay for a night or two.

She drove past the restaurant and watched for the rooming house. Three blocks later, there it was. The white sign with black lettering matched the big house partially hidden behind overgrown evergreens. A duplicate sign hung beside the front door on the wide veranda. White rocking chairs and hanging ferns depicted southern hospitality.

In the deepening twilight, the house looked huge, and had it not been for the electric candles in the front facing windows, it might have appeared menacing. As it was, the front door stood open behind a glass storm door and gave a view into the cozy foyer.

She parked at the curb, dashed up the sidewalk, and climbed the veranda steps.

~ Chapter 37 ~
Mike

Mike McNally scurried away from the bar. He fumed.

She doesn't believe that her precious Will has been lying to her. But she'll find out soon enough.

His feet pounded the sidewalk, and he delighted in stepping down hard on any insect crossing his path. A spider dashed, he smashed it; a roly-poly scuttled, he squished it; an earthworm wriggled from the edge of a yard, he sidestepped and smashed it. He was not to be reckoned with.

He's going to get a piece of my mind when he finally gets here. He's putting me off. He knows I'm due the money. I found his precious Jenna, and now he's delaying.

Good thing he hadn't come to the bar and seen Mandy. Who'd have believed she'd be there, and that she'd see me? It could have been a disaster, but I salvaged the situation by diverting her attention to Will.

He stopped at a street corner and waited for the traffic to pass before he crossed the street to the convenience store. Thoughts exploded in his head.

I don't like the looks of that cowboy she had with her. Typical jerk. Confident, cool. I should have pulled him out of that SUV and smashed his smirking face. Where'd she pick him up, anyway?

And why did she pick him up? I'm here. Aren't I good enough for her? If she's going to go alley-catting around on her dear Will, why not do it with me?

He grabbed a few candy bars from the boxes on the candy aisle and selected a bottle of pop from the cooler. He hadn't eaten supper. He'd been too tense during the drive. He wanted his money. But he'd wanted a drink more, so he'd walked two blocks to the bar.

He checked his watch. Anytime now. The man had said he'd "find" him. How hard could it be in this shithole?

Mike slammed the pop and candy bars down on the counter and dug in his pocket, hoping he had enough change to cover his purchases. He counted out the quarters and dimes and plucked a few pennies from the courtesy coin bowl next to the register.

When the employee thanked him, he grumbled, "You're welcome." He hated this town. The only reason he was here was to get the money he was owed and collect Mandy.

A motorcycle whipped around the corner, tooted its horn at him, and popped a wheelie as it sped away.

He stuck up his middle finger and waved it in the air as he walked. He didn't like it here. He didn't like the country or tiny towns, and he especially didn't like the people. The sooner he got paid, the sooner he could grab Mandy and get out of here.

Can't happen fast enough.

He trudged the last few steps past the boarding house parking lot and headed for the veranda.

"McNally." The voice spoke from the shadows.

Mike grinned and turned. "Yo. 'Bout time. You got my money?"

~ Chapter 38 ~
Mandy

Bang!

Mandy dropped to the floor of the boarding house veranda. It was the same sound she'd heard a few nights ago. A gunshot, not a car backfiring. And close.

"What was that?" A voice asked.

The middle-aged woman with stylish short white hair stood at the storm door, holding it open a few inches and peering down at Mandy.

"Did you hear that?" the woman asked again. "My husband was a hunter and that sounded like his gun going off. Did you see anything?"

"No. Sounded near." Mandy stood. "Maybe next door."

"My parking lot's over there. But I don't think that was a car. Sounded like a gun."

Mandy took the open door as an invitation to enter the house, and she stepped through as the woman backed into the foyer.

The middle-aged lady looked at her. "Did you see anyone out there? Should I grab a weapon? The fireplace poker? A butcher knife?" Her pointer finger touched her chin.

"I don't know." Mandy glanced outside again, then closed the front door. "Maybe we should stay inside for a few minutes and see if anything else happens."

The woman squinted at her and straightened her shoulders. "That's good thinking. Want a cup of tea? I can heat the kettle." She headed down the hallway toward the back of the house. "Need a room?" she asked. "I'm Mrs. Childers. I've got two open rooms right now. They're both clean, across the hall from the bathroom upstairs."

"I don't need a room," Mandy said, following Mrs. Childers to the kitchen. "I'm looking for someone. A friend of mine came into town today, and he said he was staying here. I stopped in to see him."

The landlady nodded and pursed her lips. Her peacock-blue eyes shone. "I see. And I know who you're talking about. There are house rules here. The parlor and the living room are for visitors. No non-paying overnight visitors in the guest rooms." In the kitchen, she filled the kettle with water from the tap and lit one of the stove's burners.

"I'm not an overnight guest. Just a friend. And I can wait for him down here. Mike's not really expecting me this evening. Could you let him know I'm here?"

"Mike. Yes, that's his name. He's in number 6, corner room above the back porch. I'll call up." Mrs. Childers stepped over to an intercom system on the wall and pressed the button. "Mike, you have a visitor downstairs. What's your name?" she asked, the button still depressed.

"Mandy. Tell him Mandy is here."

"It's Mandy, and she's in the parlor. Come on down."

Mrs. Childers didn't wait for a response. "Follow me." She led the way down the hall a few steps to a door, knocked, and opened it quickly. Mandy peeked in over her shoulder.

Well-used furniture, including Victorian-style walnut settees and antique tables, decorated the parlor. A pump organ stood in the corner, and an embroidered screen featuring red-vested English hunters and brown and white fox hounds shielded the fireplace. Tiffany-style stained glass lamps graced the old side tables.

"You can wait here. He should be right down." Mrs. Childers smile was polite but prim. She cocked her head. "Sure sounded like my husband's gun." She shrugged her shoulders and left Mandy alone.

Mandy waited.

A few minutes passed. Mrs. Childers appeared in the open doorway. "Still hasn't come down? Is he going to keep you waiting all night? What is the matter with men these days? Their manners have gone all to hell." She charged out of the room.

Footsteps pounded up the stairs and down the hallway above. Seconds later, they pounded back again.

"Well, he's not there," Mrs. Childers said from the doorway. "Guess he wasn't expecting you. Might try later. I'd invite you to wait here in the parlor, but somebody else might want to use it, and my guests have priority. This is their home, you know, for however many nights they choose to stay with me."

"I understand. I'll check in with him later. Thank you." Mandy rushed out of the house and down the front steps. She scanned the yard and the street. When Mike left the bar, he'd headed on foot in this direction. On the way here, she'd driven past the restaurant and a convenience store. He could have stopped at either.

Mike's car was in the garage in Tulsa for repairs, so he had most likely rented a car like she had. She'd look for a rental in the parking lot.

She crossed the lawn toward the lot where Mrs. Childers' boarders parked. A yard light near the back door illuminated the surrounding area. The gravel lot had room for about eight cars, but only two of the delineated spaces were occupied. She stepped around one vehicle to check the rear window or bumper for a rental unit number. New Mexico tag, not a rental. The other car had a Wyoming tag, and no indication of rental status.

Mike could have driven to the diner after he left the bar. She inched toward the street through the shadows, her eyes adjusting to the dimness away from the yard light. A black hump lay on the ground a few steps from the street.

Mandy leapt forward, her breath quickening.

She leaned over the crumpled body and touched a shoulder. "Are you okay?"

The body shifted at her touch, and headlights from a car on the street swept across the face.

Mike's brown eyes stared up at her, unseeing and lifeless.

~ Chapter 39 ~
Sean

Sean Wade sprinkled pepper on his chicken-fried steak, sliced it into pieces, and dipped one into the little bowl of white gravy beside his plate. He savored the bite. It'd been awhile since he'd had anything so delicious. Jenna didn't fry many dishes; she was more of a salad person. Not that he minded. She could pass for a woman in her twenties, slim and toned. She exercised and ate healthy.

And she hadn't had any children yet.

He didn't want to speculate when or if that would ever happen. It didn't look promising. He closed his eyes, still not used to the way his heart pounded in his chest, the same way it had been pounding since that night watchman had opened the door to her office and revealed that all her belongings were gone.

It was as if the past ten years had been completely erased. No Jenna. No marriage. No love.

"Can I get you anything else, darlin'?" The dark-haired waitress stopped beside his table and gave him a wide grin.

"No. This is great, thank you." He smiled back at her. His cell phone buzzed in his coat pocket. He glanced at her nametag. "Thanks again, Nancy."

He confirmed the number calling before accepting the call. "Sean Wade," he said, formally, but he knew the caller. He listened carefully, rubbing his forehead with the pointer finger of his right hand.

"That's right. I'm in the area. I'll be in touch with the locals tomorrow morning. He's close, and I suspect he will give up the rest of the gang once we've nailed him to the wall. Shouldn't take long."

He listened for another few seconds and disconnected. Who would have believed the case he'd been working for three years would finally be solved just as his wife abandoned him and in the same place where she might have gone?

He wasn't completely sure Jenna had ever grasped the full extent of his job. Yes, he worked for an insurance company. He investigated claims of theft or destruction of property. But the truth was, he was a fraud investigator.

The current case had been a hard one to crack. Paintings supposedly worth millions had been destroyed in the house fire of a Tulsa art collector. But the fire department investigator had soon determined the blaze was arson. The police and the insurance company investigated. The items destroyed were reportedly worth millions of dollars. Perhaps in excess of eight million.

Sean and a team of investigators dug through the ashes and discovered bits of the canvases. They investigated the proof of authenticity certificates the owner received upon purchase. They were forged, and likewise, so were the paintings. They'd worked through the chain of the forgery ring, moving from one link to the other. They'd landed at Yolanda's Art in Tulsa, and from there to Cha Har, a ridiculously unreadable signature of an artist who turned out to have an address in Medicine Park, Oklahoma.

And Jenna was here, too.

~ Chapter 40 ~
Mandy

"He was lying there. I don't know anything else," Mandy repeated to the sheriff. Every light blazed on the downstairs floor of Mrs. Childers' rooming house. Two other boarders huddled in the pair of wingback chairs in the parlor.

Mrs. Childers sat in a straight-backed single chair, fanning herself, repeating, "No one was ever murdered while they were staying here." She closed her eyes and fanned faster. "I feel faint, officer."

"I'll get you a glass of water, Mrs. Childers," one of the boarders said. The woman hurried from the room.

Mrs. Childers had introduced the woman to the sheriff as Missy Alfred, a long-term boarder. She'd lived upstairs for over a year and had a job at a local tourist trap on Main Street.

Mandy blinked and saw Mike's dead eyes staring at nothing.

The other regular boarder, a short man with thick glasses and a mop of dark hair, was an accountant at the bank. A pudgy single man well into his forties, he'd said the boarding house suited him fine.

Mandy didn't care where he lived, or why.

Mike was dead. He'd come here because of her.

"Now, miss, tell me again how you knew the deceased," the sheriff asked in a gravelly voice.

Mandy explained that she worked with Mike, he'd been helping her with a work project, and she was unaware he had followed her to Medicine Park until she saw him at the bar.

"Did anyone see you with him at the bar? Did you leave the bar together?"

"No. I talked to him inside, then went out to my vehicle. When he left the bar, he saw me sitting there and stopped to talk. Mike told me where he was staying and asked me to come by. A little later, I drove here. I came up on the porch and heard a car backfire, or a gunshot." She detailed her wait for Mike inside the boarding house and her search for his car in the parking lot, which led to discovering his body. Mandy knew little else to tell the sheriff about Mike.

Mrs. Childers shuddered. "She's telling the truth. I heard the shot and went to the door. She was hunkered down on the porch, her eyes big as billiard balls. I don't think she had time to fire that shot and get to the porch in a few seconds, Sheriff."

"So, what about your other boarders? Who else is here?"

"Couple of short-timers. A woman, and another man. She came in Tuesday night; he came in late today. I haven't seen either one tonight."

"I'll need their names, and I'll need to know as soon as they get back tonight. I want to talk to them." The sheriff tugged on his belt, adjusting his pants. "Anyone else who might have seen something? Any neighbors?"

"Mrs. Peabody next door sits by the windows several hours a day, unless one of her favorite programs is on the television. She has lots of favorite programs."

"Anyone walk their dogs around here, or jog, or anything that might have put them near your house earlier this evening?"

"Kids ride their bikes or scooters. But it was dark when it happened, and I don't think they'd still be out on the streets," Mrs.

Childers worked the fan faster. "I don't know about this town. I used to think it was safe."

Mandy didn't think Mike's death was a sign the town was unsafe. Someone had killed Mike for a reason. Was she the next target?

While the police searched Mike's room, Mandy paced the parlor. She didn't want to go out in the dark night alone and drive the curving road to Jandafar Hills.

One of the boarders turned on the television and selected a *CSI* rerun. Mandy closed her eyes, but the program entered through her ears. Another body, more strange circumstances. The plot wasn't any stranger than what had happened here tonight.

If she could go back a few hours, she'd let Mike into the SUV with her and Lamar. Talk to him, maybe even take him out to Jandafar. If she had, he might still be alive.

She felt immobilized. She might never leave this room. There was too much uncertainty outside. Even if she made it back to the B&B, what was to keep someone from getting into her cabin and killing her? Everyone in town knew she was at Jandafar.

"Miss?"

Mandy jumped. The deputy sheriff stood at her elbow. "We found a few things in Mr. McNally's room we need to ask you about. Would you come upstairs?"

She rose from the chair and found she could walk after all. Maybe, if she stayed in the house, she would be safe, and she was with policemen. How much safer could you get?

Mike's room was upstairs, the last door on the right.

"You were friends, you said?" The sheriff asked as she entered. The simple room had a double bed with a brass bed frame, a comfortable chair with ottoman kitty-cornered by the window, a hulking wardrobe on one wall, and a small desk and chair on the wall behind the door.

"We were acquaintances. I'd only known him about six months, when he started working at the company."

"And what does this company do?"

"Marketing. He was a creative designer, and I was in sales. We worked together on a couple of marketing campaigns for small companies in the Tulsa area."

"So, do you have any idea who these two people are? He has a whole envelope of photos of them, both together and separate. They have anything to do with a marketing campaign?"

He handed her the envelope, and she slid out a stack of photographs. Her blood chilled, but she forced herself to look at each picture. Jenna and Sean: at the park, in their yard, in their driveway, in their car, even on the deck at their Grand Lake cabin. The last picture was not only of Jenna and Sean, but her and Will in the ski boat on the lake.

Mike had told her he didn't know Jenna, but he'd obviously been following her for months even before he started work for their company.

"That's you, isn't it? You know these other three people?"

"This is Jenna Wade and her husband Sean. They both disappeared from Tulsa earlier this week. The man with me is my boyfriend Will."

"Can you explain why this fellow Mike had these pictures with him?"

She had no explanation. Obviously, Mike had known much more about Jenna and Sean, and even her and Will, than he had ever let on. A tiny headache started in her right temple.

"You don't look well. Want to sit down? I have a couple more questions," the deputy sheriff said.

Mandy sat on the ottoman by the window. "I'll help in any way I can. Mike was just a guy at work. We didn't socialize. But he helped me look for Jenna."

"And is that why you came here, and why he followed? You were both looking for this person, Jenna?"

"Yes. I left Tulsa alone. I didn't expect him to come after me."

"But he did. Were you glad to see him?"

Mandy closed her eyes. Where was this questioning going? Hadn't Mrs. Childers already told him there was no way she could have shot Mike and been cowering on the veranda seconds later?

"I wasn't *not* glad. I didn't want him to come mostly because I didn't want him to involve himself. Jenna was my best friend. She wasn't anything to him."

"She was obviously something to him. Otherwise, why all these pictures?"

"I don't know the answer to that."

"We also found this in his suitcase." He held up a plastic bag with a handgun inside. "And these." He held up topographic maps and a GPS device. "And these." Two walkie-talkies. "Looks like he was rendezvousing with someone. You?"

"I've already told you I had no idea he was coming here. If he brought those things, it was on his own initiative."

The tiny headache grew.

"Seems like you don't know a lot."

She glared at the sheriff. "I don't, and I told you that from the beginning."

"You're staying out at Jandafar Hills?"

"Yes."

"I'll be out there tomorrow to talk to you again. I'll call Dale and let her know when we're coming. For now, you can go."

But she didn't want to go. She didn't want to leave the relative safety of the house and drive to Jandafar. She didn't want to stay in a dark, empty cabin. She stood up but didn't leave the room.

The sheriff and his deputy looked at her. "Well? Is there something else you wanted to say?"

"No. It's only... I'm scared to make the drive back out to Jandafar. If someone was after Mike, they might be after me. I've already been run off the road once on the way out there."

The sheriff sighed. "Okay. Deputy Caldwell will escort you if that will make you feel better."

"Yes, it would."

But it wouldn't help her to sleep in the cabin, all alone.

~ Chapter 41 ~
Will

Will refocused his attention on the final speaker for the umpteenth time since he'd returned to the evening seminar. He was mad at himself for letting Mandy distract him. He'd used the one evening break to call her, expecting her voice to cheer him, even though he did not agree with where she was and what she was doing. He'd realized he was fighting a losing battle over Jenna. He couldn't leave here; he wasn't willing to throw away his career.

How had she determined he wasn't at the Rex? He hadn't covered his tracks, but then, he hadn't thought he needed to. It was unlike Mandy to check up on him. He should have taken that precaution. Was he losing his edge?

He focused on the front of the room and the demonstration under way. Cybersecurity was an evolving area he had to get up to speed on. The current seminar and tomorrow's morning seminar were crucial to the field work he was often assigned. He had to put Mandy out of his head.

He couldn't be the only person in the room who had a loved one to get back to. He'd been dead serious when he had talked with Mandy about moving in together. He wanted to cement their relationship. He wanted to marry her.

She'd never say yes in her current state of mind.

He'd worry about fixing that later, when they were both back in Tulsa. He'd have to tell her a few more things about his current work to regain her trust. She had to come to an understanding that secrets were necessary, both for his survival and hers.

Maybe he should quit.

The thought shocked him. He'd never considered it before.

Thinking it told him that his emotional connection to Mandy was stronger than he'd realized. Their future was a growing presence in his mind.

He was still here even though she needed him there. What did that say about him?

~ Chapter 42 ~
Mandy

The deputy agreed to follow her to the ranch. Mandy drove a mile or two under the speed limit and took the curves slowly. It helped to know the deputy was behind her, but she repeatedly checked her rearview mirror for headlights to make sure he was still there, and no one had cut between the two vehicles.

The deputy turned around at the gate.

Mandy drove on to the ranch house. The floodlight between the staff cabins revealed no vehicles parked nearby.

Lamar wasn't here. Mandy wasn't sure she could get out of her vehicle until he returned. Her shaking hands gripped the steering wheel.

Dale and Max were in the main house. She could see lamp light through the curtains and a glow—most likely a television. She slipped out of the SUV and ran for the house.

The moon had not yet risen. Stars twinkled above, much brighter than in Tulsa. Had the moon been full and the night brighter, she might not have felt so scared. As it was, the hair on the back of her neck prickled and she was sure someone was watching her from the shadows.

Mandy knocked on the door.

Max opened it wide. Holding a beer bottle in one hand, he stood in his stocking feet and looked at her. "Hi, Mandy. Can I get you a beer?" His voice was slurred.

"Is Dale awake?"

Max nodded. "She's in the office finishing book work." He took a swig of beer. "Managing this place takes it out of both of us. She gets these headaches…"

Dale came down the hall. "Oh, Mandy. I heard your knock. Everything all right? You look upset."

Dale turned into the living room and Mandy followed. Dale and Max would hear the news tomorrow if she didn't tell them tonight. There were no secrets in this town, and the death of a stranger, particularly one who had followed her here, would be a hot topic.

"Something horrible happened in town tonight," she said, her throat dry.

"Oh? Come and sit down. Tell us." Dale used the remote to turn down the television volume. She tucked her legs under her as she sat on the sofa.

Mandy sunk into an overstuffed chair a few feet away.

"What happened?" Dale tucked an afghan over her legs.

"A friend who followed me here was murdered in Medicine Park tonight." Mandy picked at a piece of lint on her jeans. Her hand shook.

Dale leaned toward her. "Not your boyfriend, I hope."

"No. A friend. But he wouldn't have come here if not for me. And somebody killed him outside Mrs. Childers' boarding house." She grabbed a tissue from a dispenser on the coffee table and swabbed at her eyes and nose.

"How horrible. You must be shaken. Can I get you something?" Dale's expression was full of compassion.

"Here's a glass of water," Max said as he entered the room from the kitchen. "You look like you need something stronger."

He handed her the glass and settled into the leather recliner.

"Did you hear what she said, Max? A friend of hers was murdered tonight in town. Someone who followed her from Tulsa."

"Really." Max glanced at Mandy before shifting his look to the television. "What happened?"

Mandy told them about the sheriff's investigation but left out the part about Jenna and Sean and the pictures they'd found in Mike's belongings. The unease she had felt since learning about the photographs grew. Mike had been stalking Jenna and using her to get information.

She closed her eyes and rested her head on the back of the sofa.

"You sure you're all right, Mandy?" Dale asked.

"Actually, no."

"Do you have any idea why someone would want to shoot your friend?" Max asked. He glanced at the television again.

"His name was Mike. And I'm not sure he was my friend. It's complicated."

Dale nodded grimly. "We don't want to pry, but I'm concerned about you."

"Someone ran me off the road the first time I tried to come here. And scary things happened in Tulsa before I left. My life might be in danger. And now Mike's dead."

Dale rubbed the back of her neck and looked at Max. He shrugged. An unspoken signal passed between the two of them, and a cold finger touched the back of Mandy's neck.

"You think I'm being paranoid," Mandy said.

"We think you're upset. There's more to this than you're saying. Neither of us think you came here to find a job. I wish you'd trust us. Maybe we can help." Dale looked worried.

Trust them. She was short on trust right now. She had trusted Mike, and she had trusted Will. Now she had no idea who she could trust. She'd been getting close to trusting Lamar before Mike had interrupted them, but she had been willing to talk to him only because of what Jenna had said to her. *Find Lamar.* And she thought she had. She'd told him about Molly, and chances were that Max would hear all about that conversation from Lamar tomorrow. She might as well explain.

"It's not that I don't trust you. It's that I'm in the dark about so much. I'm following blindly wherever I'm led. And I was led here."

"Maybe you better start at the beginning," Dale suggested softly. "And if it makes you feel any better, you can sleep in the main house tonight, upstairs. No charge. Now, tell us."

Mandy prayed she wasn't making a mistake by confiding in them.

"My best friend in Tulsa, Jenna Wade, disappeared earlier this week. I've been trying to figure out where she went, and Mike, a friend from work, was helping." They didn't need the details, only the essence. And yes, it did help to know she could sleep upstairs rather than in the little cabin, all alone. Then she remembered Moby. Surely no one would break into the cabin with the big dog inside.

"Okay. Go on," Dale encouraged.

"Jenna's secretive about her past. When I started investigating, clues led me here because of the name Jandafar. Jenna might be someone who disappeared from here years ago. One of the girls who disappeared after the fire: Molly Bergen."

Max choked on a swallow of beer.

"You all right, honey?" Dale asked him. He nodded. "Molly Bergen. The name rings a bell. Was Bergen the name of that family in the cabin fire way back when Chad and Lamar worked here?"

Max coughed again and nodded.

"So, you think your friend Jenna was one of the girls. Molly. But if she came here, where is she? We haven't seen her, and we don't get that many visitors this late in the season."

"Mrs. Childers has a couple of non-resident boarders, but neither of them was there when Mike was murdered," Mandy said.

"You think one of them might be your friend, Jenna?" Dale asked.

She'd been so focused on what had happened to Mike that she hadn't considered that possibility. Could that be true?

"Seems farfetched to believe Jenna is one of the Bergen girls," Max said. "Folks around here think those girls are long dead. Or that the crazy one set the fire and talked the other into running off. No good would have come of her. And my little brother Chad can vouch for that. She was bad news. And if your friend is Molly, she's got a story to tell and it ain't likely she wants to tell it."

Dale frowned at her husband. "We've never talked about this. Did you know those girls, too?"

"It's all over and done and better forgotten." He waved one hand in the air and focused his look on Mandy. "Have you told Lamar the truth?"

Mandy watched Dale rub her temples. The blood had drained from her face. Something felt off.

"Have you?" Max repeated.

She nodded. "Lamar told me what happened."

"The little bitch would have wrecked Chad's life if she hadn't disappeared. He was crazy about her. Hasn't been the same since. Lives in that cabin by himself. Like a hermit or something." Max drained the rest of his beer and dropped the bottle onto the floor next to the chair.

Dale stood, poked Max in the arm, and picked up the bottle. She swayed and grabbed the back of the chair. "Your brother is what he chooses to be. Don't go blaming it on anybody—especially somebody who's been gone for twenty years."

Max looked up at his wife and shook his head. "It's a waste of a man. And he's my little brother."

Dale put one hand on her husband's shoulder and turned back to Mandy. "So, the Bergen fire brought you here. But why would you be in danger? It happened twenty years ago, and you weren't here." She looked confused.

"You've forgotten about the man whose wife died that day," Lamar said from where he stood by the door. "He was suspected of starting the fire. And I wouldn't hesitate to think he might have killed both the girls, whether on purpose or by accident. He could have come back here."

"But this man who was murdered tonight had nothing to do with the fire or those women," Max grumbled. "That's ridiculous."

"Murdered? Who?" Lamar's green eyes widened.

"My friend Mike." Tears threatened to spill, but Mandy kept them in check. "Somebody killed him, Lamar, after we saw him at the bar."

Lamar blinked. Suddenly, he looked at Max. "Have you talked to Chad lately? Is he all right?"

"I guess so. Been awhile since I've seen him."

"Maybe you should send the sheriff to do a welfare check," Dale suggested in a whisper. She disappeared into the kitchen.

"We should check on Chad. Will you go with me in the morning, Max?" Lamar asked.

"We got that fence to rewire on the south pasture, one that butts up to the wildlife refuge. How we gonna get that done if we're up checking on Chad?" Max grumbled.

"One of us should go work on the fence and the other go to Chad. I'm serious, Max. You want to work on the fence, great. I'll make a quick drive up in the morning. Be back by 11 to help wrap up the fence work. I could meet you at the line shack," Lamar offered.

"Damn it. You'll go out there and find him drunk, more 'n likely. Don't say I didn't tell you. Waste of your time and mine."

"I'll leave at first light and be back mid-morning."

"Look for me on the east side. I'll be long done with that spot by the line shack by the time you get back."

Dale reappeared in the kitchen doorway.

"I've got some leftovers you could take. Last time we saw him he was nothing but skin and bones. Old bachelors aren't good at caring for themselves." Dale turned back to the kitchen.

"I'm off to bed. I'll be up early as usual, Lamar. Stop in for coffee, 'fore you leave. Night, Mandy." Max headed for the stairway. "Oh, and I'm sorry about your friend."

Lamar and Mandy were left alone in the living room.

"Am I missing something?" she asked. "What's wrong with Chad?"

~ Chapter 43 ~
Jenna

Jenna startled awake, the nightmare fresh. The darkness, the weight of his body, and the pain.

She'd thought making love would feel wonderful. Wasn't it the ultimate expression of love between a man and a woman? She'd been jealous of friends who talked about their first time and how they wanted to do it again and again after that. She'd thought she wanted it to happen. But the time had not been right.

That night, he'd raped her. She relived it weekly, if not nightly.

Jenna shifted in the pile of linens she was using as a makeshift mattress. This was the first bit of deep sleep she'd grabbed in the past four days. Life on the run, as she remembered, was not conducive to sleep.

Why had she come back here?

She closed her eyes, and the memory was imprinted on the back of her eyelids.

She loved Sean, but often the nightmare returned when she and her husband were making love. She'd clench her teeth and stiffen, and Sean would stop kissing her, stop moving, and pull back to look at her face. "Jenna," he'd say. "Where are you?"

But she couldn't tell him. It was a horrible memory, and what had happened was her fault. Her parents were dead and her sister probably was, too, and there was nothing she could do about it.

She never stopped wishing and hoping she could change the past, that she could pick up the phone and call her parents, talk to them about Sean, tell them the two of them were going to start a family, tell them life was normal.

She thought about inviting her sister to visit, asking her to bring along her husband and the kids. But that wasn't going to happen.

Her sister was long gone.

Her sister might be dead.

She could never forgive herself. And she could never forgive that man.

~ Chapter 44 ~
Mandy

Lamar studied her face for a minute before he answered. "Chad wasn't the same after that summer. Wouldn't come back to work after the fire. Didn't want to set foot on this place or have anything to do with horses or ranches. Max came back here from Texas ten years ago thinking he'd have Chad's help with this place. Instead, he has to make do with mine."

"Why was Chad so upset? I mean, what happened was horrible, but... Did he care that much, so fast, about Sharon Bergen?"

Lamar splayed the fingers of his right hand and stared at them. "He couldn't put her behind him. Started drinking way more than usual. Tried to find her. He didn't want to believe she'd had anything to do with setting the fire. He kept talking about how much she'd cared about him and what their life together could have been like. He was obsessed."

"Did he search for her?"

"Weekend after weekend. All the little towns around here, and in the Texas Panhandle all the way to Amarillo. Dropped plans to go to Texas Tech with me. When the police stopped searching for the girls, he became obsessed. He's never stopped believing she is alive and would come back."

"Does he have a job?"

"He's a mechanic, takes online courses in his spare time.

He's gotten several degrees. Not sure what in. He works at Sparks Garage. On the highway south of town."

"That's where they took my car after someone ran me off the road the first time I tried to come out here."

"You checked on your car lately?"

"Guess I should tomorrow."

"Why don't you go with me to Chad's? We can ask about your car."

Mandy considered his offer for only a second. "Great idea. Maybe he'd talk about Molly. I'd like to be certain Molly and my friend Jenna are one and the same."

"Do you have a picture of Jenna? Even after twenty years, I might recognize her."

Mandy thought about Mike's photos of Sean and Jenna and the two boarding house guests absent yesterday evening. Could one of them be Jenna?

Mike had used her to get information. Someone had hired him to follow Jenna. His employment at Empire was probably a ruse.

"Mandy?"

She came back to the present. "Sorry, I was thinking about Mike."

"Understandable. I was asking about a picture."

"I don't have one with me. Odd to go searching for someone without even a picture."

"If you're telling me the truth, you didn't have a lot of time to pack for this trip. I get that. What about pictures on your phone?"

Mandy shook her head. "She never wanted anyone to take a photo of her. She didn't do social media." She covered a yawn with her hand. "Sorry, I haven't slept much the last several nights."

"Are you sure you want to drive up to Chad's with me? I'll leave early. Before dawn. Maybe you'd rather sleep in and help Dale."

"I want to go. If we can get him to talk, I might learn something."

"Maybe. I've always wondered why he was so torn up about Sharon Bergen. Why he took it so personally. Maybe enough time has passed he'll be willing to talk about it." Lamar stretched. "Can I walk you back to your cabin, or are you staying here?"

"Guess I'll go back to the cabin. I hate to be a bother to the Hardestys. And my dog's there, after all. I'll be safe."

They crossed the veranda and stepped onto the well-lit yard. Shadows hovered at the edges, and the moist night air held the dusty odor of horse manure.

Mandy peered down the side road toward her dark cabin. Why hadn't she left a light on? She felt relaxed with Lamar standing beside her, but the thought of the empty duplex made the hair on her neck bristle.

"Maybe I should have taken Dale up on her offer and slept upstairs," Mandy said.

"I'll go in first and check it out, make sure the place is empty and the locks are secure."

Mandy wasn't about to turn down his offer, but Moby's barks as they neared the porch made it apparent there couldn't be an intruder inside.

"You have a dog?" Lamar asked before he stepped onto the wooden porch.

"A stray I'm fostering just until I get back to Tulsa." Mandy reached into her pocket for the cabin key, inserted it into the lock and shoved the door open. Moby thrust his big head through the open crack and barked again.

"Hey, it's okay. It's me." She petted the dog and pushed him back so that she could enter the cabin. Behind her, Lamar flipped the light switches, illuminating the porch light and a living room lamp. Light dispelled the room's shadows. Mandy released her breath. As Moby sniffed Lamar, his long, hairy tail swished back and forth.

"Hi, dog," Lamar said, patting the top of Moby's head and scratching his ears. "Dog sure is friendly. This breed, well, they all look alike. Good boy." He shoved Moby away when the dog put his front paws on his chest. Lamar crossed the living room into the kitchenette and turned on the light over the sink. He opened the door to the pantry and looked in before checking the bathroom.

Mandy flipped on the light in the bedroom.

The carryall she'd bought at the store lay on the bed where she'd left it. Nothing in the room had been disturbed.

"Looks fine. Nobody here but the dog." Lamar stepped up beside her. "Will you be okay?"

"I think so. Let's check the adjoining door."

The door to the other half of the duplex was at the far end of the living room. The deadbolt was secure.

"I'll be fine, Lamar. Come by in the morning, I'll probably already be up. If not, I can be ready in a few minutes."

"We'll grab coffee and toast or something at the ranch house. Dale has a pot going by 5:30."

Mandy locked the door behind him. At the window, she watched his progress to the bunkhouse porch. Even though he was bow-legged, he walked confidently. What was his story? He'd revealed nothing about himself or his relationship with Molly or Sharon. Why had Jenna wanted her to find him?

Only a few hours had passed since she'd talked to Will. Mike was dead after revealing Will had lied to her.

How many times had he lied to her before this?

Mandy let the window curtain drop and turned to the little living room. The décor could be called "Worn lodge." The fabric of the well-used pillows on the red plaid sofa featured deer and elk, the end table lamps were made of entwined antlers, and a cowhide rug covered most of the wooden floor. Rustic shelves held books and whatnots. An old TV with a VCR sat on a low coffee table, stacks of old VCR tapes piled beside it.

A few watercolors of stormy hillside scenes decorated the walls. An empty wooden fruit bowl was centered on the wooden dinette table. Other than a toaster and a four-cup coffee maker, the kitchen counters were bare.

She felt sure that if she opened the cupboards, she'd find plates and glasses. There might even be food staples in the pantry and condiments in the small refrigerator. She didn't care. She wasn't hungry. She couldn't be hungry when Mike's dead face kept appearing. Her stomach roiled.

"Here we are Moby. Need to go out? And I bet you're hungry." She unlocked the front door and stepped out on the porch to watch the animal sniff around the bushes and finally find a spot to do his business. The dog hurried back to the cabin, and she locked the door.

Back inside, she poured kibble into his bowl in the little kitchen and stood back as he ate. Her thoughts buzzed around and back to Mike. When the dog had finished eating, she stooped to pet him, glad to have the distraction.

"Okay, now where do you want to sleep?"

The dog bounded to the bedroom and up onto the bed, where he circled and settled in.

The double bed was firm, and the clean bedding smelled of lavender. Mandy's body wanted sleep, but her mind didn't. She wanted answers to all her questions, but without so much as a cell phone signal, finding those answers would have to wait until tomorrow.

Mandy dozed, then startled awake in the shadowy room. Outside, an owl hooted, and insects and birds twittered. Inside the cabin, Moby snored softly, and something scratched at a wall or floor. Mice?

In the adjacent living room, soft light filtered through the curtains. She turned on her side and stared through the open doorway at the light, hoping it might hypnotize her to sleep.

The incoming light disappeared for an instant, then reappeared. Imagination, or had someone walked in front of the window? Her heartbeat hammered and she lay still, listening. The owl and the insects were silent; the scratching had stopped.

A few minutes later, inside the cabin, something squeaked. She rolled out of bed and stepped to the living room doorway. The noise came from the far end of the living room. She squinted in the half light.

The doorknob to the other half of the duplex turned.

"Who's there?!" she cried. Moby leaped off the bed and barked.

The knob stopped turning.

"Who's there?"

Silence.

Moby panted and looked up at her.

Mandy shoved a chair in front of the connecting door, checked the front door, and the window locks. In the bedroom, she jerked the blanket off the bed. In the kitchen, she dug through the drawers until she found a butcher knife. When she returned to the living room, she sank down on the sofa and turned on the television. The dog curled at her feet.

She couldn't fall asleep again.

~ Chapter 45 ~
Sean

Sean Wade parked under the bright mercury vapor light. Something—yellow crime tape? —fluttered in the wind at the far end of the lot, where shadows hung from the trees.

He picked up his cell phone and made a call.

"Sylvester," the voice on the other end answered.

"I'm in place. Test results?" Sean scanned the parking lot as he talked.

"As expected. It's our guy. Paint pigments match, framing materials are consistent. Even the wood pulp fibers are the same. Either our guy's getting sloppy, or he thinks he'll never get caught."

"After three years, we were due for a break, Si."

"Timing is set. The buffalo jump happens Friday at sunset."

Sean grunted his agreement and disconnected. The Buffalo Jump, an escarpment where Native Americans had driven herds of buffalo to their slaughter, was only a few miles from here, in the rough granite country. He'd read all about it while they searched for the location of the forger. Sy must have also been reading up on his local history to pick that term as the code name of their raid.

He drew in a ragged breath. The timing sucked. This had all come together quickly. The coincidence of Jenna's disappearance and the chance she was also here made him uneasy. Usually, nothing made him uneasy.

What had Jenna gotten mixed up in? And if he believed Mandy, this was all part of the past his wife had tried so hard to keep from him. He knew some things about her past. He knew her tragedy, even though he hadn't heard it from her. He was fine with pretending her secret was hers alone.

She had known it was the nature of his work to learn things about people. It was all about research and connections and digging out facts people hid or intentionally omitted. Good people were not good liars. Bad people were tremendous liars.

He knew Jenna was a good person. A bad person would never have tried so hard to hide something. What people thought wouldn't matter to them. It mattered to Jenna.

As soon as tomorrow was over, he would dedicate every hour of every day to finding her.

Part 4 - FRIDAY

~ Chapter 46 ~
Mandy

When Lamar knocked on the door in Friday morning's pre-dawn light, Mandy answered the door fully dressed. Moby darted out the door and circled the porch, sniffing.

"You must be a morning person," Lamar drawled with a slight smile.

"As in, lark versus owl? Not really, but I didn't sleep much after I had my late-night visitor."

"What?"

Mandy explained.

Lamar frowned. "We don't have prowlers out here," he said. "Doobie sees to that. He'd sound the alarm."

"Doobie was in the house last night when we got back. Maybe Dale left him inside. Moby was with me, though. He barked, and whoever it was left."

"We'll tell Dale and Max. You're not spending another night out here alone. You stay at the big house, or you stay with me in the bunkhouse."

Mandy glanced at Lamar as they stepped off the porch. Was this an innocent declaration, or was he feeling something more than friendship for her? She wasn't sure how she felt about him. In the early dawn light, the firm set of his jaw seemed strong and protective. It felt good to have him concerned about her, and not in Will's sometimes-authoritarian way.

Lamar wanted to help. She might have wanted to see what could happen between her and Lamar if it wasn't for lingering thoughts of Will and an unwanted reminder that Mike—dead Mike—had seemed concerned back in Tulsa when he was lying to her. She didn't know anything about Lamar.

At the big house, the coffee was ready, but the kitchen was empty. Doobie padded over and sniffed them both as they entered the room.

"Guess this answers your question about Doobie," Lamar said as he scratched the border collie's ears. "They left him inside last night."

"Looks that way." She opened the door and let the dog out.

"You want a bagel or some toast?" Lamar asked as he moved around the kitchen.

"Toast is good. Thanks."

Lamar opened a sack of wheatberry bread and slipped two slices into the toaster.

Ten minutes later, they piled into Lamar's truck with a sack of food Dale had put together for Chad and left in the refrigerator. Lamar drove out of the gate and turned away from town into the broken landscape. The country western Top 40 blared on the radio. The road surface became gravel and Lamar dropped the truck's speed to 30 mph.

"So, what happens when you find Jenna?" Lamar asked. "*If* you find her."

The question startled her. She'd been so focused on finding her friend, she hadn't considered what would happen next. "If she needs help, I'll do whatever I can to help her," she said slowly. "After that, I don't know. I'm not sure she'll return to Tulsa. She found a strange painting in an art gallery, and it really spooked her."

Lamar turned down the radio. "What type of painting?" Lamar's look shifted away from the road. The surrounding hills and valleys glowed golden in the pre-dawn light.

"The woman in it looked like Jenna. And she was imprisoned in a glass crypt."

Lamar's look darted to her, his brow furrowed.

"Does that mean something to you?"

"Not sure." He flicked on the air vents and rolled down the windows.

An uneasy feeling settled over her. What was he hiding?

"If your friend doesn't want to go back to Tulsa, will you?" His eyebrows lifted.

"I have to decide if my relationship with Will is permanently broken. And as far as a job—I'll be starting from scratch. After the last few years in the marketing world, I don't see spending the rest of my life trying to please company owners with ulterior motives and market products with unsubstantiated claims."

"Would you consider relocating?" He smiled as he drove. Dimples popped into his cheeks.

Why did her heart thump? She didn't see anything that looked like an invitation on his face. He was being friendly.

"I might. I like this part of the state. Fond memories."

"So, you said. Tell me about your missing friend, Jenna." He turned off the radio.

She wasn't going to let him off the hook that easy. "After you tell me what you know about glass crypts. Have you seen one before?"

Lamar peered at the top of the next hill. "Only in Sleeping Beauty. Or was it Snow White? You know, the one where the prince has to kiss her?" He tossed her a grin. "So, Jenna?" he asked again.

He was evading her question. She'd bring it up again later. "She's beautiful and smart. She was the CFO at the marketing firm, but she isn't a stereotypical accountant. She has a playful side, loves to joke around. We're best friends. More like sisters. She doesn't have any living family."

"Does she think of you as a sister, too?"

"We never talk about it. Have lunch or dinner together several times a week. And Will and I get together with her and Sean on the weekends."

"Will is Sean's buddy?"

"Yeah, since high school."

"Jenna got along with Will?"

Mandy thought about that one. "They didn't *not* get along. Will liked her, but sometimes he seemed to resent the time she and I spent together. If Jenna and Sean were arguing, he took Sean's side."

"And in all that time you spent together, she never mentioned a sister or told you about her family?"

"No. She didn't like to talk about the past. Her family members were all dead, under tragic circumstances. She had no interest in contacting anyone from her childhood. Said it was too painful to talk about."

"Could be, but it seems strange to me she never mentioned her sister. When Molly and Sharon disappeared, I assumed they went somewhere together. If Jenna is Molly, what happened to Sharon?"

Lamar turned up a narrow, rutted road, the edges overgrown with tall grasses and low, spindly brush. The truck's engine roared and the suspension creaked as the vehicle dropped into and climbed over the ruts.

"Only Jenna can answer that." How many times had she wished her friend would say something about her past? It couldn't have been as ordinary as she said. "Is it much farther? Why does he live way out here, anyway?"

Lamar shrugged. "He gave up people after Sharon and Molly disappeared. Max and Dale met, married, and lived in west Texas. Didn't come back here until Max's parents died. Eventually, they sold the family ranch and Max invested his share in Jandafar Hills. Tried to get Chad to go in on it and work with him, but Chad won't set foot on the place."

Lamar downshifted to first gear. "The place looks like crap." He drove through what had once been a gate, but one post was down and broken. Overgrown cedars blocked any view of the house from the former driveway. Lamar braked to a stop and tapped the horn.

The sun had risen while they made the drive, and in the harsh glare of the morning sun, the house and yard looked bleak and uninviting.

"Chad? It's Lamar. You here?" Lamar called as he stepped out of the truck.

Mandy eased out into the overgrown grass of the former yard.

Lamar strode to the porch and rapped on the front door. "Chad? It's Lamar."

He tried the front doorknob. It swung open, and he stepped inside. Mandy waited.

A mockingbird sang his repertoire from the top of a nearby oak tree. Other birds chirped in the trees, and a hawk swooped low across the yard. Something rustled in the overgrown bushes. This area of Oklahoma was beautiful in a wild, untamed way. Standing here in this overgrown yard, with the wind blowing and clouds puffing overhead, Mandy believed it possible that a cattle drive might lumber by, or a wagon train.

Had Chad chosen to live here in this desolate place because of a broken heart?

A few minutes later, Lamar reappeared, his expression grim. "He's not here. Place is a wreck, but it always is. No sign he's even eaten a meal here lately. I put the food Dale packed in the refrigerator. This was taped outside the fridge." He handed her an old print.

Mandy recognized the family in the picture, standing on the porch of a cabin. She flipped it over. The single word "remember" had been printed on the back. "I found a picture of this same family in Jenna's things."

Lamar raised his eyebrows. "It's definitely the Bergen family, and that's Molly and Sharon."

Mandy studied the two girls in the photo. "And if I added twenty years to this face, she could be Jenna." Mandy tapped one girl in the photo.

Lamar's brow furrowed. "Then your friend Jenna isn't Molly. That's Sharon."

She'd gotten used to believing Jenna was Molly, the pretty, quiet girl unconcerned with approval and popularity. Lamar had characterized Sharon as wild, ready to try anything. If Jenna was indeed Sharon, she had changed her personality. Was that possible? Was everything she had believed about her friend wrong?

"No sign of Chad. His truck isn't here."

Mandy looked up from the picture. "Does he often disappear for a few days?"

"I'm lucky to see him once a month. He's a loner."

"You said he studies online. What else does he do when he's not at Spark's working on cars?"

"I'll show you. He's not here, so he can't be angry about it. Follow me."

Lamar led her around the house to a small building. A combination lock kept the double door latched tightly. He lifted the latch and frowned. "Now let's see, what would he use for the combination?" He spun the dial one way, then the other, and finally moved it a few clicks back in the first direction. The padlock snapped open.

Lamar unlatched the double door.

Light filled the room. Roof skylights and windows high on all four walls allowed light to pour in. An easel occupied the focal point of the small space. A white cloth covered the canvas on the easel. Elsewhere around the room, stacks of canvases leaned in rows against two of the walls. Some were in early stages, with the subjects sketched lightly in pencil directly on the canvas or sketched over a backwash of blue or yellow. A third wall held only a few draped canvases. Finished paintings?

Mandy stepped to the central easel and removed the drape from the painting.

The artist's viewpoint in the painting was higher and closer, the colors darker, but the subject was Jenna in a glass crypt, even more full of terror than in the gallery painting. The unfinished shapes surrounding her were unidentifiable.

"What the—" Lamar said.

"You didn't tell me Chad was an artist."

"Artist, painter, sculptor, welder. He's sold a few things, but he's apparently still obsessed with the Bergen girls. Who would want a painting of a woman suffocating and screaming?"

"Jenna saw a similar painting in Tulsa. That's why she ran."

Lamar looked closer at the half-finished work. "Was that painting signed?"

"Mike looked closely at the artist's signature. He said it looked like 'Cha Har,' and he asked the store clerk who that was and how he could get in touch with him."

"Cha Har..." Lamar took three steps over to the paintings covered with drapes. He uncovered the first one, a dark painting of a house fully engulfed in flames. The signature in the bottom right corner was *Cha Har*. "Chad Hardesty."

Mandy shivered.

Lamar stooped to look at the next. Another fire, but in this one, a figure stood in the open door of a burning cabin, her hair ablaze.

"He's painting scenes from that night." Mandy rubbed the gooseflesh on her arms.

"Looks like it. I had no idea."

"But you knew the combination to the lock."

"It was a wild guess. His life was divided, before the fire and after the fire, when the Bergens died and the girls disappeared. I tried the date of the fire for the combination."

Had Chad taken the painting to Tulsa, hoping to meet with Jenna at the funeral parlor? "I saw a glass crypt in a funeral parlor down the street from that art gallery. Is there a connection? Does anyone Chad knows have friends or relatives in Tulsa, in the embalming business?"

Lamar shrugged. "No one comes to mind."

"I think Jenna was meeting someone at Paducka's Funeral Parlor the day she found the painting. I found a note stuck in a book inviting her to come there. When I was snooping around, I met the owner. His name was Adam Hughes."

"Adam! I have a second cousin by that name. He married Max and Chad's sister. You say he's a funeral director in Tulsa. That's crazy." Lamar shook his head.

"And another coincidence. Chad's painting shows up in Tulsa and Jenna sees it when she's on the way to meet someone at your cousin's funeral business. I think she was meeting Chad earlier this week."

"You'll have to ask Chad about that." Lamar put the painting down and covered it once again with the drape.

Back in the truck, Lamar turned on the country western station again. They were both silent as a George Strait hit played, both lost in thought during the drive down the twisting road toward town.

Lamar passed the turn to Jandafar Hills without stopping. "Thought I'd drive to Sparks, find out about your car and whether Chad's been at work lately. Maybe we can figure out if Chad was in Tulsa earlier this week."

"Will Max be mad at you for missing out on the fence repair? I need to get back in time to help Dale with the work like I promised."

"Won't take long. And Max will agree that checking on Chad is important. He cares about him a lot more than he lets on. Can't tell you how many times he's tried to get Chad to move in at Jandafar and work for him. But Chad won't do it."

"Did they argue about something Chad can't get over?"

Lamar threw her a quick sideways glance. "They're brothers. Ever heard of sibling rivalry? That's all it is. That and too much testosterone."

Mandy wanted to talk to Max about his brother. There had to be more to this than Lamar was telling her. Either he didn't know it all or he was choosing not to tell her. Lamar was undeniably handsome, but she'd learned from her experience with Mike. Handsome didn't mean honest.

~ Chapter 47 ~
Jenna

Jenna Wade stared up at the attic rafters. Daylight seeped in around the roof vents and fell in shafts into the dark space. Dust motes floated and swirled in an occasional draft of moving air.

It was time to act, but her body was immobilized. Coming here had seemed like the right thing to do, but now she was here she seemed incapable of action. She was in limbo, unable to move forward and unable to go back.

There probably wasn't much to go back to. Sean wouldn't want her as his wife once he knew. Mandy wouldn't want her as a friend, either. She shouldn't even try to salvage anything in Tulsa. She'd have to move on. It didn't matter what happened here, didn't matter what anyone said or did.

Her thoughts darted back toward the memories again. She'd fought them for so long. She didn't want to fight them anymore. She was here, in the midst of it all, and the memories were too strong, too thick, too tied up with the smells of this place, the way the air shifted, the scent of the grass and the dust.

A sob broke free, and she slammed a hand over her mouth.

She hadn't intended to get drunk that night. But the beer had fizzed in her mouth and buzzed her head, helping her to forget that she was a fake. People thought she was one way, but she wasn't. She talked big. She'd learned the talk from the kids in the girls' bathroom—the way they tossed the sex talk around, the way they giggled, the way their eyes rolled. She'd played the part. And everyone had believed.

She hadn't intended to knock over the candle during the argument. But her father had grabbed her arm and she had whirled, hoping that Chad wouldn't see how disgusting she was, how out of control. She'd been reaching for him, wanting to leave her father behind. Daddy's little girl was no longer little or a girl. It was time to move on. Chad was so sweet. He *loved* her.

She hadn't intended to kill her parents. She wouldn't have left them there, in the burning cabin, but *he* had dragged her away. *He* had changed the course of her life. Because of him, she had lost everything, including her sister.

Was she alive? The painting made her believe so. Made her believe there was something she could still do to set things right. A way to get them to believe that it had all been a tragic accident.

Who would believe her now? She had been on the run for twenty years.

~ Chapter 48 ~
Mandy

"We got yer radiator fixed. Fixed the lamp in the busted headlight. You'll have to have that grill work done somewhere else. But the thing's drivable, although not too pretty. It'll get you where you need to go." The old mechanic winked at Mandy, nodded at Lamar.

"Thanks, Sparky." Lamar patted the man's shoulder.

"You seen that lowlife Chad out at Jandafar lately?" Sparky asked.

"Nope, I was going to ask you if he'd been in to work this week."

"Not since Wednesday. He left not long after this lady's car came in and haven't seen hide nor hair of him since. TJ came in yesterday to help out so I could work on her car. Chad's pushing his luck here, and TJ wants full time. I've half a mind to give it to him."

"If I see Chad, I'll tell him he better check with you 'cause TJ's moving on him. You ready to go, Mandy?"

She paid Sparky for the repairs and retrieved her keys.

Lamar followed her back to Jandafar.

The two dogs greeted them, barking, as they drove through the gate. Lamar followed her to the duplex. He rolled down his window and called, "I'm going to find Max. He needs to know

Chad is AWOL. Do you need me to follow you back into town to return that rental?"

"I'll see if Dale is available first. Check with me later."

Lamar rolled up his window, turned the truck around, and drove toward the narrow track that passed through the closest meadow. In the distance, horses grazed.

Mandy filled the dog bowl with kibble and set it and a water bowl on the cabin's porch. The dogs had raced away again.

Inside the main house, Dale was vacuuming. She turned the machine off as Mandy stepped in. "You still willing to help me ready the cabins?"

"Sure. Lamar took me into town. My SUV was ready. I drove it here, so I'll need to return that rental later today. Do you need to run into town? What time will your guests be here?"

"Mid-afternoon. We can go to town after lunch. There's always something I need. Can't seem to remember everything. It's these headaches."

"I'll return my rental to Champion's and help you with your shopping list."

Mandy grabbed the two empty plastic pails Dale had set by the door and the ring of keys that lay on the counter.

"Cabins 3 and 4. Dust and sweep, wipe the kitchen counters and clean the bathroom. By the time you've finished, lunch will be ready. Linens are in the storage room around the corner here, and so's the to-do list and cleaning supplies. I'm sure there's nothing on there you haven't done before."

Mandy walked down the hall to the supply room. She found the cleaning list attached to a clipboard and gathered the necessary supplies.

She took Moby with her, and in each cabin the dog found a spot for a nap and remained quiet as she worked.

If Mandy had felt any true interest in accepting Dale's open position, it had died by the time she was a third of the way into preparing the second cabin for the weekend visitors.

She dusted, cleaned countertops, swept and mopped kitchens, dinettes, and bedroom floors, cleaned the bathrooms, stocked the towels and bathroom supplies, then made beds before she filled the guests' welcome baskets with fruits, candies, and bags of 100-calorie snacks.

She checked all the light bulbs to be sure they were working and turned on the a/c systems to 74 degrees. The cabins weren't that dirty, but the tasks were tedious. She wanted to be in town, talking to the police chief about Mike and to Mrs. Childers about her other roomers. She wanted to check every possible place where Jenna could be staying, and while she was looking, she'd look for Chad, too. If Jenna was Sharon, there had been chemistry between her and Chad years ago. Had it somehow been rekindled despite her marriage to Sean?

Mandy thought of the portrait she and Mike had seen in the gallery. Had seeing it brought Jenna here to Jandafar? Had she met with Chad, the artist, her former lover? Then, why had she been so frightened Tuesday afternoon?

Mandy thought back to the handsome funeral director. She scrubbed out the tub in the second cabin and ran the water to wash the suds away. She tried to picture the funeral director's face but instead saw Lamar's twinkling green eyes and his lips.

When the second cabin was clean and ready for its tenants, she carried her supply buckets down to her cabin and set them on the porch. She needed to wash her hands and face, reapply makeup, and pull her hair back smooth into a ponytail. She could only imagine what she must look like after hours of housecleaning.

Although she was sure she'd locked her cabin when she left in the predawn with Lamar, she found the cabin door unlocked.

She stepped carefully in; Moby padded along beside her. "Hello?"

Her carryall sat on the floor in the middle of the living room. Someone had pinned a note to it. She bent over to read the unfamiliar scrawl.

"I'm fine. Please go home." The note was signed, "Jenna."

She grabbed the note and ran for the ranch house, leaving Moby inside the cabin.

"It isn't her writing," Mandy explained to Dale. "But someone wants me to think she wrote it. And the cabin was unlocked. How did someone get in?"

"I honestly don't know. I've been here all morning, getting the common areas cleaned, baking bread, cookies and muffins. Other than a couple of phone calls, I worked straight through the morning." A worry line deepened on Dale's forehead. "And believe me, I don't like the thought that somebody is roaming around in the cabins."

"There's something else I haven't mentioned. Someone was in the other side of the duplex last night. They tried to come through the connecting door. When I called out and Moby barked, they left. I was awake the rest of the night. They didn't try to get in again."

Dale pushed her dark hair off her forehead. "I should have made you stay up here last night—and I will tonight. I wish we didn't have these customers coming in, badly as we need the income. Scares me that something might happen with them here. I sure don't need a customer getting hurt. And that includes you, Mandy. Did you and Lamar find out anything at Chad's about the Bergen girls?"

"He wasn't at the house. Hasn't been at work in two days, either."

"Bet Lamar couldn't wait to carry that news out to Max."

"He did say that Max would want to know. He was headed out to tell him. Won't they be in for lunch soon?"

Dale glanced at the clock. "Anytime now. And that'll put Max in a bear of a mood, I'm afraid. If anybody can do that, it's Chad." Her voice was weary.

"Do you get along with Chad?" Mandy was sticking her nose in where it didn't belong, but Chad must be the key to finding Jenna. And she'd stay here until she did, despite the note.

"What's not to get along with? He keeps to himself. Doesn't hurt anybody or cause problems. It's my husband's ranting and raving that's unbearable. And it's been going on for years. You'd think two grown men would learn to let go of something they can't do anything about and can't change."

Dale bit her lip and turned away when Max and Lamar came through the door. Dale was right about Max's mood. He didn't speak to either of them but set about making his sandwich and choosing from a variety of salads and chips Dale had laid out on the serving counter. He scooted his chair up to the table, eyes focused outside the window on the tree-covered hills.

He'd eaten most of his lunch when Dale ventured to speak. "Mandy said Chad's not home. You gonna go look for him?"

"Do I usually? What's different this time?" He glared at his wife.

Dale glanced at Mandy and Lamar. "You know the answer to that. What's different is that Mandy has a friend who's missing who might be Molly, and she has another friend who came here to help her who was murdered."

"Don't mean either thing has anything to do with Chad."

Dale looked at her husband, but he refused to acknowledge her. Finally, she said, "Mandy and I are going into town. She's gonna take her rental back to Doug and help me gather supplies for the weekend. Cabins 3 and 4 are booked for tonight and Saturday night. We'll do a barbecue tomorrow evening. You want ribs or steak?"

Before the men left, Mandy held Lamar to one side while Max and Dale talked. She showed him the note she'd found in her cabin.

"You're sure this isn't Jenna's writing?" Lamar asked.

"I'm sure of it. I'm not going anywhere, no matter what this note says. I'm not going back to Tulsa without talking to her face to face."

Lamar nodded. "I didn't think you'd fold up camp and go. Come by the stable when you and Dale get back from town. I'll be brushing the horses, getting them ready in case the guests want to take a sunset ride after dinner. Maybe I can get Max to tell me more about Chad, and these paintings of his while we're working this afternoon."

"You stay in the cabin, Moby. And don't let anyone in," Mandy instructed the dog after lunch. She had looked for more evidence that someone had been in the cabin earlier but found nothing.

She drove the rental into town, following close behind Dale's SUV. They returned her rental, then stopped at the grocery. After buying food for the weekend, Dale drove to the police station.

"Sheriff Mark in?" Dale asked the receptionist.

"He's over at Mrs. Childers."

"If he calls in, would you tell him I'm on my way and that Mandy's with me and needs to see him?"

When they arrived at the boarding house, Mandy hopped out before Dale had brought the SUV to a complete stop. If Jenna was here, she had to see her, had to tell her about the pictures Mike had been taking before the sheriff had a chance to spring them on her.

In the parlor, a thin, dark-haired woman in her forties sat on the sofa in the living room, talking to the sheriff, while Mrs.

Childers hovered in the entry. The woman's face bore no trace of makeup, and she wore khaki shorts, a T-shirt and hiking boots. Across from the woman a dark-haired man sat hunched over, hands resting on his knees, his back to Mandy.

The woman on the sofa wasn't Jenna. Disappointed, Mandy entered the room. The man straightened and turned toward her.

It was Sean Wade.

~ Chapter 49 ~
Sean

"My God, Mandy! You're here. Have you seen Jenna?" He rushed across the room and gripped her shoulders. He eased his grip when she winced. She looked exhausted.

"I haven't seen her. I'm staying out at Jandafar, where her parents died."

Sean frowned. His mouth opened and closed. He searched for the right words. "I was there last night, looking for her. Are you staying in that duplex?"

"I heard you. I called out. When did you learn about Jandafar?"

"A dog barked, and I didn't recognize your voice. I'm sorry I scared you. Jenna has to be out there." He pondered how much to tell her. Maybe she already knew it all.

"I hate to interrupt this interesting reunion," the sheriff began, "but I was trying to get a clear picture of where Mr. Wade and Miss Bean were at the time Mike McNally was murdered last night. Both were off the property, but neither have any witnesses to corroborate their whereabouts."

"I told you, Sheriff, I was in Charon's Gardens at the Wildlife Refuge, wilderness camping," Miss Bean said. "My gear is all upstairs, Mrs. Childers saw me carrying it in late this morning."

"So, she said," the sheriff turned to Sean. "And I want to show you a photograph." He held out the candid picture of Sean and Jenna outside their Tulsa home. "Have you seen this before?"

Sean stared at the photograph. "It's Jenna and me, but I've never seen it before. Where did you get it?" Anger tasted like iron in his mouth.

"Mr. McNally had this and many other pictures of your wife, both with and without you, in his things. What do you know about McNally?"

"Absolutely nothing. He worked with her, apparently. We never interacted. I don't think he'd been with their marketing firm long." Worked with her? No. He was a spy for someone. Who?

"Were you aware he and Mandy were looking for your wife?"

"I left Tulsa unexpectedly yesterday. I haven't seen or talked to Mandy since. It's a complete surprise to find her here." Sean rubbed one hand over the back of his neck. If not for the other people in the room, he might tell the sheriff the truth, but right now he couldn't. It would jeopardize the operation.

"Why did you think your wife was here?" The sheriff demanded.

"Something scared her—that painting you told me about, Mandy."

"What brought you here, Mr. Wade?" The sheriff looked firmly into Sean's face. "Answer my question."

Sean closed his eyes again. He had to divert the sheriff. "I drove to our house. I heard someone upstairs. I thought it was a burglar and went to get our gun. The gun was gone. The door opened while I was searching, and someone shot me."

The sheriff shook his head.

"Who shot you?" Mandy cried.

"Jenna. She thought I was... someone else. When she realized she'd shot me, she became hysterical. She helped me clean my leg wound, then left. Told me she wouldn't be back. No reason for me to stay, either."

"Weren't you going to let me know?" Mandy frowned.

"Eventually. I had to get a lead on where she'd gone. Will had been checking on Jenna's past for me for several months in between other jobs."

"What jobs are you talking about?"

The sheriff crossed his arms and stood back.

The man was going to let this conversation play out. Sean's mission could remain secret for now, but it was time Mandy knew the truth about Will.

Sean released a long breath. "He's a private eye, Mandy. A special type of independent private eye. Sometimes he works for the government. He's on a case in New York, across the border from Toronto."

Mandy's face paled. Her shoulders slumped. Sean knew this information would devastate her, but he had to continue.

"Months ago, I asked him to trace Jenna through his sources. A possible connection showed up, a family named Bergen who once lived in Boulder. That connection led here, where the Bergens died twenty years ago. This was the logical place to begin searching, and Will agreed I had to start here. But he didn't want you involved. Does he know you're here?"

"Yes, and he doesn't want me here anymore than you do." She spoke in a clipped voice. "What you don't know is that Jenna called me, told me to come to Jandafar, told me to find Lamar. And it all had to be done by Saturday or it would be too late."

"Saturday is the anniversary of the cabin fire and her parents' deaths," Sean said.

"And the disappearance of the Bergens' two daughters, Molly and Sharon," the sheriff added, drily.

"Jenna's here, someplace, I know it," Mandy stated.

The silence in the room seemed to mean they were all in agreement. Jenna was here, but where?

"That painting Jenna found, the one that upset her so much... This all has to have something to do with that." Mandy crossed the room to the window.

"If you'll excuse me," the other woman said. "This conversation has nothing to do with me."

"Please stay around for the next day or so. I'm certain I'll have more questions, and I would like to get a timeline for your camping trip," the sheriff said.

"I'll be here through the weekend. We'll be hiking. Couldn't get a wilderness permit extension." She left the room.

"So, back to this painting. What was it of, exactly?" the sheriff asked.

"A woman was trapped in a big glass box, like a crypt," Mandy explained. "Blond, blue-eyed. She was screaming, terrified. But even so, there was no mistaking it was Jenna or someone who looked a lot like her."

"Like her sister," the sheriff added.

Sean shook his head. "It looked like Jenna to me." Immediately, he regretted speaking up.

Mandy stiffened. "When did you see the painting?"

Before Sean could respond, the sheriff said, "There were two Bergen daughters, Molly and Sharon. Any idea which one your wife might have been? Did your investigator provide that information?"

"Will said there was a sister, but nothing more." He looked at Mandy. "I wanted to know about her family, but she'd never discuss it. I never dreamed it was something like this." Sean rubbed the back of his neck again. He should have had Will dig deeper.

"What about Mike McNally? Did you know he was looking for your wife, too?" the sheriff asked.

Sean shook his head. The idea of McNally spying on them made his blood boil.

"I don't think I told him," Mandy added. "Will knew, though, so I'm surprised he didn't tell you. Have you talked to him in the last few days?"

"Mandy?" Dale asked quietly from where she stood near the doorway of the parlor.

"Oh, Dale, I'm sorry." Mandy grabbed Sean's arm and led him toward Dale. "This is Sean Wade. He's here looking for Jenna, too. Sean, this is Dale Hardesty."

"Nice to meet you," Dale said. "But sorry for the circumstances. Hello, Sheriff Mark. I need to go back home, Mandy, I have guests coming in. Do you want to go back with me, or could you get a ride to Jandafar after you finish here?"

Sean turned to the sheriff. "I've told you all I know. I've spent the last day and a half looking for Jenna. I don't know who would have hired Mike McNally, or who would have killed him. Jenna might know, but if she's here, she's hiding. Here's my cell number. Call if you need me. I'm going out to Jandafar."

Sean followed Dale's SUV closely as they drove, his thoughts churning. "Why did that painting cause Jenna to come here? What did it mean to her?" He looked at Mandy. She seemed tired, edgy, worried. He was certain that the information he'd revealed about Will had hurt her.

"It showed her—or someone—trapped. Kept prisoner, unable to breathe. Did she come here to save someone? Her sister? Why did they split up after the fire? They were old enough to be on their own, but barely. What happened?"

"The anniversary of the fire is tomorrow. Something is going to happen at Jandafar," Sean said.

Mandy nodded, grimly.

Trees flashed past as the car climbed the hills and navigated the curves. Sean waited for Mandy to ask the inevitable question he'd evaded back in the boarding house. Their vehicle rounded a corner.

"Sean, when did you see the painting? It blew up in the fire at the gallery not long after Mike and I were there."

Sean chose his words carefully. "I saw it a few days before she did, during an insurance assessment at the gallery. I never told her about it." He didn't need to tell Mandy it had been more than an assessment, that he'd been investigating the gallery for forgeries.

His answer seemed to satisfy her. They drove on in silence.

At Jandafar, Sean parked in front of the duplex.

"I need to run inside and let Moby out," Mandy said.

"Moby?" Sean called as she bolted out of the car.

"A dog I rescued. He was in the explosion at the art gallery." Mandy hollered over her shoulder as she ran up onto the porch.

Sean stepped out of the car and stretched. He didn't remember seeing a dog at the gallery on previous visits.

Claws scrambled and a dirty-blond curly-haired dog burst out of the cabin. He galloped toward Sean and stopped short of leaping onto him. The animal made a circle and loped back toward Mandy.

"Wow. That's a big dog." He'd seen mixed-breed poodles like it before, but this dog was much bigger than he'd expected.

"Goldendoodle, I think. Standard poodle and golden retriever. Smart." Mandy lifted her knee, knocking the animal in the chest as it attempted to leap into her arms. "No! Down. Stay down. Good boy."

"You going to keep him? Does Will like dogs?"

Mandy made a face. "It may not matter if he does or not. Meanwhile, I'm a foster parent." She snapped a leash onto the dog's collar and headed for the ranch house.

Sean followed her down the road and onto the porch, where she tied the dog to the leg of a bench. Sean patted the dog's head as he passed. He and Will had never talked about dogs. Apparently, Will and Mandy never had either. A dog was a commitment, and up until now, Will had not made many of those. This animal would either make or break their relationship, if it hadn't been broken already by the revelations he'd made.

Inside the house, Dale Hardesty was chopping vegetables on the kitchen counter.

Mandy turned to him. "Sean, I need to speak to Lamar for a minute. Will you wait for me here with Dale?"

"Sure." He relaxed against the countertop.

Dale used the big chopping knife on the cutting board beside the sink.

"Nice place you have here, Dale. How long have you lived here?" He wanted more information about this woman and her husband. They might be more connected to his wife than he'd been led to believe.

~ Chapter 50 ~
Mandy

Mandy's thoughts tumbled as she untied Moby and headed for the stables. Liars. They were all liars, every one of them. Sean. Will. Mike. Who else? Jenna, her best friend. Her heart ached with disillusionment.

In the corral, three horses roamed free. One whinnied, another pawed the earth. None had been saddled. A horse fly buzzed one of the mares. She tossed her mane.

"Lamar!" Mandy called. She strode into the stable and down the aisle to the tack room. Moby pulled her every which way, as if she was the one on the leash, not the dog. He scurried with his nose to the ground, sniffing the dirt and bits of straw.

"Lamar?" She wanted to see the cowboy. No, she *needed* to see him. She wasn't sure why. In the tack room, she passed saddles and hanging bridles. The scent of freshly soaped leather hung in the air. Where was he? Why had he let the horses in from the pasture and not saddled them? Lamar wouldn't leave that task until after dinner; saddling the horses would take too long if the guests wanted to see the sunset from a high point on a nearby hill.

Moby lapped at the water in Doobie's dog bowl near the tack room. When he looked up at her, his mouth seemed to grin. Water dripped from long, curly chin hairs.

"Come on, Moby. I guess Lamar's not here." She was more than disappointed, she was depressed. She walked back to the cabin and locked Moby inside again.

Inside the main house, Mandy found Dale perched on the arm of the leather sofa, talking to Sean in a low voice.

As she stepped closer, Dale said, "We'll find her. Maybe we can finally put the question of that fire to rest. The Bergens would want that, I'm sure."

Dale rubbed her forehead. Both she and Max had mentioned her headaches, and it was worrisome. She was either ill or stressed out from operating the ranch and dealing with the conflict between Chad and Max.

"Have you seen Lamar?" Mandy asked. "He's not in the barn. He was going to saddle several horses in case the guests wanted a sunset ride after dinner."

"He was here when the couple staying in Cabin 3 arrived. Paperwork's been signed. Must have showed them up to their cabin. The other couple isn't here yet."

"Anything I can help with? Set the tables?"

"Sure." Dale smiled at Sean. "Mandy wants to be sure she doesn't owe me anything for her stay here. She's been a great help today. I hope she decides to stay. And I'm hoping for the best for you and your wife."

Dale scooted off the arm of the sofa and looked out the window. "Back to work. I'll leave you two to talk. Check with me in the kitchen in a few minutes, Mandy, okay?" Dale left the room.

"You're thinking about staying here?" Sean crossed his arms. "Does Will know?"

"I quit my job—right before they were going to fire me. I don't want to go back to that rat race. Maybe it's more my speed in a small town." She didn't feel any regrets. Right now, she had nothing to go back to.

"And what about Will?"

"Will's lied to me from the beginning. About everything. How do you think I feel about that?" She carefully set places at a long dining table.

"Much the same as I feel about Jenna's lies. But I'm here. I still love her. The woman I married is worth loving despite anything that might have happened to her previously. I wish she would have trusted me enough to tell me the truth."

Mandy wasn't sure she felt that strongly about Will. "Trust is a funny thing. It takes so long for it to come, but it can be gone in an instant. Poof. How can you ever trust that Jenna is telling you the truth from here on out?"

"If you don't understand, then I guess what you feel for Will isn't really love." His look met hers. "And what about your friendship with Jenna?"

Her heart drummed. Maybe he was right. If she truly loved Will, would it have mattered that he hadn't been honest with her about his profession? Instead, something had broken inside her. She wasn't sure she and Will could ever mend it.

As far as Jenna, somehow, the fact that she'd hidden her past didn't matter. She was honest about who she was now. She knew Jenna's heart.

"I wonder where Lamar is," Mandy said.

"What is it with this Lamar, anyway? I haven't met him, but he seems to enter every conversation. Is there something between you two?"

She shook her head. "He's nice. Easy to talk to. And he has a caring side I rarely see with Will."

"Sounds like you've already picked out Will's replacement."

"Right," she scoffed. "Lamar's been helpful the last two days. He was here twenty years ago when the Bergens died. He's been the only one willing to talk about it and to give me a feel for who Jenna was." She could readily defend him. Lamar felt real, and honest.

"And who was Jenna?"

Was Sean ready to know? It wasn't up to her to decide. He had a right to know. "I'm leaning toward Sharon."

"Is that good?" The tone of his voice changed.

"Maybe not. Lamar thought Sharon was wild. He didn't like her behavior. Max's brother Chad fell in love with Sharon. Her sister Molly was quieter, smart but reserved. At first, I thought Jenna had to be Molly, but when Lamar saw a picture of the girls at Chad's this morning, he identified the young woman who looked the most like Jenna as Sharon, not Molly."

Sean frowned. "Jenna isn't wild. She isn't a flirt or a party girl. Her personality fits his description of Molly."

"Both young women disappeared. Something about that painting triggered Jenna to come here. I think something more than the twentieth anniversary of the fire."

Sean's eyes narrowed. "What if the woman in the painting wasn't her, but her sister, and Jenna believes her to be in danger? Maybe she came to rescue her." Sean's dark eyes sparked with a new energy.

"Sean, Jenna's a good person. You know she is."

"I want to believe that. But I don't understand why she couldn't share any of this with me."

"Or with me. Over the last few days, I've been remembering all the times she helped me. Like the time I came down with the flu. She brought me soup and checked on me twice a day, even sat with me in the evenings so I'd have company since Will was out of town.

"One time I had a wreck and I couldn't afford to pay the deductible for my car insurance so I could have it fixed. She paid it and never asked for anything even though it took months to pay her back."

Sean smiled. "I remember. I didn't want her to loan the money to you. I didn't think you were a good risk."

"Thanks for your confidence. But you know, Jenna had confidence in me from the minute we first met. I thought it was because we're both orphans and lost our parents as teenagers. Neither of us wanted to talk about it. Hurt too much. You get consumed with what-ifs, and the guilt is overpowering. You try to figure out if it was your fault, if you could have prevented it by being there or saying or doing something different. There's the pain of continuing your life without them yet thinking about them every time something happens that you would have shared with them. At times, it's unbearable."

"I can only imagine. Maybe I didn't let Jenna know how sorry I was. Maybe she would have shared more if I would have acted more interested and concerned."

"See, there you go. That guilt trip doesn't help." Mandy's throat tightened. "We need to find her. It doesn't matter if she's Sharon or Molly. Jenna is my best friend, and she wanted my help."

Forget the note in her cabin. Mandy was certain Jenna had not written it. Someone else wanted her out of the picture.

"Where does that leave me?" Sean's look was bleak. "She didn't tell me she was coming here or ask me to come. She shot me accidentally and left. Maybe she wants to leave our life behind, too."

"I don't know the answer. I wish Lamar was here to talk to you. Where is he?"

After she tucked the last napkin underneath the fork at one place setting, she looked out the window at the meadow expanse west of the house and crossed the dining room to another window facing the stable. "I don't see his truck, and he promised he'd be at the barn, saddling the horses. They're still wandering the corral." Mandy glanced at the wall clock. "It's way past time to meet him. I think I'll go up to Cabin 3, make sure he isn't sitting on the porch shooting the breeze with the visitors, or that he didn't get roped into a chore that's taken up the afternoon."

"I'll go with you."

Doobie ran up, tail wagging. He accompanied them up the road to the hillside cabins.

Behind them, engine noise broke the peaceful silence. A car drove up the road toward the main house.

"I bet that's the people who are staying in Cabin 4," Mandy said. "Let's hurry. Dale may want me to take them to their cabin after she gets them checked in."

"You like this new job of yours."

She considered that. "Doesn't feel like work. It's not like an office, where you're chained to a desk handling paperwork all day. Even in a creative business-like marketing and advertising, there's a certain chained syndrome that comes with it. This is different."

They reached the narrow road that veered off to the right to Cabins 1 through 5. At Cabin 3, a white Murano sat in the parking area. Mandy stepped up onto the porch and rapped lightly on the screen door. A man answered her knock.

"Hi. I'm Mandy, and this is Sean. We're looking for Lamar. I think he escorted you up to the cabin earlier. Did you notice where he went from here?"

"Well, the wife and I were unloading the car, but if I remember, a blue truck stopped as he was walking down the hill. He got in and the truck drove that way." The man indicated the road that passed through the meadow and on to other parts of the former dude ranch.

Mandy joined Sean again on the road. "Someone picked him up in a blue truck. Max drives a blue truck, the only one I've seen around here since I came. And if they drove up the range road, I'm sure it was Max. They must not have finished that fence project."

Sean walked silently, glancing at the trees, the meadows and hills, then back toward the cabins. "I keep thinking what it must be like to have lived through a fire that killed your parents and to have lost your only sibling. For such a peaceful place, there's lots of pain here."

Mandy knew that pain. She didn't want to experience it again.

If she thought too hard about it, she imagined she could feel a psychic scream in this place. What a horrible day that had been twenty years ago: a woman died, and a family was lost, the parents killed in a fire, their teenage daughters vanished.

Dale stepped out on the ranch house porch with a middle-aged couple. She waved at Mandy and Sean, and they hurried toward her.

"Mandy, did you find Lamar?"

"No. The people in Cabin 3 said someone picked him up in a blue truck. I guess he and Max went back to work on the fence."

Dale flicked one hand. "Max finished that. But never mind. Could you take the Johnsons up to Cabin 4? This is Judy and Rick."

"Sure." Mandy introduced herself and Sean. "We'll walk up the hill. Follow us in your car. Straight ahead and then to the right."

She and Sean retraced their steps up the hillside to the row of cabins they'd left minutes before.

After helping the couple carry their bags into the cabin, Mandy led Sean up the hillside to the burnt-out cabin ruins she'd found the previous day. "It's morbid, but I can show you where I think it happened. I found this." She handed him the earring she'd tucked into her jean pocket.

"It looks like one of Jenna's. She's been here."

"I'm sure she has. She must have snuck up here, back to the scene."

Sean studied the piles of scorched bricks and stepped over a charred timber to stand in what had probably been the living room.

"Do you think Jenna realized what Mike had been doing? Did she kill him?"

The question startled her. "I don't see Jenna capable of killing anyone. Someone hired Mike to find Jenna. He did his job. I think whoever hired him killed him. They didn't want to risk that Mike would talk."

Sean frowned. "This is very serious. A murderer is looking for Jenna. What if they find her?"

"We have to find her first. I hope we're not too late."

A crow cawed from a tree branch above them, and another answered from a hundred yards away. A third flew close to land on the ruined chimney, and a fourth flapped up to perch on the partial wall near where Mandy stood.

"Creepy birds," Mandy said. "Ravens and crows signal death to me. Maybe they can smell it. I feel sad for the family destroyed right here."

"We need to find her, Mandy. Today."

Mandy clapped her hands and the birds scattered.

"Where do we start?" She asked.

"My cabin. Supposedly she was there earlier. Or someone wants me to believe she was."

Together, they slipped down the hillside on the carpet of leaf debris. Back on the road, they walked in silence to the staff cabins. Doobie trotted along with them, stopping every few seconds to thrust his nose into the leaves and snort.

Mandy stepped onto the duplex porch.

Inside, Moby barked as she unlocked the door.

~ Chapter 51 ~
Sean

"Who lives in the other half?" The cabin looked comfortable enough, about what you'd expect for staff accommodations. The antler lamps were like nothing Jenna would ever buy.

"Nobody right now. In the summer, the female staff live here. A maid or two, maybe a cook? The men live in the bunkhouse. Right now, Dale has no staff. Come the holidays, she'll hire college kids. She said she was going to advertise."

Sean surveyed the little cabin before going to the connecting doorway. He twisted the knob. "When I tried to come in the other night, you saw this knob turning?"

"Yes. I called out without thinking. I never did get back to sleep."

"Can you open it?"

"You mean do I have the key? No."

Sean shrugged. "It's not so hard." From his pocket, he pulled a carabiner with several attached tools. After he selected one, he stuck it into the deadbolt. With a snap, the lock unlocked. His throat tightened. He twisted the knob and swung the door open.

The other side of the duplex was the mirror image of Mandy's half. A musty smell dissipated as Sean rushed away from Mandy to check out the kitchen.

Nothing conclusive there, only bits of trash in the garbage can. Remnants from the previous employees? It should have been emptied, right?

Mandy was waiting when he returned to the living room. "Nothing in the kitchen or laundry alcove," Sean said.

"I found this in the bedroom." Mandy opened her hand and showed Sean the mate to the earring she'd found at the cabin ruin. "And I noticed there's an attic trapdoor in the bedroom closet that I don't have in mine. We should check up there."

Sean's heartbeat quickened. He barreled into the bedroom and opened the closet door. After he jerked the cord on the attic access trapdoor, it dropped down to reveal a collapsible ladder. The sections of the ladder unfolded. Sean climbed into the darkness of the attic and sneezed in the dusty, musty space.

"Jenna? Honey, are you up here?" Sean called as Mandy climbed the ladder behind him. Darkness. Air vents allowed only tiny rays of light into the space.

Sean's eyes adjusted to the low light level. A thin cord hung above him, to his left. When he pulled the cord, light illuminated most of the attic.

Something huddled at the edge of the darkness. His heart pounded.

"Jenna?"

The figure moved.

Downstairs, Sean led Jenna to the sofa and dropped down to sit beside her. Moby sniffed at Jenna, then sat quietly.

Jenna stared at the floor; Sean stared at Jenna. She'd dyed her light brown hair cinnamon and streaked it with copper highlights. Her face was pale. Her eyes were sunken, but the blue-green irises were still brilliant in the light from the window.

Mandy hurried to the kitchen. Cabinet doors opened and closed. The stove clicked on.

"You two must hate me. I'm such a fraud," Jenna moaned. She wouldn't look at him.

"We're here because we love you. It doesn't matter what happened all those years ago. That person isn't who you are now," Sean said.

"No? It made me who I am. I was someone different then. Someone I'm afraid you wouldn't have liked."

Mandy carried two mugs of hot tea into the living room, handed one to Sean and one to Jenna. "Are you Sharon Bergen?" she asked.

Jenna took the mug but didn't look up. "My family died because of me."

"What are you doing here?" Sean slipped one arm around her shoulders drawing her closer. "Why did you run away from us and come here alone?"

"When I first saw that painting, I thought it was me, but the second time, I realized it was my sister. She's here, somewhere. I have to save her."

"You have a sister," Mandy repeated.

Sean saw disappointment on Mandy's face. He was not the only one who felt betrayed by Jenna's secrecy. "The second time?"

Jenna rubbed her thumbs along the rim of the mug. "I was inside the shop, talking to the clerk, trying to buy the painting when Mandy showed up outside the store. I left through the back alley after telling the clerk I'd buy the painting the next morning."

"Why did you leave town? I don't understand." Sean rubbed the back of his neck. "At the house, you could have told me, I would have done anything to help you. You didn't have to run." The walls of his stomach were twisting, and pain throbbed in his chest. Was he having a heart attack?

"I wasn't ready to tell you." His wife's eyes filled with tears. "Everything was so good between us, Sean, and I wasn't ready for it to end. You've been the best to me. I believed I could have a normal life. You gave me that gift. I didn't want to lose it. Then I saw the painting."

"But you didn't go to the gallery originally to see the painting. Someone sent you a note to meet them at the funeral parlor. Who?" Mandy probed. She sat on the edge of the chair nearest the sofa. On the floor below her, Moby wagged his tail.

Sean studied Jenna's face. Exhaustion was evident, but she was still beautiful even though the dark hair dye had washed all the color out of her face.

"I thought Chad had asked me to meet him. I couldn't imagine how he found me, but I trusted him, and I thought he might know where my sister was. But after I found the painting, it was clear to me it wasn't Chad I was meeting, but someone else. I'm afraid of what he's done to her!"

"What who's done to her? What happened?" Sean insisted. He tightened his arm around her shoulders and scooted closer.

Jenna's eyes were full of terror. "Oh, my God." She rocked, and tea sloshed out of her mug.

Mandy stepped over to kneel in front of them. "It's going to be okay. Sean and I are here to help you. But you've got to trust us."

"I don't know how he found me." Jenna's voice quivered.

"I think I do," Mandy said. "Mike McNally was working for someone. I thought he was helping me, but he was in it for himself. He was photographing you and Sean, and he was using me to find you."

Jenna's eyes widened. "Mike McNally? That guy you work with? But I don't even know him."

"Whoever he was working for probably killed him," Sean said. "They shot him last night."

Jenna covered her face with her hands. "He must have murdered my sister."

"Who?" Mandy and Sean asked in unison.

Jenna closed her eyes. "I need to start from the beginning. I have to make sense of this." She took a long sip of tea and sat back on the sofa, shaking. Sean took her mug and set it on the table. She uncovered her eyes and dropped her hands to her lap.

~ Chapter 52 ~
Jenna

Jenna Wade looked at her husband, Sean, and her best friend, Mandy. She had to trust them. They'd proven they loved her. They'd found her, and that couldn't have been easy. And now, she had to tell them her deepest secrets and hope they didn't walk out of her life. She wouldn't blame them if they did.

She cleared her throat and glanced out the window before she began. "It was hot that week. Cicadas droned in the trees all day. I had dreaded that family vacation. My parents irritated me. They were old-fashioned, and I wanted excitement.

"My family had come to Jandafar several summers over the years and my parents always talked about how much fun it was. And it had been fun, when I was younger. It wasn't the same that year. Molly and I were too old for a family vacation. We were both spoiled brats and bored. By the end of each day, Mom would go quiet. And Dad would stare into the distance." Jenna sniffed.

"Go on, honey," Sean prodded.

"When I got here this week, my memories were strong. It could have happened yesterday. But so much time has passed. Everything is different. *I'm* different.

"I understand how my parents must have felt. Life never stays the same, and yet we hunger to keep it the same. Even if it means we shut things out to keep our world like it used to be.

"Last night, I wondered if I was wrong about the painting. Maybe there was no message. Maybe it had nothing to do with Jandafar. Maybe it was the time of year that made me think that painting was Molly, and that she was still alive. I've been so convinced she had to be dead."

She took a long swallow of tea. Sean stared at her with rapt attention. Mandy frowned.

"After the fire, when I was in the wind, alone and uncertain what to do, I read a news story about the fire, my parents' deaths, and how my sister and I had disappeared. I was sure I would be blamed for what happened to Mom and Dad if I returned. And I left without my sister. I was so young and so stupid." A sob escaped her throat. "If I went back to Boulder, I was afraid they'd label me a nutcase and lock me up. I couldn't go back. I could only go on, alone. My sister would have to fend for herself." Jenna wiped her nose with one hand. "If she survived the fire."

"Tell us what happened that day," Sean urged.

Jenna stared up at the ceiling and closed her eyes. "I've pushed these memories aside for so long. It hurts so much to remember." Tears ran down her cheeks.

"Molly and I signed up for the morning trail ride, along with a dozen other guests. Chad and Lamar, the cowboys, had been flirting with us all week, and so had some of the men."

She explained the rules of the trail ride: single file, no racing, no gait faster than a trot. Those who broke the rules had to walk back to the lodge.

"We reached a meadow. Most of the group had been riding all week, so Chad said we could lope across the meadow. I kicked my horse, and in four strides, she was loping. The woman riding beside me kicked her horse and kicked me. Our horses took off in a fast gallop, racing.

"I hung onto the saddle horn and tugged on the reins. My horse eventually slowed to a trot. The horses scattered across the meadow. My horse reared up and staggered on her hind legs. Not far from me, a horse screamed." She closed her eyes, and the scene was there on the back of her eyelids.

"One horse was down; one rider was down. A hysterical man shoved at the downed mare. The two cowboys ran to the animal. I couldn't see who was underneath the horse. I was frantic, afraid it was my sister. I tried to control my horse.

"When I spotted Molly across the meadow, I rode to her. 'You were racing that woman!' she yelled. 'Her horse fell on her.'

"The horse kept screaming. My horse bucked again. I calmed her down, and we all waited, watching the thrashing horse. Finally, the animal got up, but the woman didn't move.

"Lamar lined us up and led us across the meadow to the trail. At one point, I turned and looked back. My sister said, 'I think she's dead.'"

Jenna closed her eyes. Her mouth quivered. Sean slipped his arms around her. Her heart raced. The story was far from over. She had to finish. Jenna gently pushed him away and opened her eyes.

"At dinner, the ranch owner announced that the woman had died. He called it an 'unfortunate accident.'"

Jenna grabbed her mug and swallowed the remaining tea. "As if that wasn't bad enough, what happened that evening was worse." Her voice cracked.

"We want to know, Jenna. But we need to get you away from here," Mandy said. "I'll walk over to the house and let Dale know we're leaving. I hate to let her down, but we need to find the sheriff and let him know you are all right."

"Dale? Who's Dale?"

"Dale and Max own the B&B."

Jenna's face froze. "Max? Do you mean Max Hardesty?" The blood rushed from her face and her heart plummeted.

~ Chapter 53 ~
Sean

"Max is Chad's older brother. You know him?" Sean asked. His wife's eyes were wide, her expression scared. He wanted to bundle her into the car and drive her away from this place.

"It was Max," Jenna whispered.

"What do you mean?" Sean enclosed her free hand in his.

"The man who raped me that night. The man who set the fire. The man who killed my parents."

Sean threw his arms around her and pulled her to him. Jenna was shaking.

Mandy scooted closer. "Max Hardesty. Are you sure?"

"I was there, wasn't I? I've been running from him for twenty years," Jenna whispered.

"Lamar told me Chad was in love with you," Mandy said. "He was upset when you disappeared. Everyone—Dale, Lamar, and even Max—said he went crazy after you disappeared. He's been a recluse since."

Jenna ducked out of Sean's grasp. He reached for her again, but she folded her arms across her stomach and swayed. A tear traveled down her cheek. "It wasn't entirely because of me. It was what his brother Max did. He showed up drunk that night when Chad and I were making out. I thought he was handsome, and I wanted to make Chad jealous. I was drunk, I flirted." She paused and took a deep breath.

"Max took my hand and led me outside. We kissed. He got rough, pushed me into the woods, threw me down on the ground, and raped me. When I finally got away and ran, he chased me to my cabin." Mandy reached for her hand.

"Chad was already there, hoping I'd gone back to my cabin and looking for Max. Dad was threatening to call the sheriff. Max barged into the cabin right behind me, calling me horrible names. My mom was crying, and Dad was yelling. Chad demanded Max apologize, but he wouldn't, so Chad told him to leave. Max laughed."

Sean clenched his fists. Jenna had kept this bottled up inside her for twenty years. Could he have said or done anything differently so she would have trusted him enough to tell him what had happened?

"My sister came in and tried to talk sense into Max. He slapped her, shoved her across the room. She slammed into the fireplace and fell. Max hit Dad, and then threw Mom to the floor when she tried to knock him over the head with a lamp. He grabbed me. Mom and Dad lay on the floor, not moving. Max was crazy, yelling at Chad. He was choking me. Molly wasn't moving. I tried to get away from him and over to her. I knocked a candle off the table."

She sobbed again.

"It's okay, Jenna. You don't have to go on." Sean stroked her hair, but she pushed his hand away.

"The tablecloth caught on fire. Max dragged me out to his truck. He shoved me inside and drove off into the country. I pleaded with him to let me go, but he just laughed. He slapped me. A little later, he jerked me out of the truck, took me inside a building, and raped me again. I fainted. When I woke up, Max was gone. I ran." Jenna covered her face with her hands. Sobs shook her body.

Sean stared into his wife's eyes. "You're all right now, honey. You're safe."

Mandy crouched on the floor in front of the Jenna. Moby whined.

The cabin door slammed open and Dale burst into the living room. "There's been an accident at the line shack." Dale looked shaken, her eyes wide. "Lamar called on the walkie-talkie. They need another pair of hands and..." She saw Jenna on the sofa beside Sean. "I didn't realize anyone else was here. Sorry to bust in."

"It's all right, Dale. This is Jenna—my wife," Sean said. He wiped the tears from Jenna's cheek with his finger.

Moby barked one and leaped across the room to Dale. She patted the dog's head absently. Her face blanched. "They found you. I'm... so glad." Her voice dropped. "But I have four guests," she said to Mandy. "I need help. Have to serve dinner, and I don't know what's happened up there."

"Tell me how to get to the line shack. I'll go and see what they need," Sean said. He glanced at Jenna. "Will you be okay for a bit here with Mandy?"

"The shack's twenty minutes from here. The roads are rough, you'll need the four-wheel drive." Dale handed the keys to the SUV to him, giving directions as she shuffled outside.

Sean took mental notes. Hours of daylight remained. It shouldn't be any problem to find them.

"I've got to get back to the main house and get things ready for dinner." Dale stepped off the porch, rubbing her forehead. She swayed as she crossed the grassy lawn.

"I'll be back as soon as I can," Sean assured her.

Sean stepped back inside the cabin. Jenna stared beyond him, through the empty doorway.

"Jenna? Maybe we should all go, if you feel up to it. It's Lamar, and Max," Sean said. Jenna looked terrified. He reconsidered. "Maybe you don't want to..."

"I can't go with you. I'm not ready." She closed her eyes, stood, and lost her balance.

Sean grabbed her arm and eased her down onto the sofa. "You're shaking."

"I think he must have taken me to the line shack. While the cabin and my parents burned. I ran from there. That glass crypt in Chad's painting was in the line shack."

Mandy stood. "Oh, Jenna, how horrible. I'll go with Sean. You stay here. Lock the door and don't let anyone in. Lamar is on our side. That'll be three against one," Mandy said.

"Three against one," Jenna repeated in a strangled voice.

"Are you sure you'll be all right?" Sean asked. His wife was so pale. But he wanted to find Max. The man deserved prison for what he'd done. His gun and his handcuffs were in his car.

He and Mandy left the cabin and Jenna locked the door behind them.

He didn't know what they'd find up at the line shack, but he did know one thing. He'd have to force himself to take Max Hardesty to the police when he'd much rather kill him himself.

~ Chapter 54 ~
Mandy

Mandy and Sean rushed to the main house where Dale's SUV was parked.

"I don't think Dale knows what Max did." She couldn't get past the loving looks she had witnessed between the couple during her brief stay. "She doesn't seem afraid of him. They seem normal."

"You've spent the last few days with her. Don't ask me if she knows her husband was responsible for Mr. and Mrs. Bergen's deaths, as well as raping my wife." Sean scowled as he slid behind the wheel.

"Dale met Max after the fire. She was vague about her past. She's not the only person in the world who didn't have a perfect childhood." Mandy thought about Dale's constant headaches. Could there be a connection to her past? "If she knew about any of this, she's blocked it out. And if Max killed Mike, he gave no indication last night. No sweat, cool as a cucumber, drinking his beer. But there was something odd." She remembered the exchange of looks between the husband and wife; they had suspected she was not who she said she was.

They got into the SUV and headed out on the dirt track road through the pasture.

Mandy stared out at the waving grasses, watching for the first fork in the road, where they would turn right and begin to navigate the hills toward the line shack. Hot air hung over the yellowing grassland. Grasshoppers and butterflies flitted among the grass stems.

Her head filled with images of Jenna's rape and the cabin fire. She tried to put herself in her friend's place. Could she have kept such a secret for twenty years? She imagined Jenna's loneliness, and her fear. Had Jenna truly believed she would be held responsible for that fire, for abandoning her sister, and for her parents' deaths?

Twenty minutes later, Sean turned the SUV to the right at the final fork. It rumbled down the rutted road and took another curve. Mandy spotted the small building between two oak trees. Max's blue pickup was parked in front of the shack.

They jumped from the vehicle and ran to the door. When Mandy knocked, the unlatched door creaked open. Inside, Lamar and Max sat at a wooden table across the room, their chairs turned to face the door. A walkie-talkie lay between them on the table.

"Hey there, Mandy," Max sneered. "This must be your friend's husband." A smug smile curled his lips.

Lamar didn't look up. His hands remained in his lap. A beer can sat on the table beside him.

"What's going on? Dale said there was a problem." Mandy stepped into the room, but Sean remained in the doorway. The room smelled of beer, dirt, and sweat. Empty beer bottles and dirty plates were stacked on the counter in the small kitchen as if someone had been living here.

"Problem? Yes, there is," Max said. "You know too much. I have to take care of that."

Alarm bells rang in her head. She took a step back toward Sean.

"Maybe it's not what you actually know," Max continued, "but what you're getting too close to figuring out."

Sean's eyes narrowed. He glared at Max. "You son of a bitch."

Max startled. "Whoa! Maybe I'm wrong, and you *do* know! Did Sharon talk about me? After all these years, she's still talking about how great a lover I was, isn't she?"

"You don't know her at all," Sean replied.

"Maybe *you* don't know your *wife*, after all," Max snickered.

Lamar tried unsuccessfully to shove his chair back and grimaced. His hands were tied together in his lap, his feet bound at the ankles.

The door behind Mandy and Sean slammed open, knocking Sean to the floor. The man who entered shoved Mandy toward the table, stomped brutally on Sean's hands and kicked his head.

"Oh, let me do the honors." Max laughed. "Chad, this is Amanda Lyons. And that mess on the floor is her friend Sean Wade. He's married to Sharon, only he knows her as Jenna. This is my brother, Chad."

The man wore a full beard and his long brown hair was pulled back into a ponytail and tied with a strip of leather. With crazed blue eyes, he checked the room. His look locked on Mandy.

"Hey," Chad said. He motioned with a gun for Mandy to move into the room to the right, where a double bed had been pushed up against the wall. Mandy cringed. The dark paneled walls, the single shuttered window high on the wall behind the men were familiar. This room was the setting for the picture Chad had painted.

"The sheriff knows I'm looking for Jenna Wade, and he met Sean last night. If we suddenly disappear, he'll come here," Mandy stated. She rubbed her clammy hands on her jeans.

"Who says you disappeared?" Max said. "Maybe you gave up. Went back where you came from. Tulsa, was it? Interesting downtown. I was just there earlier this week." Max balanced the chair on two legs and rubbed his beer belly. "Now, if something were to happen to you during that drive, say, you go off the side of the road on a bridge or hit a culvert, well, sad to say, it happens all the time. Sometimes people survive, sometimes they don't."

"Your wife's waiting for us to come back, and there's someone else waiting too," Mandy said. "There's no way your plan will work." Her brain tumbled with thoughts. What could they do to turn the tables on Max and Chad? Sean lay still on the floor. She glanced at Lamar, wanting to find hope there, but his eyes were closed. What had Max done to him?

"You think Dale will turncoat on me? She's listened to Chad blather on his nonsense for twenty years, and she never believed it. Why would she suddenly decide not to trust me now?"

"Chad told her what you did?"

"What I did? Hmmm. Seems like you've got your story wrong. What we all wanted to do, and enjoyed it, we did." Max smiled at Lamar and at his brother.

Mandy felt the blood rush to her face and then just as quickly rush out as Max leered at her.

"Well, no point dilly-dallying. Let's get to it—and get on down to the ranch house to visit with the guests."

Max lunged toward her.

~ Chapter 55 ~
Jenna

Jenna Wade peered through the vertical slit between the window shade and the window frame as the evening shadows began to lengthen. The cicadas droned louder, and somewhere, horses whinnied. Outside the window, the hillside was quiet. Inside the cabin, Moby panted.

She paced the room. Being back here was like finding a time warp to the late nineties. Not much had changed. Same old stores, a few more empty, a few more full of antique junk. She'd seen enough as she came into town to convince her nothing important had changed. Her memories were still there, too, along with suffocating loss and fear.

The matter of getting out to the ranch had taken thought. She hadn't wanted to drive the rental car—it would be too obvious someone else was on the property. In the end, she'd borrowed/stolen a bicycle and pumped her way up the road, stopping frequently, pulling over and hiding in the trees whenever a vehicle neared. It had taken her most of the first day to get to Jandafar. And every mile she'd pedaled had strengthened her resolve. She had to end it now. Twenty years of her life had passed. She'd either find her sister or find out where she was buried. But first, she had to find Chad.

Jandafar hadn't changed much either. The sign said it was now a bed and breakfast, but it still smelled like horses, grass, and dirt. And the horses probably still whinnied when people drove up.

They had not greeted her, because she walked in after leaving the bicycle in the bar ditch down the road from the entry gate.

She remembered the ranch from all those family vacations. She had explored it twenty years ago, sometimes while hiking but mostly on horseback. Galloping through the trees had been thrilling. And she hadn't minded the hikes with Molly that much. They'd kept her from being bored to death during those summer visits. Molly had carried that book with her and looked up every flower and bird she saw.

Usually, Molly preferred to read a book or walk in the woods. Sharon had looked for other things to do, and she'd focused on Chad.

Vacations were a chance to get away from Boulder and the high school drama queens, even though Sharon often interacted with that crowd. Neither she nor her sister wanted to be one of them. You did what you had to do to survive high school.

Her thoughts had swirled around those memories of high school and vacations at Jandafar as she crept onto the property, crossed the meadow and headed for the ruins of the cabin. She didn't want to be here. If it hadn't been for the painting, she wouldn't have been.

The painting brought it all back, like it had happened yesterday. But she wasn't sure she had the facts right in her head. Odd parts were missing. She couldn't recall them and trying to remember made her sick to her stomach. But she'd seen the painting and the artist's signature and known it was Chad. He'd talked about wanting to be an artist. She'd laughed. That was about as far from a rough-and-tumble bowlegged cowboy as you could get.

Sean wanted her to tell him about her past. But how could you talk about something you didn't fully remember or even want to remember? What she did remember made her want to be sick and left her feeling ashamed and dirty. She'd run from it rather than face it. She'd run for twenty years, alone. And she hoped her sister had been running in the opposite direction. That hope was better than what could be true: that he'd killed Molly the same night he'd killed her parents.

The painting had changed things. After she saw it, she had this feeling her sister was still alive, but in danger. She couldn't run this time, couldn't turn her back, couldn't live with herself if there was any possibility Molly was alive.

When a vehicle motor roared outside, she peeked beneath the shade. The blue truck parked by the ranch house. There were only two people inside; no second vehicle followed. Jenna let the blind drop over the window and turned to the room. Cheap old red plaid sofa, worn cowhide carpet. Still, it was better than the green shag carpet up in the line shack, carpet so used that the nap looked like a thousand drunken caterpillars. She could still feel it beneath her bare bottom.

The two lamps in the shack had been fitted with forty-watt bulbs, but that was strong enough. Dimness didn't disguise age and misuse or keep the place from being a torture chamber.

No one in town had recognized Jenna this week, not that they had seen her often as a teenager. She only encountered a few people, and when their gazes met hers, she'd turned away rather than risk seeing a spark of recognition. She'd parked the rental car and gone into the café. The waitress had taken one look at the dark-haired woman with half-moon smears under her eyes, wearing a tank top and sporting a tattoo on her left bicep and asked nothing more than that she pay in cash.

Even Jenna hardly recognized herself in the cabin's mirror. The cinnamon-brown hair dye had washed all the color out of her face, and gray eye shadow smudged beneath her eyes and on her eyelids had emphasized the exhaustion of the past seventy-two hours. The tattoo was the best she could find of the wash-off variety. And it had done the trick.

She paced the room, certain that Mandy and Sean had walked into a trap. Jenna hoped they wouldn't be dead when she got there. She shouldn't have left Mandy that message, but she'd been in such a panic, so afraid to do this alone. She'd wanted backup, and Mandy was a good friend. Mandy had never cared about her secrets, never seemed to need to know anything Jenna wasn't willing to tell. And the two of them had such shared grief from being orphaned at a young age.

Jenna should never have told Mandy about the painting without explaining. No doubt when Mandy saw the painting, she thought it was Jenna. She didn't know Jenna had a younger sister who looked a lot like her. People usually overlooked the subtle differences between their appearances.

Sean might never forgive her—if he was still alive after tonight. Her secret past had eaten at him throughout their marriage, and even more lately. He wanted to have children, but Jenna didn't want to until she knew for sure about her sister. Maybe now she'd get answers and be able to move on with her life.

She'd done so well for so long at not getting attached, not forming relationships. Wouldn't you know it was when she'd had a few years of normalcy that everything would blow apart?

Jenna glanced at the window shade. The sun was dropping. If she was going to do this, it had to be at dusk or later. They wouldn't expect her. Sean and Mandy were still at the line shack. Were they dead or alive?

She grabbed the small drawstring bag she'd kept with her since leaving Tulsa.

This was it.

"Good-bye, Moby." She flicked the porch light on as she exited through a window on the far south end of the duplex. They would assume she was still there. Dale might have told her husband Jenna was waiting in the duplex. Well, she wasn't waiting, and she didn't think Sean and Mandy would return of their own volition.

Jenna slipped down the hillside toward the stable, ducking low so the shadowy underbrush covered her movement. Her tennis shoes made only the slightest sound on the grassy hill.

The flashlight in the bag bumped her hips; she wouldn't turn it on unless necessary. Dale and the guests would finish dinner, and the men would come out and head back up to the line shack. She had to play her cards right. Timing was everything.

Jenna slipped into the tack room and grabbed a bridle, then ambled through the barn. A horse whinnied. At the stall, the animal made its way to her. The horse nickered, and she petted its velvety nose. "That's a good horse," she crooned. She hoped she remembered how to ride. It had been so long. But that wasn't something you forgot, was it?

She closed her eyes and stroked the velvety muzzle, felt the horse's lips searching for something sweet. "Sorry, no treats tonight, but if this all works out, you'll have lots tomorrow."

Voices carried into the barn. She slipped into the horse's stall and crouched in the dark. Truck doors slammed. Surprised, she exited the stall and peered out one of the barn's few windows. The blue truck's headlights came on. The vehicle backed up and headed toward town.

It was time. They hadn't come to find her. Maybe Dale hadn't told them she was there. Jenna hustled back to the stall. "Okay now, boy. Let's see if I can remember how to do this." She left his halter on and slipped the bridle over the animal's head, easing the bit between his teeth. "That's the way."

She debated about the saddle. She would be more comfortable with it, but she had often ridden without. She had loved the feel of the horse's muscles moving beneath her. But she needed to ride fast. She opened the gate to the stall and led the horse out into the barn to throw on the saddle.

The barn light flashed on. Dale Hardesty stood in the doorway.

~ Chapter 56 ~
Mandy

Mandy became slowly aware of the floor beneath her. Gradually, with her eyes open, she noticed light filtering from above, falling in a straight line, coming in around a door or window.

She tried to move, but her wrists were bound together, and so were her ankles. A sour smell of sweat and something else hung in the air.

"Sean?"

Someone moaned off to her left.

Mandy moved like a caterpillar across the floor. "Sean?" Whoever it was she rolled into was warm and alive.

"Mandy?"

"Yeah. What happened?"

"I don't know. My head feels like I've been slammed in a door."

"You took a beating. He kicked you."

"Yeah. I feel like I've been stomped. Everywhere. Where are we?"

Something rustled. Sean was trying to move.

"There's light coming from above. Maybe we're in a basement. Did the line shack look like it had a basement?" he rasped.

"No. Any chance you can get your hands apart or undo your feet? My cell phone is in my pocket, but I can't reach it."

Mandy pulled at the plastic ties that bound her wrists. There was no give at all.

There was more rustling. Sean's breathing quickened, he groaned with his efforts, and let out a long breath. "Too tight." They lay back on the cold floor, side by side. Sean's body was warm.

How long would they be here?

Had Max gone after Jenna?

~ Chapter 57 ~
Jenna

Jenna's heart pounded in her ears, pushing adrenaline through her body along with her blood.

She glanced at the woman beside her, still not believing.

Together, they rode down into a gully and up the other side, moving across country toward the line shack. The horses huffed air from their noses and sweat glistened on their withers. At the top of another rise, the ground leveled out. Tall grass reached to the horses' flanks.

The two women kicked their horses into a gallop. The animals pounded past a copse of persimmon trees, and then the oak forest thinned. When they reached a wide meadow and a rustic split rail fence, Jenna and Dale turned their horses and followed the fence, keeping to the right and moving along the line of trees. Finally, when all that remained between them and the line shack was cleared land, the women stopped. Jenna and Dale slipped off their horses and tied their mounts to trees a few yards into the forest.

"Ready?" Jenna whispered.

Dale lifted her hand. "More ready than you know."

Now. Jenna ran as fast as she had back in high school on the track team, dashed across the grass towards the shadowy side of the shack, Dale right behind her. Slowly, she rounded the corner of the building. Jenna stepped onto the porch and stopped to catch her breath. Adrenaline had kicked in, and it wouldn't fade until this was finished.

"Are you ready?" she whispered over her shoulder.

Beside her, Dale lifted her hand. "Of course."

The wind picked up, swooshed through the trees, and whispered *remember*. Her hand was on the doorknob, but for another instant, Jenna was frozen in time.

The fresh scent of the meadow grass, and the cicadas, droning louder, softer, louder. The memories were strong, but not as strong as the heartache and the pain. The air had crushed out of her and her spirit had broken as he lay on top of her, grinding and thrusting, tearing her apart.

"Your turn, Chad. You've wanted this all week. Come and get it."

The voice seeped through her brain as if it was happening now.

"It's okay, Sharon. We'll take care of this." Her sister Molly spoke into her ear.

~ Chapter 58 ~
Mandy

Mandy and Sean lay on the cold floor, shivering, hearts pounding. Their shallow breaths quickened as minutes stretched on. They jumped at every little sound. Something rustled in the corner, something else scratched at the wall. Mandy's throat dried out. She struggled to keep panic at bay in the dark.

Then, above them, hurried footsteps crossed the wood floor. A latch clicked. The trapdoor lifted and light poured into their prison.

Mandy stared up, terrified. They were sitting targets. She had no doubt Max meant to kill them, but doubted he'd do it without first raping her and torturing Sean.

"Mandy, Sean, are you down there?" Jenna's voice called.

"Jenna? We're here. Max tied us up."

"I'm coming down." The trapdoor ladder screeched against the hard floor. A flashlight beam cut through the darkness.

"We don't have much time," Jenna said. "They could be back any minute."

Light filled the room. For the first time, Mandy was able to look around their dark prison. Windows high on the walls had been painted black to minimize daylight. Two upholstered chairs with sagging seats had been placed side by side against one wall, a small wooden table between them.

She and Sean lay on the floor, next to a platform.

Jenna's flashlight beam reflected off the crystalline crypt that filled the center of the basement platform. Prisms danced on the dark walls of the room.

Dale cut the ropes binding Sean's hands and feet while Jenna turned to Mandy to do the same.

Mandy studied the two women's faces as they worked side by side. She found similarities that time had not eroded. "Jenna? Is this...?"

"No time to explain. We need to get out of here. Let's go." Jenna helped her stand, then motioned to Sean to climb the ladder. Mandy followed. Soon after, Dale climbed into the cabin, and last, Jenna. They pulled up the ladder and dropped the trapdoor. Outside, a truck engine roared.

"Hide. They'll head for the trapdoor, and maybe we can get them down there before they realize what's happened," Jenna instructed.

They scattered. The room was hardly big enough for any of them to feel hidden, but the men wouldn't expect them to be in this room; they would be focused on the prisoners trapped below.

The door flew open. Max stormed in, carrying a flashlight, and didn't bother to turn on a lamp as he crossed the room to the trapdoor.

Max lifted the trapdoor, and his flashlight beamed down. "Where are you? Tell me where you are, damn it!"

Mandy felt sure Max could hear her breathing. She squatted scarcely six feet away in a dark corner and beneath a table, partially covered by a floor rug.

"Damn!" Max cursed as he descended the ladder. "Where are you?" he bellowed.

Heart pounding, Mandy dialed 911 as Jenna left her hiding place and dashed to the trapdoor. Sean and Dale joined her to stare down at Max.

"How do you like it down there?" Jenna called.

Dale glared down at her husband. "You thought my memory would never come back, didn't you? Were you drugging me? The headaches and confusion... How could you?"

Mandy joined the trio at the trapdoor, her anger building. This man had raped Jenna, and he was responsible for the family tragedy. Never before had she wanted to kill someone, but she did now.

"Oh, come on, Dale. You wanted me more than you wanted a sister. You always have." Max sneered up at them.

Dale grabbed an empty beer bottle and pitched it down on her husband.

Max cursed as he ducked. He pulled a gun from his waistband.

"Get back," Sean pulled Dale away from the trapdoor as the gun blasted.

Mandy and Jenna darted away from the trapdoor, and then began pitching everything they could down into the basement room. The man below scrambled away from the ladder when a lamp, pots, and pans rained down, followed by glassware and dishes. Another shot rang out and pinged off a light fixture in the upstairs room. After more dishes were pitched down the ladder, Sean grabbed the trapdoor and shut it. He scooted the sofa over the door and piled the rest of the furniture on top of it.

Below, Max shouted obscenities. He had climbed the ladder and was now pounding on the closed trapdoor.

Dale's face was pale, her eyes dark. She sank to the floor.

"I shouldn't have left you. I'm so sorry."

"Shh. It's going to be all right now," Jenna soothed.

Headlights flashed into the cabin.

"Finally." Mandy rushed to open the door to the police. "In here," she yelled.

Doors slammed. The sheriff and three men hurried into the cabin. "What's going on? You said it was life or death." The sheriff looked from Mandy to where Dale sat on the floor.

Mandy explained what had happened as quickly as she could. Dale stayed on the floor, her face pale, her eyes looked dazed.

"Dale, we'll get you in the truck and down to the ranch in no time," the sheriff said. "We'll call an ambulance to meet us back at your place. Think you can handle the trip?"

"I don't need an ambulance. I'm not sick. And I'm not injured. Just get me back to the ranch. Can you take care of the horses?" Dale asked Jenna.

"Yes. We'll ride them back down. I'll take care of them." Jenna's eyes glittered with tears.

The sheriff glanced around the room. "Where's Max?"

"In the cellar." Sean gestured at the trapdoor.

Mandy grabbed Sean's arm. "What happened to Lamar? And to Chad?"

~ Chapter 59 ~
Jenna

Jenna led the way across the pasture to the horses, then helped Mandy into the saddle. "Sean and I can ride together." Her head was spinning. Her sister Molly was alive, and she'd been married to Max Hardesty for twenty years. Questions fired into her brain, as guilt waves passed through her. If only she hadn't run. If only she had stayed and found Molly that night. Twenty years.

She swung up into the saddle of the second horse and reached down to give Sean a hand up. He groaned as he swung himself up and settled in behind her on the horse's rump.

"Are you okay?" Jenna asked.

"Chad kicked me, knocked me out. Otherwise they never would have got us down in that basement."

"Don't be so sure. Max is very strong, and very smart." Jenna turned her horse toward the road. "This road won't be as fast as going cross country, but it'll be easier on you. Are you okay, Mandy? Can you handle the horse?"

"Sure." Mandy's voice was soft.

The horses picked their way through the grass to the road in silence. Jenna knew she owed them an apology for her deceit. What would happen next? Would the sheriff arrest her?

Jenna cleared her throat. "I'm sorry I didn't tell either of you what happened to me, and to my family. A lot of my memory is fuzzy. Dale doesn't remember everything either. Maybe, eventually, we'll work through what happened."

The horses shook their manes and snorted as they stepped up on the road.

"How did you and Dale wind up coming to the line shack? Didn't Max and Chad go back to have dinner with the guests?"

"After you left, I waited in the cabin. The truck came back, but you didn't. I knew something had happened. Then, Max and Chad drove away from the ranch, toward town. In the stable, I saddled a horse, hoping I could get up to the shack before they returned and find you. I was about to leave when Dale showed up at the barn."

"How long did it take you both to realize the truth?" Sean rubbed Jenna's arm and hung on as the horse stumbled and then righted itself.

"She asked if I was going up to the shack and said you probably needed help, that Max might have done something bad. We looked at each other, and I knew she was Molly." Jenna's voice broke. "I recognized her voice, and her eyes. But she looks so different. She's filled out, and her hair color ages her. I look different, too. Once, we were both blondes."

Jenna peered at Mandy, but her friend's face was hidden in shadow. The horses walked on. Her heart heaved in her chest. Even now, she couldn't believe she'd found her sister. She couldn't believe that her running was over. She closed her eyes for a minute. This time tomorrow, would she be in jail?

"So, she decided to go to the line shack with you?" Sean asked.

"Yes. We knew we had to hurry to get to you before Max and Chad went back there. We talked as we saddled the horses."

"Has she had amnesia?" Mandy asked. "I know she has lots of headaches."

"Yes. Migraines probably caused by the head injury the night of the fire. Your questions about the fire triggered memories.

Nightmares. But she couldn't make sense of what was in her head, and when she asked Max, he told her she was hallucinating."

Jenna's voice broke. Her poor sister. "She's been married to Max for twenty years. She loves him. And he'd been giving her pills, supposedly for her headaches, but I think they were something else. Something to keep her in a fog." Jenna tried unsuccessfully to swallow a lump in her throat. She choked.

"I'm not sure I get it. You said Max assaulted you and killed your parents. How did he end up with Molly?" Mandy asked.

"I hope our parents were dead before the fire consumed them. My parents had challenged Max, and he couldn't tolerate it."

Crickets chirped and an owl hooted. Seconds passed.

"What did Molly say happened after the fire?" Sean asked.

"She is still sorting it all out, but apparently, after I escaped, Max took my sister. Chad had pulled her out of the cabin and taken her to the bunkhouse. Max picked her up there and left for Texas. Days later, they were in Midland and he got a job at a feed lot. He convinced Molly she'd been in a car accident and he'd rescued her. He made up a story about her past and told her that her name was Dale." She paused. Anger seethed inside her. "What little she remembered seemed more like a nightmare than reality. Max was so loving, so kind to her, she never imagined he was lying to her. He got on at a ranch, bought a little house and they got married. She didn't have any idea what Max had done.

"I guess that after Max took Molly away, Chad got it into his head that Max had killed us both. He didn't talk to Max again until his parents died ten years later. Max and Dale came back here, but Chad rarely saw them. Dale doesn't think he ever realized who she was. I'm guessing Max began to think the only way to convince Chad we were alive so he would return to normal was to bring me here. Reunite the sisters and shake Chad up."

Sean tightened his grip around her waist. "There's more to the story of those brothers. Now's not the time to go into it, but

Max is a criminal in many ways." Sean kissed the back of Jenna's neck.

"I was so ashamed of the person I was," Jenna blurted. "I caused my parent's deaths and left my sister behind. I knew she was probably dead. I changed who I was, for her. Can you both forgive me for not telling you?"

"Don't apologize. You were young and scared. I probably would have done the same thing," Mandy said, quietly. "Max is evil."

Sean nodded in agreement. "Yes, he is evil. I'm here with you, and I'm not going anywhere without you."

They rode on in silence for a few minutes. An owl called in the distance.

"Tell us about the painting, Jenna," Mandy asked. "Why did it frighten you so much?"

"I knew Chad had painted it. But it wasn't me. The forehead and eyebrows were my sister's, not mine. I wondered why he painted her imprisoned in the glass crypt. Now, I think Chad must have finally realized Dale was Molly and his brother was keeping her a prisoner."

"Chad created that crypt and painted the picture?" Mandy asked.

"Yes, he did," Sean said. "It's another way he makes a living besides painting depressing pictures no one wants to buy, like that one in the gallery. He also creates forgeries of master painters, and his brother Max set up an entire network of places that offer them for sale to the highest bidder, as originals."

"So, Chad had nothing to do with that painting being in Tulsa?" Mandy asked. "Was Chad there earlier this week? You thought he sent you a note, didn't you? You were going to meet him."

Jenna wished that they were sitting some place with a glass of wine while she explained this to Sean and Mandy. As it was, she couldn't see Sean's face, she couldn't gauge her husband's reactions. She didn't want to hurt him anymore than she already had.

"I did get a note, and I initially thought Chad had sent it. It had been twenty years. I'm tired of running. I thought he might explain things, might tell me what had happened to my sister. Then I saw the painting in the gallery. I didn't want to believe he'd painted it to scare me. Truthfully, I don't think he meant for it to ever be on display."

"Here's my take on what happened," Sean began. "We'll have to hear from Chad and Max before we know for sure. I think Max included it in a shipment of paintings to be sold at the gallery and hoped you would see it. His spy, Mike McNally, had located you and determined you were Sharon Bergen. And you're probably right that he wanted to bring you back here to shock Chad back to reality and prove he hadn't killed you."

Jenna swallowed hard. It was hard to hear, hard to know that Max had been so conniving, and that someone who worked for her company had been his spy.

Her legs ached. She was ready to get off the horse. The beams from the rising moon glistened off the crushed rock of the all-weather road. She glanced ahead, watching for signs of the ranch complex and cabins.

"There's more to this than a simple shipment of Chad's paintings," Sean said. "I've been working to uncover an art forgery operation in Tulsa. I've connected it with Medicine Park. Max is the ringleader; Chad is the artist."

"Chad is forging paintings? How?" Mandy asked.

Jenna's horse stumbled and then righted itself.

"Several ways. Duplicating paintings from the Baroque period and forging papers of provenance. I have a team in place here. The plan was to round them up tonight. But our criminals were otherwise engaged. Couldn't happen. I'll have to explain everything to my team tomorrow."

"What do you think would have happened if Jenna had gone on to meet Max at the funeral home?" Mandy asked. Her horse was lagging several steps behind Jenna's.

"Because of what I know, I think you would have been kidnapped if you hadn't seen the painting in the gallery and returned to your office," Sean explained. "The funeral home was also storing forgeries and shipping them in caskets to other galleries around the United States."

Jenna shook her head. "I can't believe it. Chad would never have gotten involved in something like that on his own. Max had to have taken advantage of him." The memories she had of Chad were of a kind, sensitive young man. He loved animals, and he loved art. And he had fallen head over heels in love with her in a very short time. She'd loved him, too, but not so desperately.

"Who blew up the gallery and Arnie's that night? It WAS because of Mike and me, wasn't it?" Mandy kicked up her horse so that she was riding next to Jenna again.

Sean shifted on the horse's rump. "I suspect it was Max. Your friend Mike probably knew those things were going to happen. He even expected the drive-by shooting, but not getting grazed by a bullet. That was an accident." Jenna reached around and patted his thigh.

"Are you doing okay? I know it's not comfortable."

"I'm fine, honey. Almost there." The mercury vapor light was a speck in the distance, about another mile ahead. Sean kissed her neck. "Mike must have been angry at Max after that. Probably demanded more money. Max wasn't planning to pay him anyway. Mike was dispensable."

"Once he'd located me, Mike didn't matter," Jenna added. "He didn't bargain on the fact that I'd tell you about the painting, Mandy, and that you would enlist Mike to help you find it and be such a bloodhound on the case. He thought his scare tactics would stop you."

"But he didn't know what a good friend you were," Mandy said. "I couldn't let you slip out of my life without knowing why."

Jenna's throat was dry, and tears pricked her eyes. "Max didn't count on that. Lucky for me you felt that way. We both wanted a sister. You didn't know that I already had one. And I had to find her."

Without warning, Jenna's horse shied and bolted into the underbrush beside the road.

"Whoa! Hold up!" Jenna held the reins tightly to slow the horse's mad dash. Sean's grip around her waist made breathing difficult.

"We're okay. Calm down now." She patted the horse's withers as she spoke over her shoulder to Sean. "You okay?"

"What caused that?" he asked.

"Everything all right?" Mandy called from fifty yards away.

"Something spooked him. See anything in the grass?" Jenna circled the horse back to where Mandy waited on the road. "Might have been a rodent or something."

Mandy urged her horse to the edge of the road. "I don't see… wait. Oh no!" Mandy vaulted off her horse.

~ Chapter 60 ~
Mandy

Mandy dropped to her knees in the tall grass beside the huddled figure. Sandy hair glinted in the moonlight. She held her breath. This couldn't be happening.

Jenna and Sean road up beside Mandy and hopped off, one after the other.

"What is it?" Sean asked.

"It's...Lamar." Mandy was afraid to touch him, afraid he was dead.

Jenna stooped next to the man. She touched his shoulder, shook him. "Hey, wake up. Lamar?"

His face was bloodied and bruised, his hands still tied with rope. His denim work shirt was covered with dirt and torn at the shoulder.

Jenna leaned over him, her ear to his mouth and nose.

"Is he breathing? Is he... dead?" Mandy's heart raced.

"He's alive." Jenna shook his shoulder again. "Lamar. Wake up. Lamar, it's me, Sharon."

One eye had begun to purple with a bruise, and his puffy lips oozed. His shirt was soaked in blood.

Mandy squatted beside Lamar. "He's been beaten, maybe shot. We've got to get him to the hospital."

Jenna unbuttoned Lamar's shirt and peeked at the wound. "He's bleeding, but it's not arterial. The gunshot caught him near his collarbone. Went clear through."

"Can we lift him?" Sean grabbed Lamar beneath his armpits and tried unsuccessfully to lift him. Lamar was bigger than Sean. Moving him was not going to happen while he was unconscious.

Lamar groaned.

"Lamar. Wake up. Please, wake up." Mandy got to her feet and stepped close to Sean, close to where Lamar's head rested on Sean's shoulder, his body awkwardly leaning against him.

Lamar shifted and groaned louder. His eyelids fluttered.

"Lamar. Wake up. It's me, Mandy." Her heart fluttered with his eyelids. "Open your eyes. You're going to be all right." She patted his back. "We'll get you to the hospital."

Sean lowered him to the ground; the cowboy looked around, confused. His eyes rolled in his head. He blinked.

"Where am…?" His gaze rested on Jenna. "I'm dreaming." He closed his eyes and sank to the ground. "Maybe I'm dead."

"You're not dead," Mandy said. "It's my friend Jenna, the woman I've been searching for."

Lamar focused on Mandy. "Your friend. You found her." He touched Mandy's arm. "It's over then. You're both okay."

"Yes. But you aren't. We need to get you to the hospital. Think you can walk a little way to the house??"

"No hospital. Nothin's broke. Shot. Bruised, a bit."

"But it looks bad," Mandy insisted. "You need medical attention." He looked like a car accident victim. There was blood everywhere.

"Dale can see to it. No worse than being thrown by a bronc. Happened plenty of times. Just ask her."

"Can you stand up? We're not far from the ranch house. Can you ride? Might be easier than walking." Sean extended one arm and Lamar grabbed his hand.

"I can make it."

Lamar slowly got to his feet. Mandy took one side and Sean the other as they helped him over to Jenna's horse and shoved him up into the saddle.

~ Chapter 61 ~
Dale

Dale Hardesty sat on the porch of the ranch house, rocking in the glider. She heard the clopping of the horse's hooves on the road long before the animals plodded through the night into the pool of brightness below the yard light.

Ever since the sheriff had left with Max in the backseat of his cruiser, she'd been rubbing her hands together and staring into the southern sky at pinpricks of stars.

She picked at her memory.

The horses stopped near the porch. The woman who was her sister and Sean walked beside them. Together, they helped one rider slide off. Lamar? The four of them stepped into the pool of light surrounding the porch.

"You look bad, Lamar." Dale's eyes widened as she stared at the cowboy. She had been afraid something had happened to him when Max and Chad returned to the ranch house for supper without him, but neither man would answer her questions. Then, she'd expected to find Lamar at the line shack with Mandy and Sean. His absence had set off alarm bells in her brain, but the memories were sparking by that time, and it was all she could do to stay upright and put one foot in front of the other. The memories slammed back into her brain, too fast.

"Come inside. I'll try to patch you up," Dale said. He looked horrific, bloody and bruised. He needed more than her limited experience patching up animals. But she owed him her best. Her husband Max had done this to him.

She opened the door and Lamar limped into the house. "Have a seat," she said to the others, tossing the words over her shoulder. "I need to talk to you." She followed Lamar into the house. Her stomach pitched.

Twenty minutes later, she returned to the porch. Her hands shook. *Could she really talk about this, now?* She had no choice.

"He's resting. Don't think anything's broken, but he's shot, bruised, beaten." Dale settled into one of the Adirondack chairs. Confusion buzzed in her head, but she was determined to get things straight. She had to speak it out loud.

Dale watched Jenna cross the porch to sit in the chair beside her. Her sister was still thin as a rail. She never had eaten right, and she was an exercise fanatic. It didn't look like that had changed. She didn't like the color of her sister's hair. Then, she reasoned, it was probably a disguise. She had recently realized her own hair color was a disguise as well, something Max had insisted on.

When she'd gotten back from the line shack, she'd had a good look at her hair roots. Max had always said she was prematurely gray when he met her twenty years ago, and he wasn't ready to accept a wife who looked older than he was. She was faithful to go to the hair salon every week for him, to have her roots done. Now that she remembered her former life, she knew she was a blonde.

Max had hidden her from herself and from her sister, shrouding her memories with drugs. Memories were flooding back unhindered, now. Many of them were better left forgotten. But not her sister. She was here. She was alive.

"All these years, so many nightmares." Dale took a long sip of water. "Without the medication Max has been giving me, my head is starting to clear. I don't know if I am remembering correctly. Twenty years have passed. These are teenage memories, interpreted by a teenage mind. Perhaps the reality of what happened is a combination of what both Sharon and I think we remember." She rubbed her eyes for a minute and then stared out into the starry night.

"I didn't remember what happened that summer, only bits and pieces of *something*. Then Mandy started asking questions about the fire. I tried to break through the brain fog, tried to talk to Max about it last night. He gave me three headache pills instead of the usual two, said I was suffering from 'the power of suggestion.' I pretended to take the pills. I couldn't sleep. This afternoon, I started to remember everything." She grabbed Jenna's hand.

"I remember that night, everyone who was staying at the ranch that week ate together, like we do here," she began. "Sharon left the table without Dad's permission when she'd finished eating. Fifteen minutes later, she hadn't returned. I asked to be excused and went to find her."

Jenna squirmed in the wooden chair. Dale kept her focus on the stars.

"Outside, I searched. It was a hot night, typical August. Someone giggled near the bunkhouse where the cowboys lived, so I walked over. Sharon was on the porch in the shadows, her arms wrapped around a man; he was kissing her face. I called to her, but she pulled his head down to her and pressed against him. It made me angry. Chad was in love with her, but that hadn't been enough, it wasn't Chad she was kissing. It seemed callous. A woman was dead, and she was making out with another cowboy?" Dale closed her eyes. Why did the memory still upset her?

"I went back to the dining hall and then to the barn dance with my parents. Sharon never showed. When my parents and the other older people left, several men, friends of the ranch owners, came in and the real party began. They'd been drinking. One of them introduced himself to me as Chad's brother, Max.

"He asked me to dance. We started off slow as he taught me the two-step. Soon we were following the other couples, circling the room. Max had been staring into my eyes all evening, telling me I was beautiful, telling me all the things a young woman wants to hear. I fell in love. Max said he had beer in his truck. I didn't care about the beer. All I wanted was to touch his hair, close my eyes, and let him kiss me.

"Out in the truck, Max watched me drink the beer, then took my empty glass and slid his hand up my arm to my chin. 'You're so pretty,' he said."

Dale's voice cracked. The memories crowded in. They'd been locked inside her brain for so long. Now, feelings rushed back with the memories. Max had been her husband for so long, but she'd never remembered that night before. He'd said they met in Texas, that she'd been in an accident. He'd repeated that story to her over and over again for twenty years. It was a lie.

"Our lips met, and time stopped for me. I wanted to kiss him forever. But when he touched my breast, I pushed him away and told him I had to go inside. It was late. I got out of the truck and ran to our cabin. My heart was beating so fast."

Dale looked at Jenna. Her face was the color of spaghetti. "What's wrong?" She squeezed her sister's hand.

"I wasn't there. I don't know about your kiss. But you're mistaken about who I was with at the bunkhouse."

"Lamar, wasn't it? Who else would it have been?"

"Max."

Dale withdrew her hand. A lump filled her throat. "No, Max chose to be with me at the dance. Then we went to the truck. We kissed. It was late and I left him in the truck and went back to the cabin." She rubbed her head. Why would Sharon lie and say she'd been with Max? It didn't make sense.

Sharon had been with Lamar that evening, she was positive. But the man had been in the shadows. Wearing jeans, and a t-shirt. What had Max been wearing? She couldn't remember.

"Go on, Molly," Jenna said, her eyes wide, her face pale. "I want to know what you remember."

The rest was harder, she'd buried it the deepest. Even now, she didn't want to remember. Dale wasn't sure she could speak the words.

"I was in my room at the cabin. Mom and Dad were in the living room. I heard someone come in, heard someone else's voice. Dad yelled, and then I heard Sharon. She sounded hysterical. A door slammed." Dale pinched her eyes shut. *Am I remembering this right?* "I heard Max. Dad yelled. Something crashed. I rushed out to the living room. Max had a hold of Sharon. I tried to get to Max, to talk to him. Mom and Dad were on the floor in the hall.

"Sharon and Max struggled. She knocked the candle off the table. The tablecloth caught on fire." She rubbed her head. "I... I don't remember what happened next."

Dale closed her eyes and sat quietly. Her memory was foggy again. She wasn't sure...

"Maybe I passed out from the smoke. I couldn't breathe. Then I was outside with Chad. I begged Chad to take me back to the cabin, back to my parents. Told him I wanted Max, but he carried me down the hillside to the bunkhouse. The sky was lit up with the flames from the cabin fire." She stopped. "That's all I remember."

She peered at Jenna. Her sister's eyes drooped, and heavy tears rolled down her cheeks. "Is that what you remember?"

An SUV drove up the driveway. As it neared, she could make out the insignia on the door, and the combination black and white paint job. The vehicle parked and the sheriff climbed out.

"Dale. Mr. Wade," the sheriff began. He nodded at Mandy and Jenna. "Interesting evening. I need to talk to each of you, individually. Inside?"

"Of course, Sheriff." Dale stood. She swayed.

Why was he here again? Had something happened to Max? Had he told the sheriff who she really was? Was the sheriff going to arrest someone?

"I'll go first," she offered. "Then I have a patient I need to check on."

The sheriff followed her into the house.

~ Chapter 62 ~
Mandy

"What do you think he wants to talk to us about?" Mandy asked.

"It's obvious," Sean said. "What happened tonight. He's probably already interviewed Max at the police station. He has a few details, what we told him at the line shack. But now he's heard Max's side of things. No telling what he said. But I'm guessing it wasn't the truth."

Mandy rubbed her neck. "We're all exhausted. Do we have to do this tonight?"

"Better to get it over with," Jenna said. "Tell him the truth. You didn't know what you were getting into. You were trying to help. You did nothing wrong." Jenna bent over, elbows on her knees. She closed her eyes. "He'll arrest me."

"No, he won't, Jenna," Sean said. "You did nothing wrong, either. You didn't kill your parents. It was an accident. He'll see that."

"Sean's right, Jenna. Max will go to jail, not you. Tell the sheriff you're filing charges for rape."

Jenna shook her head. "For a rape twenty years ago? There's no proof, and Max will certainly deny it. He won't be charged with that, or with my parents' deaths. He'll get off Scott free."

"No. He won't," Mandy said. "Your sister can charge him. He's kept her a virtual prisoner all these years, giving her those pills."

Jenna sighed. "I wish that were true. But I don't think my sister will file charges against the man she's been married to, and loved, for twenty years." She stared at the floor of the old porch.

"But Max lied to her. He raped you. When you tell her that, she'll never forgive him."

Jenna rubbed her palms together. She stood and paced the length of the porch.

"We'll tell the sheriff the truth about tonight, and I'll be sharing with him what I can of our investigation into the forgery ring. Whether Max goes to prison for rape, murder, imprisonment or some other charge, I don't know, but I can guarantee he'll go to prison for forgery."

The sheriff appeared in the doorway. "Jenna Wade? Could I speak with you inside, please?"

Jenna stepped into the house.

~ Chapter 63 ~
Jenna

The sheriff led her across the living room to the table by the window and motioned for her to sit. "Mrs. Wade, it's my understanding that your real name is Sharon Bergen. Your parents were killed in a cabin fire here twenty years ago. Is that correct."

"Yes, sir, it is. And Dale Hardesty is my sister, Molly."

The sheriff scratched his head. "Do you wish to have counsel present?"

"Am I a suspect? For committing what crime?" The chill she'd been fighting for the last few minutes grew icier.

He squinted. "Nope. I just want to be sure I got everything straight. Your face has been on a Missing Persons poster in my office for twenty years. I'm glad to be able to write 'found' across that poster and file it away."

Jenna sighed in relief. "I know it was wrong to have left the scene, and to have left my sister behind. I've regretted it every day of my life. And I've regretted I didn't do more to try to save my parents."

"Your sister has told us what happened. Unless your version of that evening differs greatly from hers, I think we can finally mark that incident as an accidental fire. I'm sorry you lost your parents in the blaze."

"The blaze was accidental, but my parent's deaths were not. Max Hardesty knocked them both unconscious before the fire started. Then he left without trying to help."

"Your sister didn't tell me Max was responsible."

"My sister didn't see everything that happened before the candle fell and caught the tablecloth on fire. I did."

"So, you allege that your sister's husband killed your parents? You realize there is no way to prove a crime was committed at this late date? I will check the files, but your parents remains— cremains—were buried in Boulder, CO. I was here that day with the investigative team. I remember. There wasn't much left. Dental records were used for identification." He leaned toward her.

Jenna flinched. "I… didn't… know." She remembered her parents as she'd last seen them crumpled and lying on the cabin floor. At least they hadn't been awake when the fire took them.

"I'm sorry if I shocked you. Will you tell Dale the truth?"

His question startled her. She considered her answer before she responded. "I'm sure that learning what her husband has done all these years to block her memory upsets her. Why add to that trauma? Max imprisoned my husband and my friend Mandy, intending to kill them. I'm sure both will file charges."

The sheriff stood. "Well, that's another thing. We can't find Chad. We've searched his cabin, and other than finding a whole lot of photos and paintings of you, we found no clues as to where he might have gone. But he's definitely gone."

Jenna sank back in her chair. Despite what Chad had helped Max do to Sean and Mandy, she would have liked to look him in the eye to see if anything was left of the gentle cowboy she'd fallen in love with. Now she'd never have the chance.

Her husband would do everything he could to see to it that Chad was caught. Sean was a good investigator.

Mary Coley

Part 5 – SATURDAY

~ Chapter 64 ~
Jenna

Jenna rolled over on the soft mattress and stretched. When she opened her eyes, Sean lay beside her, watching her.

"You're awake."

"What time is it?" She looked around the unfamiliar room and found the radio alarm clock on the bedside table. "10 a.m.! I never sleep this late."

"I think you were overdue. I'm going to ask Mrs. Childers if I can bring up a breakfast tray. Service downstairs was at 9."

"You don't have to do that. I can get something later."

"I want to do it. I want to spend every minute of this day with you."

"What about the takedown? The art forgers? Max and Chad Hardesty?"

"Max is already in jail. Chad is missing. I have the day off. The investigation is far from over, but my team is working with the police, combing through Max's office and Chad's cabin and studio right now. I'm confident we'll find more than enough to cement the forgery charges in court and send them both to jail for a long time."

Jenna sighed. "I can't help feeling sorry for Chad."

Sean frowned. "Seriously? He should never have gotten involved with his brother's forgery ring. He was a pawn at his brother's beck and call, but he participated, unconcerned about the outcomes and who might get hurt. Max is the real criminal, but Chad must be held accountable. We'll find him."

Jenna nodded and laid her head back on the pillow. Her mind turned over the events of the previous evening. Her heart ached. Molly had been at Max's mercy, too, for so many years. He'd poisoned her thoughts with lies about the night of the fire.

Sean interrupted her rolling thoughts. "Mandy called. She woke up early and drove out to Jandafar with your sister. Invited us to come out when we can."

Jenna sat up. "I want to see her, but I'm in no hurry to go back to Jandafar. Could they come here?" She picked at the thick comforter. Being at Jandafar had brought everything back–the shame and the fear. She'd found her sister; she didn't need to go back to Jandafar again.

"I can ask. And another thing. Will is here. He came in late last night. He's out at Jandafar, too."

"I didn't expect that. Maybe he really does love her. Though I'm not sure she can forgive him for lying to her about everything." She looked up at Sean, knowing how her own lies had jeopardized her marriage. "I hope you can forgive me."

He sat down on the bed and leaned over to kiss her. "I understand why you lied. And while we're on that subject, I must tell you that your secrets were not quite as secret as you thought. Will investigated things. I connected some dots."

He kissed her lightly. Her heart jumped. *Sean already knew.* She choked back a sob as a tear spilled onto her cheek.

"Mandy has a lot to consider. She and Will haven't known each other as long as we have. And there's another thing that must be thrown into the mix. She has feelings for Lamar." He gently pushed a lock of hair behind her ear with one finger.

"She does? I'll ask her about that."

Jenna rolled out of bed and slipped a robe on over her nightgown.

"You think Molly's been brainwashed by Max, don't you?" Sean asked.

"Yes, and I'm not sure I want to set her straight about what happened at the cabin. At the same time, I can't listen to her defend Max when she doesn't know everything he did that night."

"Surely she won't want to stay on at the ranch."

"I'll ask her in a few days, when she's feeling better. Meanwhile, she should go home with us."

"Home? Remember what happened? We have an empty house. Nothing to return to. You resigned. We were going to relocate."

"Oh, yeah. I don't have a job. You don't want to go back to Tulsa?"

"I'm open."

Jenna crossed the room to the window. She lifted the sash and hot August air flowed into the room. She closed her eyes and let it blast her face. Lightness filled her. She was no longer burdened by her past, and she'd found her sister. Many things still had to be resolved, and it would take time for the two of them to get to know one another again. But thankfully, she no longer had to look over her shoulder, no longer had to be prepared to run from the police. She could go anywhere, do anything.

"I'm free," she said.

Sean stepped up behind her and slid his arms around her. "You are. Now what do you want to do with your life?"

Chapter 65
~ Mandy ~

Mandy Lyons sat on the porch swing, elbows propped on her knees. Will sat in one of the Adirondack chairs.

"Well, when are you coming back to Tulsa? I asked you to move in with me, remember?" Will's voice was deep and forceful.

Mandy looked up, but she didn't look at Will. She glanced at the green lawn, the fenced stable yard and the barn, the horses grazing in the meadow, and the two dogs leaping and charging one another as they played near the driveway.

Moby looked her way and raced to her, his tongue hanging out and his eyes sparkling. He stopped just short of leaping into her lap but swiped his tongue across her forearm instead.

"You're not planning on keeping that dog, are you? He'll have to learn manners." Will sat back in the chair and crossed his arms.

"I love it here." Mandy ruffled the curly hair on Moby's head and the dog playfully backed away and then lunged at her.

Will stared. He sat forward. "Okay. Here, boy. Come on over here." He stuck a hand out toward Moby.

Moby wagged his long tail and sat beside Mandy. She scratched his ears and under his chin, his favorite spot.

"Are you playing a game? I need to get back to Tulsa. You've found Jenna and everything is good. We don't have to hang around, do we? I love you, Mandy." Will continued to try to get Moby to come to him, but the dog refused.

Mandy was listening to the conversation going on inside the house. Lamar and Dale were trying to speak quietly, but she could still hear them. She wanted Will to stop talking so she could make out every single word.

So far, she had heard bits and pieces that told her the gist of their conversation. Dale was filing for divorce and wanted to sell the B&B and the ranch property. She was offering a first option to Lamar. Dale wanted to be with Jenna; wherever she and Sean decided they would make their next home, that's where she was going. And Lamar was making excuses for why he wasn't qualified to own a place this big, either as a ranch or a B&B.

She bolted up out of the swing and into the house. Lamar and Dale looked up as she burst in with Moby close behind. The dog trotted over to Dale, tail wagging.

"Mandy, when did you find Shah, Chad's dog? He's been missing a while."

"What?" Mandy couldn't process what Dale had said about the dog. She felt a stab of worry at Lamar's bruised face. His arm was in a sling. Broken ribs, she guessed.

"Lamar, you are passing up a great opportunity," Mandy lectured. "You love this place. You would do a fabulous job of running it. And I'll help! I like to cook, I love the area, and if we hire maids and a couple of cowhands, we can do it together." The words spilled out before she could stop them.

She'd quit her job. Jenna wasn't going back to Tulsa either. And she knew they'd stay in touch. What reason did she have to be anywhere but here?

Lamar's face was a mass of purpling bruises, but she could still see the handsome underneath. His sandy hair was tousled. He stood and crossed the room to stand in front of her.

Her eyes glistened with unshed tears when Lamar's own sparkling eyes studied her. Dimples popped out in his cheeks.

"Well now, are you proposing to me, Mandy?"

Mary Coley

About the Author

Mary Coley splits her life between Tulsa and north central New Mexico. A certified interpretive guide, naturalist and environmental educator as well as a writer, she occasionally blogs about writing and nature at www.marycoley.me. She is a recognized professional both in the environmental education field and as an author. Her book, *Environmentalism: How You can Make a Difference,* published through Capstone Press, received a first-place award for Best Juvenile Book from the Oklahoma Writers Federation, Inc. A frequent winner in annual OWFI contests, Coley has also published two volumes of short stories, including several stories previously published in anthologies.

She is a member of The Tulsa Nightwriters, the Oklahoma Writer's Federation, Mystery Writers of America, Sisters in Crime and the Society of Children's Book Writer's and Illustrators and is a frequent participant in the Around the Block Writer's Collaborative workshops.

Coley is available for speaking engagements and writing workshops. Topics include: The Writing Life, How to Write (and Edit) for Mysteries, Where Do Ideas Come From?

She is also available to speak about her books at book clubs, schools and libraries in Oklahoma. Contact her at writer@marycoley.com.

Awards Received by Mary Coley's Mysteries

Chrysalis – Silver Falchion Finalist, Killer Nashville International Mystery Writer's Conference, 2019. First Place Winner, OWFI Mystery/Suspense category 2018.
Blood on the Cimarron – The Hillerman Award Winner, New Mexico/Arizona Book Awards, 2018. First Place Winner, OWFI Mystery/Suspense category, 2016.
Ant Dens – Oklahoma Book Awards Finalist, 2016. Delta Kappa Gamma Creative Woman of Oklahoma award, Best YA Fiction, 2016.
Cobwebs – Delta Kappa Gamma Creative Woman of Oklahoma award, Best YA Fiction, 2015. First place winner, OWFI Mystery/Suspense category.

Contact Information

Visit https://marycoley.com to learn more about Mary's writing life and each of her books. All books are for sale on her website.

All of her books are available in trade paperback and e-book from all online booksellers, including Amazon, Barnes and Noble, and Books-a-Million. In addition, her first book, **Cobwebs**, is available as an audiobook from Audible.

Facebook: www.facebook.com/marycoleyauthor

Pinterest: www.pinterest.com/marycoleymysteries

Blog: www.marycoley.me

Crystalline Crypt

Mary Coley

Made in the USA
Coppell, TX
17 February 2020